DANIELLE STEEL

Family Ties

A Novel

RANDOM HOUSE
LARGE PRINT

Copyright © 2010 by Danielle Steel

All rights reserved.
Published in the United States of America by
Random House Large Print in association with
Delacorte Press, New York.
Distributed by Random House, Inc., New York.

Cover design: Shasti O'Leary Soudant
Cover photograph: © Ron Chapple Stock

The Library of Congress has established a
cataloging-in-publication record for this title.

ISBN: 978-0-7393-7742-0

www.randomhouse.com/largeprint

FIRST LARGE PRINT EDITION

Printed in the United States of America

10 9 8 7 6 5 4 3 2 1

This Large Print Edition published in
accord with the standards of the N.A.V.H.

To my beloved, precious children,
Beatrix, Trevor, Todd, Nick,
Sam, Victoria, Vanessa,
Maxx, and Zara,
of whom I am so proud,
to whom I am so grateful,
for whom I live my life,
with whom life is a joyful adventure!
May the ties that bind us be
ever gentle and ever strong!

with all my love,
Mommy/D.S.

Family Ties

Chapter 1

Seth Adams left Annie Ferguson's West Village apartment on a sunny September Sunday afternoon. He was handsome, funny, intelligent, fun to be with, and they had been dating for two months. They had met at a Fourth of July picnic in the Hamptons, and he was as excited about his career as Annie was about her own. He had graduated from Harvard Business School two years before and was enjoying a meteoric rise at a Wall Street investment bank. Annie had graduated from Columbia Architecture School six months before, and she was reveling in the excitement of her first job with an important architecture group. It was her dream come true. And the handsome pair had spotted each other across a crowded room, and it was infatuation at first sight. It had been a great summer so far, and they were already talking about renting a ski house together with some of their friends. They were falling in love and looking forward to good times ahead.

Annie was having the time of her life: weekends with Seth, passionate lovemaking, happy times on the pretty little sailboat that he had just bought. She had it all, new man, new home, first big step in the career she had worked so hard for. She was on top of the world, twenty-six years old, tall, blond, beautiful. She had a smile that could have melted the world, and a lot to smile about. Her life these days was everything she had dreamed of.

She had to force Seth to leave that afternoon after another perfect weekend on his boat, but she had work to do. She wanted to spend some time on her first big project for a client meeting the following day. She knew she had to blow their socks off, and the plans she had been working on were meticulously done, and her immediate supervisor had shown a lot of respect for her ideas and was giving her a chance to shine. Annie was just sitting down at her drafting table when her cell phone rang. Although he had only left the apartment five minutes before, she thought it might be Seth. He called her sometimes on his way home, to tell her how much he already missed her.

She smiled, thinking of him, and then saw from the caller ID that it was Jane, her older sister by ten years. The two sisters were crazy about each other, and Jane had been like a mother to her since their parents had passed away when Annie was eighteen. Jane was happily married, lived in Greenwich, Connecticut, and had three adorable children. The two sisters looked almost like twins. Jane was a slightly older version of Annie, and she was looking forward to meeting Seth. He sounded like a keeper to her. All she hoped for Annie was that she would find someone as wonderful as her own husband Bill and be as happily married one day. Jane and Bill Marshall had been married for fourteen years and still acted like they were on their honeymoon. They were role models Annie hoped to emulate one day, but for now she was focused on her brand-new career, in spite of the delightful distraction provided by Seth for the past two months. Annie wanted to be a great architect one day.

"Is he there?" Jane asked conspiratorially, and her younger sister laughed. Jane was a freelance illustrator of children's books and a proficient artist, but she had always been more interested in her husband and children than in her career. Bill was the publisher of a small but respected publishing house. They had spent the weekend in Martha's Vineyard, closing up their summer house, and enjoying a romantic weekend away from their three kids.

"He just left," Annie answered.

"Why so early?" Jane sounded disappointed for her.

"I have to work. I have a big presentation tomorrow, to an important client, and I wanted to work on the plans."

"Good girl." Jane was infinitely proud of her little sister. She was a star in her eyes. "We'll be home in a couple of hours. We're just leaving now. Bill is pre-flighting the plane. It was gorgeous here this weekend. I hate to close the house." They loved the Vineyard, and so did their kids. They'd bought the house when their oldest, Lizzie, was born. She was twelve now, and the portrait of her mother. Ted was eight and looked just like Bill, with the same sweet nature and easygoing style. And Jane liked to say that her youngest, Katie, came from another planet. At five, she had opinions about everything, was incredibly bright, and was fearless. She was an old soul in a child's body, and she always said that she and her aunt Annie were best friends. "How's the weather in New York?" Jane asked her conversationally. It was hurricane season, but the weather at the Vineyard had been good.

"It's been hot and sunny all weekend, but they say there's a storm coming in tonight. It doesn't look like it to me," Annie answered.

"They're expecting a storm here too—the wind picked up an hour ago, but it looks okay so far. Bill wants to get home before it starts." He was waving to her from the plane then, and Jane grabbed her styrofoam cup of coffee and walked toward him, as she wound up the conversation with Annie. "I'll call you when I get home. Don't work too hard. . . . I love you. Why don't you bring Seth out to dinner next weekend?"

"I'll try. I may have to work, depending on how the meeting goes tomorrow. I love you too. Call me later," Annie said comfortably as they hung up and she went back to work. She spread out the plans and studied them carefully. She could see a few adjustments she wanted to make, just subtle ones, but she was a perfectionist and wanted everything to be flawless the next day. She began slowly and meticulously making the changes she had thought about all weekend.

Jane got into the plane that was her husband's pride and joy. He had been a Navy pilot, and in love with planes all his life. This was the biggest one he'd had. It was a Cessna 414 Chancellor that seated eight. It was perfect for them, their three children, and their babysitter Magdalena when she came to the Vineyard with them, which left room for two friends, or the mountain of shopping bags and suitcases that Jane always dragged back and forth between Greenwich and the Vineyard. The plane was a luxury, but it meant more to Bill than their house and was his most beloved possession. Jane always felt totally safe when Bill was flying, more so than on any commercial flight. He kept his license current and was instrument rated.

"Get your ass in here," he said jokingly, as she pushed one more shopping bag into the plane. "There's a storm coming, and I want to get us home before it hits." The sky was darkening as he said it, and Jane's long blond hair was flying in the wind. She hopped in, and he leaned over and kissed her, and then concentrated on the dials in front of him. He had clearance to leave, and they had instruments if the weather got socked in. Bill put the headphones on and talked to the tower as Jane pulled a magazine out of her bag. She loved trashy gossip magazines and reading about famous actresses and their romances and breakups, and discussing them with Annie as though the celebrities were their friends. Bill loved to tease them about it.

He carefully watched the sky as they took off in a stiff wind, and he rose quickly to the altitude he'd been assigned by the tower. They would be landing at Westchester County Airport in roughly an hour. It was an easy flight, and he had to pay attention to the traffic around Boston. He chatted amiably with the tower several times and smiled at Jane. They'd had a nice weekend. As much as he loved them, it was nice to get away from the kids and have her to himself.

"Annie sounds serious about her new guy," Jane reported as he laughed.

"You're not going to be happy until you marry her off." He knew his wife well, and they both knew he was right. "She's still a kid, and she just started her first job."

"I was twenty-two when I married you," she reminded him. "Annie is twenty-six."

"You weren't as serious about your career as she is. Give her a chance. She's not exactly an old maid." There was no way she ever would be. She was young and beautiful, and men were always pursuing her. But Bill was right—Annie wanted to get her career as an architect squared away before she settled down, which sounded sensible to him. And she loved being an aunt, but wasn't ready to have kids.

Jane noticed that Bill was looking distracted then, and concentrating on the darkening sky. The air got choppy, and Jane could see that they were heading toward a storm. She didn't say anything to Bill, she didn't like to bother him when he was flying, so she looked out the window and then opened her magazine and took a sip of her coffee. A moment later, it splashed in her lap as the plane started to bounce.

"What was that?"

"There's a storm coming up," he said, with his eyes on the dials, and he let the controller know they were hitting a lot of chop, and got clearance to drop to a lower altitude. Jane could see a big airliner flying above them on their left, probably coming in from Europe, heading to Logan or JFK.

Their plane continued to bounce even at the lower altitude, and within minutes it grew worse, and Jane saw a bolt of lightning in the sky.

"Should we land?"

"No, we're fine," he smiled reassuringly, as it started to rain. They were over the Connecticut coast by then, and Bill turned to say something to her just when an explosion hit their left engine like a bomb, and the plane tipped crazily, as Bill concentrated on the controls.

"Shit, what was that?" Jane said hoarsely. Nothing like that had ever happened before, and Bill's face was tense.

"I don't know. It could be a fuel leak. I'm not sure," he said tersely, as his jaw clenched. He was fighting to control the plane as they lost altitude rapidly, and with that the engine caught fire, and he guided the plane down looking for a clearing to land. Jane said not a word. She just watched as Bill fought to level them out again, but he couldn't. They were listing badly and heading down at a frightening speed as he called in to the controller and told him where he was. "We're going down, our left wing is on fire," he said calmly, and Jane reached out and touched his arm. He never took his hand off the controls, and he told her he loved her. They were his last words as the Cessna hit the ground and exploded in a ball of fire.

Annie's cell phone rang again just as she was erasing a change she had spent an hour making on the plans. She didn't like it and was delicately changing it back. She was concentrating intensely, and then glanced at her phone lying on the drafting table. It was Jane, they had obviously gotten home. She almost didn't answer it, she didn't want to break her concentration, and Jane always wanted to chat.

Annie tried to ignore it, but the ringing was annoying and persistent, and finally she picked it up.

"Can I call you back?" she said as she answered, and was met by a flood of Spanish. Annie recognized the voice. It was Magdalena, the Salvadoran woman who took care of Jane and Bill's kids. She sounded frantic. Annie knew these calls well. Magdalena had her number for when Bill and Jane were away. She usually only called Annie when one of the kids got hurt, but Annie knew that her sister would be home within minutes, if she wasn't already there. She couldn't understand a word Magdalena said in rapid Spanish.

"They're on their way home," Annie reassured her. Usually it was Ted who had fallen out of a tree or off a ladder or bumped his head. He was an active boy and accident prone. The girls were a lot more sedate. Lizzie was almost a teenager, and Katie was a fireball, but she was more verbal than athletic and had never gotten hurt. "I talked to Jane two hours ago," Annie said calmly. "They should be home any minute."

With that, Magdalena exploded in another torrent of Spanish. She sounded as though she was crying, and the only word Annie understood was **la policia**. The police.

"What about the police? Are the kids okay?" Maybe one of them really had gotten seriously injured. So far it had only been small stuff, except for Ted's broken leg when he fell out of a tree at the Vineyard and his parents were there. "Tell me in English," Annie insisted. "What happened? Who got hurt?"

"Your sister . . . the police call . . . the plane . . ."
Annie felt as though she had been shot out of a
cannon and was spinning in midair. Everything
was in slow motion, and she could feel herself reeling at the words.

"What did they say?" Annie managed to grind
out the words through the shards of glass in her
throat. Every word she formed was a physical
pain. "What happened? What did the police
SAY?" She was shouting at Magdalena and didn't
know it. And all Magdalena could do was sob.
"TELL ME, DAMMIT!" Annie shouted at her, as
Magdalena tried to tell her in English.

"I don't know . . . something happen . . . I call
her cell phone and she not answer . . . they say . . .
they say . . . the plane catch fire. It was the police
in New London."

"I'll call you back," Annie said, and hung up on
her. She finally got a police emergency number in
New London, that referred her to another number. A voice asked her who she was, and after she
told them, there was an interminable silence on
the other end of the phone.

"Are you nearby?" the voice wanted to know.

"No, I'm not nearby," Annie said, torn between
a sob and an urge to shout at this unknown
woman. Something terrible had happened. She
was praying they were only hurt. "I'm in New

York," she explained. "What happened to the plane?" She gave them the call numbers of Bill's plane, and a different voice came on the phone. He said he was a captain, and he told her what she didn't want to know and never wanted to hear. He said the plane had exploded on impact and there were no survivors. He asked her if she knew who was on the plane.

"My sister and her husband," Annie whispered, as she stared blindly into space. This hadn't happened. It wasn't possible. This couldn't happen to them. But it had. She had no idea what to say next so she thanked the captain and hung up. She told him he could contact her at her sister's home in Greenwich and gave him the number. And then she grabbed her purse and walked out of the apartment without even turning out the lights.

Later, she could not remember getting into her car or traveling to Greenwich in a driving rain. She had no memory of it whatsoever. The promised storm had hit New York. She left her car in the driveway in Greenwich and was drenched when she got to the house. Magdalena was crying in the kitchen. The kids were upstairs watching a movie, waiting for their parents to come home. And when they heard the door slam as Annie walked in, they came running to see their mom and dad, and what they saw instead was her, standing dripping in the living room, her hair plastered to her head, the tears running down her face like rain.

"Where are Mom and Dad?" Ted asked, looking confused, and Lizzie stared at her with wide eyes. The moment she saw Annie standing there, she knew, and her hand flew to her mouth.

"Mom and Dad . . . ," Lizzie said with a look of horror, and Annie nodded as she ran halfway up the stairs to them and put her arms around all three. They clung to her like a life raft in a stormy sea, as the realization hit Annie with the force of a wrecking ball. Now all three of them were hers.

Chapter 2

The next days were a total nightmare. She had to tell them. Lizzie was devastated. Ted hid in the garage after he heard the news. Katie cried inconsolably. And at first Annie had no idea what to do. She went to New London to speak to the police. The wreckage of Bill's plane was charred beyond recognition. There were no bodies, they had been blown to bits.

Somehow she managed to make the "arrangements." She held a dignified funeral for them, and half of Greenwich came. Bill's publishing associates came out from New York to pay their respects. And Annie had called her office and explained that she needed to take a week or two off and couldn't make the presentation.

She moved into Bill and Jane's house and went back to the city to get her things. The new apart-

ment she loved was history. It had only one bedroom, and she didn't want to uproot the children
so soon, so she'd have to commute to the city.
Magdalena agreed to move in. And Annie had to
adjust to the idea that suddenly she was a twenty-
six-year-old woman with three children. Jane and
Bill had talked to her about it, that if anything
happened to them, she would have to step in for
them. Bill had no close relatives, and Annie and
Jane's own parents were dead. There was no one to
take care of them now except Annie, and all four
of them had to make the best of it. There was no
other choice. And Annie's vow to Jane the night
before the funeral was to devote her life to their
children and do the best she could. She had no
idea how to be a mom, all she had ever been was a
fun aunt, and now she would have to learn. She
couldn't even imagine stepping into their shoes,
and she knew she was a poor substitute for parents
like Bill and Jane, but she was all they had.

Seth had the grace to wait until a week after the
funeral before he came to see her in Greenwich.
He took her to dinner at a quiet place. He told her
he was crazy about her, but he was twenty-nine
years old, and there was no way he could take on a
woman with three children. He said he had had a
terrific time with her for the past two months, but
this was way, way over his head. She said she un-

derstood. She didn't cry, she wasn't mad at him. She was numb. She said nothing after he explained the situation to her, and he drove her back to the house in silence. He tried to kiss her goodbye, and she turned her head away and walked into the house without a word to him. She had more important things to do now, like bring up three children. They had become a family overnight, and Seth wasn't part of it, and didn't want to be. She couldn't imagine a man who would. She had grown up instantly the moment the plane had hit the ground.

Nine months later, in June, at the end of the school year, Annie moved them into the city, to an apartment she had rented, not far from the one she had just moved into when her sister died. This one had three bedrooms. And she signed the kids up in school in New York. Lizzie had turned thirteen by then, Ted was nine, and Katie six. Since she had been with them, Annie had done nothing but rush from work to home, to be with the kids. She spent the weekends taking Katie to ballet and Ted to soccer games. She took Lizzie shopping. She started Ted at the orthodontist and went to school meetings when she wasn't working late. The architecture firm she worked for had been understanding about it. And with Magdalena covering for her, she managed to stay on top of her projects. And eventually she even got a promotion and a raise.

Bill and Jane had left their children comfortably provided for. Bill had made some good investments, the house in Greenwich sold for an excellent price, and so did the one on Martha's Vineyard, and there had been an insurance policy for the children. They had what they needed financially, if Annie was careful with it, but they didn't have a mom and dad. They had an aunt. They were patient with Annie while she learned. There were some bumps and some sad times for them all at first, but in time they all got used to the hand they'd been dealt. And Magdalena stayed.

In time, Annie got them through high school, through their first romances, and helped them apply to college. By the time he was fourteen Ted had decided to go to law school. Lizzie was obsessed with fashion and wanted to be a model for a while. And Kate had her mother's artistic talent, but unlike the rest of them, she marched to her own drummer. She used her allowance to get her ears pierced at thirteen, and then her belly button, to Annie's horror. She dyed her hair blue and then purple, and at eighteen she got a tattoo of a unicorn on the inside of her wrist, which must have hurt like hell when she got it. And she was a talented artist like her mother. She got accepted at Pratt School of Design and was a very capable illustrator. She looked like no one Annie had ever known. She was tiny, fiercely independent, and very brave. She had strong beliefs about everything, including politics, and argued with anyone who didn't agree with her, and wasn't afraid to stand alone. She had been a handful in her teens but eventually settled down once she got to college and moved into the dorm. Ted had his own apartment by then, and got a job after college, before he went to law school. Liz was working for **Elle**. Bringing up her sister's children had been Annie's vocation and full-time job. She had no other life but theirs and her work.

At thirty-five, Annie had opened her own architecture office, after nine years with the same firm. She loved what she did and preferred residential jobs to the big corporate ones she had done for years. After four years in her own firm, she had found her niche. And she was stunned by how much she missed the children when they moved out. It gave the term "empty nest" new meaning, and she filled the void in her life with more work instead of people.

She hadn't had a date for the first three years the

children lived with her, and after that there had been some minor relationships, but never a serious one. She didn't have time. She was too busy taking care of her nieces and nephew and establishing herself as an architect. There was no room for a man in her life. Her closest friend, Whitney Coleman, scolded her for it regularly. They had been friends since college, and Whitney was married to a doctor in New Jersey, with three kids of her own, younger than the Marshall children. She had been a source of endless support for Annie, and invaluable advice, and now all she wanted was for Annie to think of herself. She had thought of everyone else for thirteen years. The time had moved like a bullet in the night. The early years had been a blur, but after that, Annie had truly enjoyed the children she had raised. She had lived up to the vow she had made Jane and she had gotten the children grown up, and all three were doing well.

"Now what?" Whitney said to her after Kate moved into the dorm. "What are you going to do for yourself?" It was a question Annie hadn't asked herself in thirteen years.

"What am I supposed to do? Stand on a street corner and whistle for a guy, like a cab?" She was thirty-nine years old and not panicked about being single. She didn't mind. Things had turned out differently than she'd planned, but she was happy.

The kids were all good people, her architecture firm was a success, and she had more work than she could handle. She was doing well, and so were they. Ted had just applied to law school and had gotten a new apartment with a friend from college, and at twenty-five, Liz had just landed a job at **Vogue**, after working for three years at **Elle**. Each of them was on a career path. Annie had done her job. The only thing she didn't have was a life of her own, other than work. They were her life, and she insisted that was all she needed.

"That's ridiculous!" Whitney said irreverently. "You're not a hundred years old, for chrissake. And you have no excuse not to date now—the kids are grown up." She had fixed Annie up with several blind dates, none of which had worked out, and Annie said she didn't care.

"If I'm meant to meet a guy, it'll happen one of these days," she said philosophically. "Besides, I'm too set in my ways now. And I want to spend holidays and vacations with the kids. A man would interfere with that. And it might upset them."

"Don't you want more in your life than just being an aunt?" Whitney asked her sadly. It didn't seem fair to Whitney that Annie had sacrificed her own life for her sister's children, but she didn't seem to mind, and she was happy as she was. Her own biological clock had run out of batteries years before, without a sound. She had three children she loved and didn't want more.

"I'm happy," Annie reassured her, and she seemed to be. The two women met for lunch when Whitney came into the city, usually to go shopping. And Annie went to New Jersey for the weekend once in a while, after the kids were gone, but most of the time she was too busy working on weekends to go anywhere. And her work was beautiful. There were several handsome townhouses on the Upper East Side that she had renovated, spectacular penthouses, and several beautiful estates in the Hamptons, and one in Bronxville. And she had turned a number of brownstones into offices for clients. Her business was booming and continued to grow. She had just turned down a job in Los Angeles, and another in London, because she said she didn't have time to travel. She was happy working in New York. And basically she was happy with her life, and it showed. She had done exactly what she wanted and what she'd promised. She had accompanied her nieces and nephew from childhood to young adulthood, and she didn't mind the sacrifices she'd had to make at all. And by the time she was forty-two, Annie was one of the most successful architects in New York, and loved practicing on her own.

It was the day before Thanksgiving, on a freezing-cold morning, as Annie walked through the gutted interior of a townhouse on East Sixty-ninth Street with a couple who had hired her two months before. The house represented an enormous investment for them, and they wanted Annie to turn it into a spectacular home. It was hard to visualize as they climbed over the rubble the workmen had left after taking out several walls. Annie was showing them the proportions of the newly enlarged living room and dining room and where the grand staircase was going to go. She had a unique talent for combining ancient and contemporary designs and making it look both avant-garde and warm, although it was hard to imagine right now.

The husband was questioning her intensely about the costs, and his wife was looking anxious now that she saw the state of total chaos the house was in. Annie had promised them it would be complete in a year.

"Do you really think you can get us in by next fall?" Alicia Ebersohl said nervously.

"This contractor is very good. He's never let me

down yet," Annie said, smiling pleasantly at them. She looked calm and unruffled, as she stepped over several beams. She was wearing gray slacks, stylish black leather boots, and a heavy coat with a fur-lined hood. She still looked considerably younger than she was.

"He'll probably bring it in at twice the price. I had no idea we were going to destroy this much of the house," Harry Ebersohl commented with a look of dismay.

"We're just making room. You're going to need these walls for your art." She had been working closely with their interior designer, and everything was in control. "Three months from now you'll start to see the beauty of the house emerge."

"I hope so," Alicia said softly, but she no longer looked so sure. They had loved their friends' house that Annie had done, and had begged her to take this job, and once Annie saw the house she couldn't resist, although she already had too much on her plate as it was. "I hope we didn't make a mistake with this house," Alicia said, as her husband shook his head in despair.

"It's a little late to be saying that now," he grumbled as they went back downstairs and headed toward the front door. When they opened it, they stepped out into an icy blast, and Annie pulled the fur hood up over her blond hair. Both Ebersohls had already commented to each other how pretty she was, and that she apparently was good at what she did too, from everything they'd heard.

"What are you doing for Thanksgiving?" Annie said easily, as she walked them to their car with the plans under her arm.

"Our kids are coming home tonight." Alicia smiled. Annie knew that both of them were in college, one at Princeton, and the other one at Dartmouth, a girl and a boy.

"So are mine." Annie smiled happily. She couldn't wait. All three had promised to stay with her over Thanksgiving, as they always did. Her favorite times were when they came home.

"I didn't know you had children." Alicia looked surprised as Annie nodded. She never talked about her personal life, just the job. She was the consummate professional in every way, which was why they had hired her. The information that she had children startled both Ebersohls.

"I have three. Actually, they're my nieces and nephew. My sister died in an accident sixteen years ago, and I inherited her kids. They're grown up now. The oldest is an editor at **Vogue**, my nephew is in his second year at law school, and the youngest is in college. I miss them like crazy, so it's a treat for me when they come home." Annie was smiling as she said it, and the Ebersohls looked amazed.

"What a wonderful thing to do. Not everyone would have taken that on. You must have been very young." She hardly looked thirty now, but they knew her age from her credentials on her website.

"I was very young." Annie smiled at them. "We all grew up together, and it's been a great blessing for me. I'm very proud of them." They chatted for a few more minutes, and then the Ebersohls got in their car and drove away. Harry was still looking worried, but Annie had promised him the work would come in at the price she'd quoted them, and Alicia was talking excitedly about the grand staircase when they left.

Annie glanced at her watch as she hailed a cab. She had five minutes to get to Seventy-ninth and Fifth to meet with a new client. Jim Watson had just bought a co-op and didn't know exactly what he wanted. All he knew was that he wanted it to be fabulous, and he wanted Annie to make magic with it. She was meeting with him to give him some ideas. Jim was recently divorced and wanted a fantastic bachelor pad. It was a shift of mental gears as she rode uptown, and just before she got there, her cell phone rang. It was Liz. She sounded nervous and rushed. She always was. She had recently become the jewelry editor at **Vogue**, and she had just gotten back from Milan. She had come home to be with Annie and her siblings for Thanksgiving. It was a sacred date for all four of them. Annie was going to cook the turkey as she did every year.

"How was Milan?" Annie asked her, happy to hear her voice. She worried about her. Liz worked so hard, and she was always so stressed. She never had time to eat and had been much too thin for the past three years. It was the look everyone aspired to at **Vogue**.

"It was crazy but fun. I ran around for four days. We spent the weekend in Venice, which is dismal in the winter. And I spent a day in Paris on the way back. I picked out some great pieces for the shoot I'm doing next week." If possible, she worked even harder than Annie, or just as hard. "Can I bring Jean-Louis tomorrow?" she asked Annie, and knew she would say yes. The question was just a formality, out of respect. Annie had welcomed their friends and significant others for all the years they'd lived together and since. "I didn't know he was coming. He just flew in today. He has a shoot here this weekend." They had met while working together in Paris, and Jean-Louis kept a loft in New York for his frequent visits. He was a successful photographer and almost identical to all the men Lizzie had had in her life. They were either photographers or male models, always

29

handsome, never too deep, and Liz never got too attached. Annie often wondered if losing her parents had made Liz gun-shy about getting too close to anyone. Her romances never lasted long. She was surprised that Jean-Louis had been around for a while. Lizzie had been going out with him for six months.

"Of course you can bring him." Annie had only met him once. He seemed nice enough, but she hadn't been too impressed.

"What time should we come?"

"Same as every year. Come at noon, lunch at one. Or you can come home tonight if you want. Ted and Katie are spending the weekend."

"I promised Jean-Louis I'd stay with him," Liz said, sounding apologetic. "I'm going to help him with his shoot, unofficially. I'm pulling some jewelry for him today."

"He's a lucky guy," Annie said, and meant it, and not just because Liz was helping him with his work. Liz always gave better than she got. The men she got involved with were always selfish and spoiled, and Annie worried that she sold herself short. She was a beautiful, talented, intelligent young woman. It shocked Annie sometimes when she realized that at twenty-eight, Liz was two years older than she had been when she inherited all of them. And in some ways Liz seemed so young.

And she never seemed to think about marriage or settling down. Annie realized that she hadn't set them much of an example on that score, since all she did herself was work, and take care of them when they were young. They had rarely if ever seen her with a date. She had kept the few men in her life well away from them, and there hadn't been many anyway, and none she had cared about seriously. The last man she had been crazy about had been Seth, sixteen years before. She had run into him once a few years ago—he was married, lived in Connecticut, and had four kids. He had tried to explain to her how bad he felt that he hadn't stepped up to the plate for her when her sister died, and she had laughed and brushed it off and told him she was fine. But it had given her a little flutter to see him. He was as handsome as he'd been before, and she had told Whitney about it. It all seemed like ancient history now.

Liz was in the process of apologizing to Annie that Jean-Louis hadn't brought decent clothes with him, since he'd be working, and Annie assured her it didn't matter. None of the men in Liz's life ever owned a suit. Whether successful photographers or famous models, they always showed up in ragged clothes, with long hair and beards. It was the look she seemed to like, or the one most prevalent in her milieu. Annie had grown used to it over the years, although she would have loved to see her with a decently dressed guy with a haircut, just once.

In contrast, Liz was always stylish beyond belief and gave Annie fashion tips and even occasionally brought her clothes. It was always fun to see what Liz would wear. Annie's style was simpler and more practical than hers. She felt too old now for wild clothes, and she had to wear things she could get around her job sites in without freezing or falling on her face in stiletto heels. Liz was tall, like her late mother and her aunt, and never wore anything less than six-inch heels. They were considered running shoes at the magazines where she had worked.

"See you tomorrow," Lizzie said, as Annie arrived at the address on Fifth Avenue and took the elevator up to the top floor where Jim Watson was waiting for her, looking slightly dazed. He was suddenly terrified that the place was too big for him, and he said he had no idea how to decorate it without his ex-wife's help. Annie assured him she would take care of everything for him, and she took some sketches out of her briefcase, and as he looked at them, he smiled. Annie had imagined the perfect bachelor pad for him, even before he knew what he wanted himself. He was thrilled. And she walked through each room describing it to him, and bringing her ideas to life.

"You're amazing!" he said happily, and unlike Harry Ebersohl, he wasn't worried about the cost. He just wanted something that would impress his friends and the women he wanted to date. And better than that, Annie was going to give him a home. She promised him a delivery date of nine months. And they stood on the terrace together looking out at Central Park as it started to snow.

He was forty-five years old, and one of the richest men in New York. He was looking at Annie with interest, as she talked to him about the apartment. She was completely oblivious to the way he was looking at her. Any other single woman her age would have been doing her best to charm him, but she was always professional with her clients. All he was to her was a job. It made no difference to her whatsoever that he had a yacht in St. Barts and his own plane. She was interested in the apartment, not the man. Annie was friendly but totally businesslike in her manner. He suspected that she had a husband or boyfriend, but he didn't dare ask.

Annie left an hour after she arrived. She promised to send him plans within two weeks and wished him a happy Thanksgiving. She was totally clear on what he wanted and what she was going to do for him. He told her he was leaving for Aspen that night, to spend the holiday with friends. And he stood at the window, watching the snow fall on Central Park after she left.

The apartment was silent and empty when Annie got home, just as it was every night. It was so different now than when the children still lived there. There were none of Kate's clothes on the floor, strewn around the living room. Ted's TV wasn't on. Liz wasn't dashing in and out, brandishing a curling iron, late for whatever she was doing, with no time to eat. The fridge wasn't full. Kate's briefly vegan meals weren't left all over the sink. The music wasn't on. Their friends weren't there. The phone didn't ring. The house was empty, neat, and clean, and Annie still wasn't used to it, even three years after Kate had left for college. Annie suspected that it was a void she would never be able to fill. Her sister had given her the greatest gift in life, and time had slowly taken it from her. She knew that it was right for them to grow up and leave, but she hated it anyway, and nothing made her happier than when they came home.

She went out to the kitchen and started organizing things for the next day. She had just stacked the good plates on the kitchen counter, getting ready to set the table, when she heard the front door slam and what sounded like a load of bricks being dumped in her front hall. She gave a start at the wall-shuddering sound and stuck her head out the kitchen door, as Kate dumped her backpack on the floor where her books lay. She had an enormous artist's portfolio in one hand and stood grinning at Annie in a black miniskirt, a black hooded sweatshirt with a shocking pink skull on it, and silver combat boots that Annie knew she had found at a garage sale somewhere. She was wearing black-and white-striped tights that made her look like a punk Raggedy Ann, and her short jet-black hair stood up all over her head. What saved the whole look was her exquisite face. She came bounding across the living room and threw her arms around Annie's neck. The two women hugged as Annie beamed. This was what she had lived for, for sixteen years.

"Hi, Annie," Kate said happily, then planted a kiss on her cheek and bounded toward the fridge. The look of bliss on her aunt's face said it all.

"Am I happy to see you! Are you vegan this week?" Annie teased her.

"No, I gave it up. I missed meat too much." She helped herself to a banana, sat down on one of the kitchen chairs, and smiled lovingly at her aunt. "Where's everyone?" she asked as she peeled the banana and stuffed a chunk of it into her mouth. The way she did it made her look about five years old instead of twenty-one.

"Ted should be here any minute. And Lizzie is coming tomorrow. She's bringing Jean-Louis." Katie looked unimpressed, went to get a CD out of her backpack, and put it in the machine that had been silent since the last time she'd been there. It was one by the Killers, which sounded like the rest of her music to Annie.

"I got a new tattoo, wanna see?" she asked proudly as Annie groaned.

"Can I still ground you at twenty-one?" Annie asked as Katie pulled up her sleeve to show off a colored Tweety Bird on her forearm. "You should get one too," Kate teased her. She knew how much her aunt hated them. "I designed it myself. I did some designs for the tattoo parlor, and they gave me this one for free."

"I'd have paid you double not to do it. How are you going to feel about having Tweety Bird on your arm when you're fifty?"

"I'll worry about it then," Kate said, looking around the familiar kitchen, and obviously happy to be home. "I'll set the table," she volunteered. And when Annie went to get the tablecloth out of a drawer in the dining room, she saw Katie's belongings spread all over the front hall. It looked good to her. The house was much too pristine without them. She loved the mess, the noise, the music, the funny hair, the silver boots. It was everything that she missed.

They were setting the table together when Ted walked in half an hour later. He was wearing a heavy parka, a gray crew-neck sweater, jeans, and running shoes and had come straight from school. His hair was short, and he was clean shaven, a tall, handsome boy with dark hair and light gray eyes. He looked preppy and wholesome and of no possible relation to Katie, with her wild clothes, row of pierced earrings, and brand-new Tweety Bird tattoo. She showed it to him, and he made a face. The girls Ted went out with were always blond and blue eyed and looked like his mother and aunt. It was hard to believe that he and Katie had grown up in the same house.

He gave his aunt a warm hug and turned the TV on to a hockey game. He didn't want to miss the end. They ordered pizza for dinner, and the three of them laughed and chatted at the kitchen table when it came. Ted talked about law school, and Annie showed them some of the work she'd brought home in her portfolio, and it was very good. She had real talent. The TV and music were both on. The table was set for Thanksgiving, and as Annie looked at the two young people in her kitchen, all was well in her world. Katie's things were still in a heap in the front hall at midnight, when Annie finally picked them up and took them to her room. There was a time when she would have complained about it and scolded Kate for the mess she made. Now it warmed her heart to see it, and she was just happy to have them home.

Chapter 3

Annie was up before dawn the next morning, moving silently around the kitchen, as she made the stuffing, put it in the turkey, and then slid the huge bird into the oven. She checked the dining room, and the table she and Katie had set the night before looked lovely. She was back in bed by seven, and decided to get a little more sleep before they all got up. She knew that Ted and Katie would sleep late.

Annie managed to get two more hours' sleep before her friend Whitney called and woke her at nine.

"Did I wake you? You're lucky. The boys have been driving me crazy for the past two hours. They've already had two breakfasts, the one I made them, and the one they made themselves." Annie smiled when she heard her and stretched in

39

her bed. She even slept better when the kids were home. She could no longer imagine what her life would have been like without them. Whitney always said that without her two nieces and nephew, Annie probably would have been married and had kids of her own. Annie wasn't as sure. She might have just concentrated on her career. Since Seth, no Prince Charming had ever come along. At least not so far. Just a few men she had gotten briefly involved with but never fallen in love with. And within a short time the relationships had fallen apart. She had too much else to do to devote herself to a man, and their existence in her life always interfered with her main commitment, to her sister's children. There had been no room for them and a man too. "Are all three of them home?" Whitney asked her.

"No, just Ted and Katie. Liz is staying with her boyfriend."

"Is this one serious?" She would have loved to have a daughter and envied Annie the two girls. All her boys wanted to do was play sports. She missed having a daughter to fuss over, but hadn't dared try again for fear of having a fourth son, and always said that that much testosterone under one roof would have done her in. Three sons and a husband were enough for her.

"He looks like all the others," Annie said, referring to Jean-Louis. "He commutes between New York and Paris, and Liz works so hard she doesn't see him much. She's focused on her career."

"Guess who she takes after," Whitney teased her. "You've set a lousy example to these kids. It's about time you gave them a healthy role model and found a guy."

"I keep writing my name and phone number in public bathrooms, but no one calls."

"That's pathetic. Fred has a friend I want you to meet. He's a really nice guy. A surgeon. Why don't you come on New Year's Eve? He'll be here."

"That's not a night for blind dates. Besides, I don't want to leave the kids." It had been her battle cry for years.

"Are you kidding? They'll probably all be out with friends. They don't want to spend New Year's Eve with you. At least I hope not."

"I don't know their plans," Annie said vaguely. She didn't want to meet a stranger on New Year's Eve. It would be too depressing. Annie had had too many blind dates over the years, and none of them had panned out. Friends had been fixing her up with losers for years.

"Well, keep it in mind, because they're going to ditch you for their friends, I promise. I'd be surprised if they didn't. You can spend the night with us." Whitney and Fred gave a New Year's Eve party every year, but it was never fun for Annie. Everyone was married, except for the creeps they set her up with. And as much as she loved Whitney, and had for years, being the wife of a doctor in New Jersey didn't make for an interesting social life. Annie always wound up feeling like the odd man out at Whitney's parties, or a freak for being single at forty-two. People just didn't understand how busy she had been for all those years. And now that the kids were grown up, she was busy with her business. She had no time to go out looking for a man and no longer really cared.

"You've done what you promised your sister. Now give yourself a break. Come to New Year's Eve."

"I'll let you know," Annie said vaguely. She had the unpleasant feeling that Whitney was going to insist. She usually did. "So who's coming to Thanksgiving?" she said, trying to change the subject and distract Whitney from her own nonexistent personal life.

"The usual suspects. Fred's sister and her husband and kids, and his parents. Her twins destroy my house. You're lucky yours are civilized and grown up."

"Believe me, I miss the stage you're at with yours," Annie said nostalgically, with a wistful tone in her voice.

"You just don't remember what it was like. God save me from teenage boys." Whitney sounded rueful, and they laughed. "I'll come in for lunch next week. And I want you to think about New Year's Eve. He's a great guy."

"I'm sure he is. I just don't have time." Or the desire to meet another one of Fred's dreary friends. They just weren't fun, and there was no reason to think that this one would be any different. They never were. If she was going to fall for a man, Annie wanted it to be someone great. Otherwise, why bother? She had decided years before that she'd rather sit home alone than go out with a dud, just for the sake of going out. And everyone tried too hard on New Year's Eve and drank too much, including Fred. Whitney thought he walked on water, which was nice. Annie's role models for relationships were her late sister and brother-in-law, who had been madly in love until the end. She didn't want less than that for herself or even for their kids. She had talked about them a lot to their children over the years, and there were photos of Jane and Bill everywhere. She had kept their memory alive for all of them.

Annie got up to go check on the turkey, and Ted wandered in a few minutes later in pajama bottoms and a T-shirt, looking like an overgrown boy. At twenty-four, he was a handsome man, like his father. And when she checked, the turkey was looking good and turning brown.

"Do you need help?" Ted offered, as he poured himself a glass of orange juice and handed one to his aunt.

"I think I'm fine. You can help me carve."

"That's good. It's great being here. I get tired of living with three guys at my apartment. They're all such slobs."

"Like your sister," Annie said with a rueful smile as they sat down at the kitchen table.

"Actually they're worse than Kate." Ted grinned.

"That's scary," Annie said, as her younger niece walked into the room. Her spiky hair was standing up straight, and she was wearing a flannel night-gown with skulls all over it.

Annie made them both scrambled eggs and then basted the turkey, as the two young people thanked her for the breakfast and devoured it.

"It's nice to be home," Kate said happily, as Annie smiled at her and leaned over and kissed her.

"It's nice for me too," Annie said softly. "This place is a tomb without you."

"You need to meet a guy," Kate said firmly, and Annie rolled her eyes.

"You sound like Whitney. She says hi by the way."

"Hi to her," Kate said easily, and then Annie saw that she had Tinkerbell on the other forearm.

"What is **that**?" Ted commented with a look of disapproval that his sister was familiar with. "A tribute to Disney?"

"You're just jealous," Katie said, and then put her plate in the dishwasher. "I think Annie should get a tattoo. It would give her a whole new look."

"What's wrong with my old look? Besides, it would scare my clients."

"I'm sure they'd love it," Katie insisted. "Don't listen to Mr. Clean here. He wouldn't know style if it bit him on the ass. He's stuck in 1950. Leave it to Beaver."

"That's better than the cartoon fest on your arms. What's next? Cinderella or Snow White?"

"I think I should get an eagle on my chest," Annie said pensively, as Katie grinned.

"I'll design it for you if you want. You could do a butterfly on your back. I did a great one for the tattoo parlor last week. They've already used it for two people."

"There's a career goal for you," Ted commented drily. "Tattoo artist. I'll bet Mom and Dad would have loved that."

"What do you know?" Kate looked annoyed by the comment. "Maybe they would have thought law school was boring. They had more pizzazz than that."

"They would have been proud of you both,"

Annie intervened in the discussion, and basted the bird in the oven again. "We should probably get dressed." It was eleven o'clock by then.

"No rush. Liz will be an hour late and act surprised. She always does," Katie commented.

"She has a lot to do." Annie defended her.

"She just can't tell time. Who's she bringing?" Ted asked with interest.

"The photographer she's dating. Jean-Louis."

"Oh. A frog. He can watch football with me."

"Lucky guy," Kate teased her older brother. "Football is such a redneck sport." Ted looked murderous for a minute, and then he laughed. Katie had known how to get his goat ever since she could talk, and it was no different now.

A few minutes later they all disappeared to their rooms and emerged again at noon. Ted was wearing gray slacks, a blazer, and a tie and looked heartbreakingly like his father to Annie. They were almost clones. And Katie looked like a more dressed-up version of herself. She was wearing a black leather miniskirt, a black fur-trimmed sweater that Annie had bought her, and black tights and high heels, and she'd put gel on her hair to spike it more, and wore makeup, which she rarely did. She looked beautiful, while still being faithful to her very individual style. And Annie was wearing a soft brown cashmere sweater-dress and high heels.

It was nearly one o'clock when Liz walked into the apartment. She was wearing black leather pants, a white Chanel jacket, and towering high heels. Her blond hair was pulled back in a sleek bun, and she was wearing small diamond earrings that she had borrowed from the shoot, and they were glittering fiercely on her ears. The man who walked in behind her looked like a homeless person she had picked up on the street. He was wearing torn sneakers, jeans with holes in them, and a black hooded sweatshirt with holes in it too. His uncombed hair was pulled back in a ponytail, and he had a beard. He was smiling and relaxed as he walked into the room, and he had brought flowers for Annie. His manners were impeccable, and his appearance was totally out of sync with Liz's. She looked like one of the models from the magazine, and he looked like he had been shipwrecked for a year. And his French accent lent charm to his appearance. He kissed Annie and Katie on both cheeks and shook Ted's hand. He was personable and friendly, and within minutes, they all forgot how he looked. He was one of the most successful young photographers in Paris, and in great demand in New York. He didn't seem to care at all about what he wore, nor did Liz. She was obviously happy to be with him, as Annie silently wished her niece didn't have a weakness for men who looked like that. They all stood around the kitchen while Ted carved the turkey, and then they sat down in the dining room, as Kate lit the candles, and Liz and Annie brought in the food. It was a feast. And by the time they got up from the table, they could hardly move.

"I think it was your best Thanksgiving ever," Ted complimented Annie, and she beamed. The turkey had been perfect. She had improved her culinary skills over the years, mostly by trial and error.

Ted turned to Jean-Louis then and invited him to watch football with him. The young photographer was only a few years older than Ted but was far more sophisticated. He had talked about his five-year-old son at dinner. He had never been married to the boy's mother but had lived with her for two years, and they had remained friends. And he said he saw the boy as often as he could. He was planning to spend Christmas with him. And Liz was meeting Jean-Louis in Paris the day after. She had a major jewelry shoot there after the first of the year, and she was going to spend a week with Jean-Louis between Christmas and New Year's. Annie was intrigued to hear he had a son and wondered how Liz felt about it, but she didn't seem to mind. It seemed so grown-up for Liz to be dating a man with a child. But she was old enough to take it on if that was what she wanted. Annie wasn't quite sure. Liz seemed no more serious about Jean-Louis than she had about the look-alikes who came before him. And he seemed no more serious about her, although he was very flirtatious with her, and Annie found them kissing passionately in the kitchen. She suspected the relationship was about sex and enjoying each other's company. It made her feel old to see it. And for a moment she wondered if Whitney was right. Annie had put that part of her life away on a shelf and forgotten all about it. But it seemed like too much trouble to remember. Those games belonged to youth. Watching Jean-Louis and Liz suddenly made her feel ancient. She had traded her own youth for surrogate motherhood to her sister's children. Even now it seemed like the right thing to do, and a fair trade, and she didn't regret it.

Ted and Jean-Louis went to watch TV in the living room, while Jean-Louis extolled the virtues of soccer, but he seemed to enjoy the American sport too. There was much hooting and cheering and yelling from in front of the TV, while the three women cleared the table, and Liz commented to her aunt and sister what a nice man Jean-Louis was. Kate was inclined to agree and liked his looks, and Annie admitted he was a little too scruffy for her, but she knew that was the desirable look of the moment. She had seen enough of Liz's friends to be aware of it, and it no longer shocked her, but it didn't appeal to her either. She preferred Ted's clean-cut style to Jean-Louis's.

The three women stood in the kitchen and talked while they cleaned up, and by the time they finished, the football game was over. Jean-Louis commented about what a fantastic meal it had been, the best he had ever eaten. And he won Katie's heart by admiring her tattoos. They all agreed it had been a perfect Thanksgiving, and Jean-Louis seemed to revel in the warm atmosphere. And he touched Annie by saying what a wonderful woman Liz was. It was obvious that he was very taken with her, and he charmed everyone. After they left, Ted, Annie, and Kate watched a movie on a DVD, and it was midnight when they finally got up to go to bed.

Annie came in to say goodnight to Kate a few minutes later and was surprised to find her lying on her bed, still dressed, talking on the phone. She sounded animated and looked happy, and Annie discreetly left the room. She went to say goodnight to Ted, and he kissed her and thanked her for the wonderful Thanksgiving. He seemed grateful to be home. And when she went back to Kate's room, she was off the phone, with a mysterious expression. She looked like the proverbial Cheshire cat.

"New romance?" Annie asked her. She didn't like to pry, but she tried to keep abreast of what was happening in their lives. Kate nodded vaguely in answer and didn't meet her eyes.

"Maybe."

"Do I know him?"

"No. Just someone I know from school. It's not a big deal." But her eyes said something different. Kate had always been very private and somewhat secretive, and more inclined to serious relationships than casual ones. She had gone out with the same boy all through high school, but they broke up when he went to college on the West Coast. She hadn't had a serious boyfriend in three years, but something told Annie that this one might be. Katie looked dreamy eyed as she kissed her aunt goodnight.

"Happy Thanksgiving," Annie said as she kissed her niece, and Katie just smiled.

Chapter 4

As it had been for several years now, it was an adjustment for Annie when her nieces and nephew left after the Thanksgiving weekend. Ted went back to his apartment, and Kate to her dorm on Sunday night. The house felt like a tomb, and the only thing that cheered her was knowing that they would stay with her again over Christmas, which was only a month away. After so many years of living with them, and as her main focus and only personal life, she lived for the times when they were together. She hated to admit it to anyone, even Whitney, but it was true.

It was a relief to get back to work on Monday morning. She had four client meetings set up in one day and visited two of her job sites during lunch. And she didn't get back to the apartment until eight that night. She was so tired, she looked at some plans and notes she'd made during meetings with clients, and then took a bath and went to bed. She was almost too tired to miss the kids, never bothered to eat dinner, and barely noticed the darkened rooms and silence in the apartment. It was the drug she had always used to counter loneliness and pain, total immersion in work.

The Monday after the Thanksgiving weekend was a busy day for Liz too. She had an important jewelry shoot for the March issue, and she had pulled major pieces from all over the world. The theme was Spring, and all the jewelry she was using was in flower designs, leaves, and roots, from their most important jewelry advertisers, and some new designers that Liz had found herself. There were three armed guards at the shoot, and four of the currently most important models in the world. One of them had agreed to pose naked, literally covered in jewels. And the photographer they were using was major too. They were having fun on the set, trying things on and playing with them during breaks.

Jean-Louis stopped by when he finished his own shoot. Liz and her group were working late.

"Pretty shot," he said admiringly from the sidelines, as he stood next to Liz. She was wearing black leggings and a T-shirt, her long blond hair pulled back in a ponytail, no makeup, and high-heeled Givenchy sandals they had made especially for her. She looked tired and stressed. They had been working since eight o'clock that morning, and she'd been at the photographer's studio at six to set things up. Usually she would have had an assistant do it, but the pieces they were using were of such enormous value that she felt she should be there herself.

Jean-Louis put his arms around her and kissed her. They had been dating for months, with frequent breaks since they lived in separate cities, and they both traveled constantly for work. They tried to get together in Paris or New York once or twice a month. It seemed to work, and neither of them had time for more of a relationship. They were both rising stars in their fields.

Liz's secret dream was to be editor of **Vogue** one day, and she knew that getting there was still years away. She had to make her mark as an outstanding editor first. And the stories she did now were key. Jean-Louis was successful but more relaxed about his work. He told her that she took life too seriously, but Liz always had. Life had gotten very serious for her on a September Sunday when she was twelve. And she had been intense about everything ever since. The one thing she never did was relax. She never took anything for granted, and she never got too attached. The only people she felt she couldn't live without were her brother, sister, and aunt. The men in her life came and went. Jean-Louis had accused her several times of being cool and detached. The Ice Princess, he called her. She wasn't, but she was standoffish with men. It was easy to understand why. She had told him she had lost her parents as a child, but she never went into detail. Her night terrors afterward, the nightmares she had had and sometimes still did, the years of therapy to get over the loss, were none of his business. All she wanted from Jean-Louis was to have fun, and she liked that they worked in the same field. The men she went out with were always related to fashion. Other people didn't understand the crazy world in which she lived, and how passionate she was about her work. Her aunt Annie felt the same way about what she did and had been a role model for Liz as she grew up. Her directive to Liz had been to follow her dream and do whatever it took to do it well. Liz had always tried to live by those rules and was highly respected in the world of fashion as a result. Her ideas were innovative, bold, and fresh.

It was nearly midnight when they took the final shot. Jean-Louis had gone home to his loft by then, and Lizzie promised to come by when they finished. There was a cheer in the studio when the photographer shot the last roll and gave a war whoop of satisfaction with the last shot. The pictures they got were going to be great.

It took Liz and two assistants another hour to wrap up all the jewels and mark the boxes. The three armed guards accompanied her back to her office, where she put everything in the safe. She got to Jean-Louis's place at two. He was listening to music and drinking a glass of wine as he waited for her. And he was standing naked in his living room, with his long, lean splendid body, when Liz helped herself to the key he kept behind the fire extinguisher outside his door and walked in. He hid it there because he was always losing it. Half the models in town knew where to find that key. But for now the key was only for her. She didn't mind how little time they spent together, but the one thing she cared about was that they were exclusive to each other and slept with no one else. And Jean-Louis had agreed. He had no need for a long-term commitment. When he wanted a different woman, he left and found one. But neither of them had any desire to go elsewhere for now. However inadequate Annie thought he was for her, Lizzie was satisfied. Jean-Louis fit perfectly into her high-flying, fast-moving, glamorous world, and he was just as comfortable with her.

He smiled as she walked in, and silently held out a glass of wine. And as she came to him, and he stripped her thin layer of clothes off, he became rapidly aroused. He lowered her gently onto the couch, and they made love there. They were both breathless and sated when they were through.

"You drive me crazy," he said happily, his head thrown back, as she ran a graceful finger along his beard, down his neck, and then let her fingers drift slowly down. "Don't . . . ," he said, catching her hand and smiling at her. "If we make love again, I'll die."

"No, you won't," she whispered, and kissed him where it mattered most. They worked hard, played hard, and the sex was great. Better because they weren't together all the time. There was still excitement and mystery and hunger between them, which fueled the fires of their passion. He had never told her that he loved her, and she never wondered if he did. She wasn't ready for that, with anyone, and never had been. She cared about him and liked him and enjoyed him, but at twenty-eight she knew she had never been in love. Something always held her back. The fear of loss. This way she had nothing to lose if he ever left her, except great sex. She would have missed him, but she never wanted to experience the wrenching agony of real loss again, and she did everything to avoid it. She called the kind of relationship she wanted "intimacy without pain," but her therapist said that there was no such thing. Not real intimacy, or love. There is no love without risk, she had said, which was precisely why Liz had never loved any man. She was committed but never owned. And when it no longer felt right, or got too close, she moved on. Her aloofness was a challenge to most men, and to Jean-Louis. They wanted to possess her and to make her fall in love. She never did. Or not yet. She wondered if one day she would, or if that part of her had died when her parents' plane went down when she was twelve, the part of her that was willing to be vulnerable and take risk.

"I'm crazy for you, Liz," Jean-Louis said, as they started to make love again in the candlelight in his loft.

"Me too," she said softly, her blond hair falling like a curtain across her face, with one enormous blue eye peeking through at him. She was happy he hadn't said he loved her. It was a step she didn't want to take. He wasn't in love with her either, he was in like and lust with her, which was all she wanted from him. She put her lips on his then, and they kissed. They fell asleep in each other's arms afterward, on the couch, as the candles flickered and gently went out, as Liz lay against Jean-Louis and sighed peacefully in her sleep.

Ted's Monday after the Thanksgiving weekend was not a happy one. It was one of those days when everything went wrong. The water had been turned off in his building for an emergency repair, so he couldn't take a shower when he got up. His roommates had finished the coffee and not replaced it. He missed two buses and then a subway, when he tried that to get to school, and was late to class. And when the assistant professor handed back their papers on a quiz from the week before, he had gotten several answers wrong and got a miserable grade. The guy sitting next to him had BO, and by the time class was over, he was in a rotten mood, from the lousy grade on the quiz he had actually studied for, and the unpleasant seat.

He was leaving the class with a glum expression, when the teacher signaled him. The professor who normally taught the class was on sabbatical, writing a book, and she had taken over his duties for a year. Her name was Pattie Sears. She was an attractive woman with long curly hair who wore jeans and Birkenstocks with socks and T-shirts that showed off her breasts. He had noticed it when he was bored in class. She looked to be in her early thirties and was sexy in a wholesome, natural way.

"I'm sorry about the grade on the quiz," she said sympathetically. "Contracts are a bitch." Ted smiled at what she said. "I flunked them the first time I took the class myself. Some of the rules just don't make sense."

"I guess not. I studied for it. I have to read those chapters again," Ted said diligently. Throughout his entire school and college career, he had always had good grades. And other than the recent quiz, he was doing well. He was in his second year at NYU Law School.

"Would you like some help? Sometimes if you prepare it with someone to give you some guidance, it helps. I don't mind." She had warned them of a quiz the following week, and he didn't want another bad grade.

"I don't want to bother you," he said, looking embarrassed. She had put on a heavy jacket and a woolen hat. There was something homespun and friendly about her. He could easily imagine her chopping wood and building a fire in Vermont, or making soup from scratch. "I'll read the chapters, and if I feel like I'm not getting it, I'll ask you after the next class."

"Why don't you come by tonight?" she said, and

her eyes were warm and kind. Ted hesitated, and now he felt even ruder turning her down. She was offering her help, and he didn't want her to feel that he didn't appreciate the gesture, but it seemed strange to go to her house. They had never spoken to each other outside of class. "My kids are asleep by eight. Why don't you come by at nine? We can knock out the prep for the quiz in an hour. I'll give you some pointers about contracts, and show you some things that are key."

"All right," he said hesitantly, not wanting to intrude on her private life. She had already jotted down her address on a piece of paper and handed it to him. He saw that she lived in the East Village, not far from the university, in a run-down neighborhood. "You're sure you don't mind?" he asked, feeling like a kid. She seemed so motherly to him, although she probably wasn't that much older than he was. "I won't stay long."

"Don't be silly. Once the kids are in bed, I'll have plenty of time." He nodded and thanked her again, and his day went better after that. He was relieved that she had offered to help him, he knew he needed it in this one class. He had another class afterward, then went to the library to do some studying, and stopped to eat dinner in a diner, before his appointment at the assistant professor's house at nine. He arrived at her building five minutes early, and it was freezing outside so he went in. The building smelled of urine and cabbage and cats, and he rang the bell and took the stairs to the third floor two at a time. Seeing the building made him realize how little money she must make at her job, and he wondered if he should be offering her some kind of tutoring fee for helping him, but he didn't want to insult her. He rang the doorbell, and he could hear children laughing inside. Apparently they hadn't gone to bed on time, and Pattie looked flustered when she opened the door to him. She was wearing a pink V-neck sweater, jeans, and bare feet, and her long curly blond hair made her look younger than she was. And the little girl standing just behind her looked like a miniature of her, with ringlets and big blue eyes.

"This is Jessica," Pattie said formally as she smiled at him. "And she doesn't want to go to bed. She had cupcakes after dinner, and she's on a sugar high." She was seven and the cutest kid Ted had ever seen, and as he talked to her for a few minutes, her brother Justin whizzed past them, "faster than the speed of sound," he said as he flew by. He had on a Superman cape over his pajamas, and Jessica was wearing a pink flannel nightgown that looked well worn.

"It's my favorite," the little girl explained, and then followed her mother and Ted into the living room, where Justin flew over the couch and landed on the floor with a loud thud.

"Okay, you two, that's it. Ted and I have to do some studying, and I don't care how many cupcakes you had, it's time to go to bed." It was already an hour past their bedtime, and the living room looked a shambles, with toys all over the place. The apartment was small. There were two bedrooms, the living room, and a kitchen, and Pattie said it was rent-controlled. The university housing office had found it for her, and she was grateful to have it. She said the babysitter she used lived downstairs, and since the divorce it was a perfect arrangement. She promised to return in five minutes after she put the kids to bed. And in the end it took half an hour, while Ted read his contracts book and made a list of questions for her.

By the time he finished his list, Pattie had reappeared. Her hair fell around her face in soft curls, and her cheeks were flushed from playing with the kids. "Sometimes they just don't want to go to bed," she explained. "They were with their father for Thanksgiving. We have joint custody, and there are no rules at his house, so when they get back here, it's always a little nuts. By the time they calm down and shape up and get sane again, they go back to him. Divorce is tough on kids," she said, as she sat down next to Ted and looked at his list. The questions were intelligent and made sense, and she had a clear answer for all of them. She showed him examples and flipped through the book to point out what he needed to study and learn by rote. She clarified some important points for him and an hour later Ted sat back on the couch, looking immensely relieved.

"You make it seem so simple," he said with admiration. She was a good teacher, and he liked her style. She was an easy, warm person, a bright woman, and obviously a good mother from what he had seen. She was like Mother Earth as she tucked her feet under her, and smiled at him. She had a lush body and seemed limber and graceful and explained to him that she had done yoga for years. She taught it privately sometimes and said that she did everything she had to to make ends meet. Her ex-husband was an artist and couldn't even pay child support. She was carrying it all herself. Ted admired her for her openness and courage. She didn't say anything nasty about her ex-husband, and she seemed to accept her life as it was, and it had been kind of her to help him. He felt like he should pay her something for the tutoring help but didn't know what, and he didn't want to insult her.

He was about to get up to leave, so as not to impose on her further, when she offered him a glass of wine. He hesitated for a moment, not sure what he should do. She somehow made him feel boyish and inept, and next to her he felt awkward. And so as not to offend her, he accepted the glass of wine. She poured him some inexpensive Spanish red wine and poured another glass for herself.

"It's pretty good for cheap wine," she commented, and he nodded. It was good, and it was pleasant sitting there with her. He stretched his long legs out under the coffee table, and she brushed against him as she set down her glass on the table and turned to smile at him. "You're young to be in law school," she said warmly. "Did you come right in after college?" They both knew that that was rare—most law students worked for a few years before entering law school.

"I'm not that young. I'm twenty-four. I worked as a paralegal for two years. I had a great time and it convinced me I wanted to go to law school."

"I clerked for a family law judge during law school. It convinced me I wanted to teach. I'd never want that kind of responsibility, screwing up people's lives and making decisions for them."

"I'd like to be a federal prosecutor when I grow up," Ted said, half teasing, and half serious.

"That's pretty tough stuff. I'm thirty-six, and all I want to be when I grow up is happy and able to stop worrying about how to pay my rent. That would be great," she said, and took another sip of wine. Their eyes met over the glass, and there was something smoldering in hers. He didn't know what it was, but it was mesmerizing, as though she had the secret of the ages in her possession and wanted to share it with him. As he looked at her, the difference in their ages disappeared like mist.

They didn't say anything for a long moment and Ted was about to thank her again for her help with the contracts class, when without a word she leaned toward him, put an arm around his neck, and pulled him close to her. She kissed him then, and as she did, he felt as though his lips and soul and loins were on fire. He had never felt anything like it before. He started to pull away and then found he couldn't stop. It was as though he had been drugged. She was the drug, and he wanted more. When they finally drifted away from each other, all he wanted was to go back, and he slipped a hand under her sweater and touched her breasts. She didn't seem to mind at all, and her hand was resting lightly on his crotch, which bulged at her touch. He felt as though he had suddenly gone insane. Pattie was smiling at him, as she pressed closer to him and kissed him again.

"What about your kids?" he asked as he reached hungrily into her jeans and devoured her mouth.

Worrying about her children was the last sane thought he had.

"They're asleep," she whispered, and he was aware of silence from the second bedroom. They had finally worn themselves out. But Pattie and Ted had come alive, as though they were being held together by an electric current that was drawing them to each other. He couldn't keep his hands off her, and she unzipped his pants and was cradling him in her hands. "Let's go to bed," she whispered, and without hesitating, he followed her to her bedroom. It was the only place he wanted to be, as Pattie locked the door and literally tore his clothes off him, as he peeled off hers. All he wanted now was to be inside her, and he couldn't get there fast enough as they fell onto her bed, and she teased and taunted him unbearably until she let him get there, and then suddenly she turned around and swallowed him whole, letting him pleasure her, and then she turned again and took him into her, and Ted felt as though he had been sucked into another world and turned inside out. He had never known sex like that in his life. He was dizzy and light-headed when they finished and lay panting on the floor, where they had wound up.

"Oh my God . . . ," Ted said. He had been so

excited that he almost felt sick, and all he wanted was more. She was a drug. "What happened?" He sounded as dazed as he felt as he squinted at her in the dark, and they climbed back into her bed. His long athletic body was glistening with sweat, and so was hers. Hers was full and lush, and every inch of her was like a heady, warm embrace, like some kind of magic elixir that he could no longer live without.

"I think they call that love," Pattie said softly in the dark. They had tried not to make too much noise so as not to wake her kids, and they were whispering now. He wasn't sure he agreed with her word choice. He didn't know her well enough to love her, he didn't know her at all, but it was the wildest sex he could ever have imagined and an experience he knew he would never forget.

"I'm not sure that's love," he said honestly, "but it's the best sex I've ever had." He ran a hand down her stomach and between her legs and touched the place that had just welcomed him so warmly and given him so much joy.

"Is that all it was for you? Just sex?" She sounded disappointed, and he laughed softly in the dark.

"It was some kind of world-class explosion," he tried to describe it. "The Hiroshima of lovemaking, or Mount Vesuvius or something." It had never happened to him like that before. He could only imagine that it must be how people felt on psychedelic drugs, which he had never tried.

"I've wanted you since the first time you walked into my class," Pattie whispered, and as he saw her in the moonlight streaming through her bedroom window, she suddenly looked like a little girl, with masses of soft curly blond hair and huge eyes. She looked innocent and sweet, not like the femme fatale who had taken him to the heights of seduction only moments before. She seemed to have many faces and facets, which only helped intrigue him more. He was surprised to hear that she had noticed him in class.

"I didn't think you even knew who I was." There were two hundred students in the class, and Ted was always low key and often sat in the rear.

"I knew exactly who you were," she said as she kissed his neck and pinched his nipple at the same time. It aroused him faster than he thought. The little girl was morphing into the sex goddess again, and moments later they were rolling on the bed, and he tried every position that Pattie directed him to try until he could stand it no longer and they exploded violently at the same time. Afterward he could hardly speak.

"Pattie . . . what is this?" he said weakly. "What

are you doing to me? I think you have me under your spell."

"I told you . . ." Her laughter was a tinkling sound like tiny bells. "This is love . . ."

"I think it may kill me if we don't stop for a while." But she was relentless, she aroused him and teased and tormented him and satisfied him again and again. They didn't stop till dawn, until he finally fell asleep with his head resting on her breast, and she gently caressed his hair, as she would have a child. She tucked the covers around him and gently kissed the top of his head. It was the most incredible night he had ever spent.

Chapter 5

When Ted awoke the next day at noon, Pattie had already left. There was a pot of coffee for him, some bagels, and a note, "See you in class. I love you, P." He realized with dismay that he had missed two early classes that morning, and when he staggered to the kitchen, he could hardly walk. He had no idea what had happened to him the night before. She had bewitched him. She had the effect of a sorceress on him. She looked and seemed so motherly and wholesome, and with one kiss she turned into a tigress, and after that a child. He told himself that it couldn't happen again. It was too trite to be sleeping with his professor, and yet as he drank the coffee, all he could think of were their acrobatics of the night before, and he was aroused just thinking about her. He felt temporarily insane.

He took a shower then and got dressed,

smoothed out the covers on the bed, grabbed his coat, and ran down the stairs of her foul-smelling building. He didn't even care. He was almost late to her class and was the last person in as he hurried to his seat, and he found himself staring at her during the lecture, remembering the night before. She was wearing the same pink sweater she had worn the previous night, and she turned several times to look at him, with a glance that flicked over him and ripped right through his soul. He had an erection all through her class and waited for it to calm down before he got up to leave. When class ended, she walked over to him with a smile and looked down at him. He could feel everything tighten when she spoke. They were the only ones left in the classroom, and for a crazy moment he wanted to make love to her right there. She took his hand and pressed it between the legs of her jeans. He grabbed her and looked at her with utter amazement. Overnight she had turned him into someone he didn't even know. He was a stranger to himself as much as he was to her.

"You must be a witch," he whispered as he looked up at her, and she shook her head.

"No, I'm just yours. You own me now, Ted." She said it so simply that it would have touched him if the words weren't so odd. Suddenly everything around him was new.

"I don't want to own anyone," he said honestly, trying to keep a grip on sanity before he lost it again with her. "I just want to be with you again." He felt like a kid with her, until he entered her and turned into a man he had never even dreamed he could be. This was a part of life that went way, way beyond the ordinary experiences he had had till then. He had broken up with a girlfriend six months before, because he didn't want to get serious with her. Now this was a whole new world, with a woman who was much, much more experienced than he. It was a heady feeling, as she leaned over and gently rubbed the bulge in his jeans and pulled him to his feet. He stood with his arms around her, clinging to her, like a child lost in a storm.

"I love you, Ted." She said it so fiercely that it unnerved him, and he was almost beginning to wonder if this was what love was. Maybe she really knew.

"Don't say that. You don't know me yet. Let's get to know each other and find out what this is." He tried to reason with her, but nothing that was happening made sense.

"This is love," she whispered in his ear, and he was willing to believe her if it would get him to her bed again. "Let's go home," she said as they walked out of the room.

"What about your kids?" He was worried about

them. He didn't want them to become aware of what he was doing with their mother, and it unnerved him knowing they were there. He had forgotten it eventually the night before, but he didn't want to do that again. It didn't seem right to him.

"They're with their dad tonight," Pattie said with a girlish grin, and Ted looked at her and smiled. "He picked them up at school. They'll be with him for two days." It was good news to both of them, and she and Ted walked home to her place at an ever-quickening pace and raced up the stairs to her apartment. He was already slamming her against the door as she unlocked it, then kicked it closed, and they both flew into the living room and fell on each other on the couch. The night they spent together was even wilder than the one before. And the next day, neither of them went to school. They both called in sick and made love night and day. Pattie commented that you had to be Ted's age to make love as often as that, but she was there with him every time. As their bodies writhed and joined and blended together, neither of them thought or cared about their age. All Ted wanted now was her.

When Pattie's children came back from their father's, Ted went to his apartment for the first time in three days. The nights he had just spent with her felt like a tidal wave, and he had been washed up on the shore. He looked like he'd been on a three-week drunk when he finally got home. He was grateful that none of his roommates were in. He hadn't been to school in three days. Pattie had promised to give him an A in her class no matter what he did, but that didn't feel right to him. He had to get back to school. She had finally gone back to work that afternoon.

She called him an hour after he got home. He was lying with his eyes closed on his bed.

"I can't stand it. I have to see you." Pattie's voice sounded ragged on the phone, and he smiled, thinking of her.

"We may have to go everywhere like Siamese twins." The day before he had actually carried her to her kitchen, still deeply plunged into her. He fed her grapes and strawberries, sat her on the kitchen counter, and finished it there. There was nothing they hadn't tried in the past three days. Thanks to Pattie, his sexual education was now complete, or maybe it was just beginning.

"Can I come over?" She sounded desperate.

"Where are the kids?" He always worried about them. He didn't want them to be upset in any way because of his wild affair with her.

"I can leave them with Mrs. Pacheco downstairs for a couple of hours. What are you doing?"

"Lying on my bed. My roommates should be home soon, but you can come over if you want." He had his own room, although the walls were paper thin. It didn't even occur to him that they might be startled by her age. He had stopped thinking about the difference in their ages the first night. Sex had leveled the playing field between them.

She was there half an hour later, after dropping the kids off and taking a cab to his place. She got there before his roommates, and they made love frantically for two hours before she had to leave. They had never left his bed or his room. They hardly talked to each other, except when they were too exhausted to make love again, but Pattie said they were kindred spirits, and he believed her. What other explanation could there be for this? He could think of no other.

"See you tomorrow," she said dreamily as she left, and he kissed her. He was so exhausted that five minutes later he was sound asleep, and he never got to all the studying he had to do and had promised himself he would do that night. He'd have to make up for it the next day. He had so much catching up to do now.

Ted caught up on some of his work for the next two days, and they were both miserable. But she had papers to correct too. She wanted to come over for a couple of hours, and he wouldn't let her. He knew they wouldn't be able to tear themselves away again, and he had to study for final exams in a couple of weeks. He had promised to take her to dinner at the Waverly Inn on Friday, and they were both looking forward to it. He wanted to spend a normal evening with her, talk to her across a dinner table and get to know her, not just have wild abandoned sex wherever they could on every surface in her apartment. He wanted to have a relationship with her and try to figure out what this was. Was it just an animal attraction they couldn't control, or was it what Pattie kept saying, that it was love? Ted wanted to find out, and he wanted to take her to dinner and act like a civilized adult with her, not just a sex maniac on a rampage. Pattie was touched that he wanted to take her out, and the kids were back at their father's for the weekend. With their joint custody arrangement, the children went back and forth every couple of days, which gave Ted and Pattie time to be together, and a little breather in between.

Their dinner at the Waverly Inn started out perfectly, with a nice table and a good dinner. Ted ordered wine for them. He was showing off a little and wanted to demonstrate how sophisticated he was, but Pattie didn't care. She never took her eyes off him all evening, and they were both aching to go home long before dessert.

"Maybe we're just not ready to go out yet," Ted said, as they hurried home. The idea had been good, but practically they couldn't keep their clothes on, stay out of bed, and keep their bodies away from each other long enough to have a decent meal or get to know each other. Ted locked the front door behind them, and they never made it a step farther. He spun her around, gently laid her down on the carpet, and shoved her skirt up. She was begging for him as he took her right there, and then carried her to the bedroom with their clothes strewn across the floor. They didn't leave the apartment again after that for two days, until her kids came home. Ted left five minutes before Pattie's ex-husband dropped them off, and he went back to his own apartment, exhausted and happy and missing her.

Annie called Ted several times over the weekend, but his phone always went to voice mail. She finally called Liz and Kate, who was out with friends.

"Have you heard from your brother?" she asked them both the same question. He usually checked in with her every few days, and this week he hadn't, and she thought it was strange. "I hope he's okay." Maybe he was sick. But he was never too busy to call her, and she hadn't heard a word from him since the Sunday after Thanksgiving when he'd left. Kate said he hadn't called her, and Liz said the same and that she'd had a busy week herself. They all had, and things were going to be even busier before Christmas and over the holidays.

"I'm sure he's fine," Liz reassured her. "He's probably just busy with school. He was complaining about it the other day. Law school is really tough."

"Maybe he has a new girlfriend," Annie suggested, sounding pensive, and Lizzie laughed.

"I don't think so. After he broke up with Meg, he's been pretty careful not to get too involved with anyone. I think it's just school."

"I guess you're right." The two women chatted for a few minutes, and Liz said that Jean-Louis was going back to Paris over the weekend. She was flying over to meet him the day after Christmas, spend a week with him, and then she had to work. She was trying to get him assigned to her shoot. It would be fun working with him if she could. "Is this getting serious?" Annie asked, and Liz just laughed at her.

"I don't know what you'd call it. Neither of us goes out with anyone else, so it's exclusive, but we're not making plans for the future or anything. We're too young for that." Annie wasn't so sure. Some women were ready to settle down at twenty-eight. Others weren't. Lizzie wasn't. And Jean-Louis didn't seem to want to settle down either. They were having too much fun in their own lives. And Jean-Louis had apparently not felt too young to have a son, since he had a five-year-old at twenty-nine. It made Annie nervous to realize that he had been Ted's age when he had a child. She couldn't even imagine it. Ted still seemed like a kid to her. And so did Kate at twenty-one. And Annie couldn't see Liz with Jean-Louis long term. He just didn't seem like the right man to her. He was no better or worse than the others Lizzie had gone out with. She always went out with someone who, like her, wanted no commitment. Annie had other dreams for her, like a serious man who would take care of her. And Annie couldn't imagine Jean-Louis as anyone's father, nor as the husband Lizzie deserved. And at twenty-eight it wasn't unreasonable to be thinking about her future. Annie didn't want her to end up alone like her. It worked for her, but she wanted something more for Liz. Jean-Louis wasn't it. Ted and Kate were far too young to worry about long-term partners yet. They were still just kids, and still in school, but Liz was an adult.

Annie finally reached Ted on Sunday night, when he got back to his apartment, and she was relieved to hear him, although he sounded a little sick.

"Are you okay? Do you have a cold?"

"I'm fine." He smiled at her concern. He couldn't help wondering how she would react to Pattie, but he wasn't ready to share the news of her arrival in his life yet, so he kept it to himself. "I'm just tired. I've been working really hard all week." He certainly had, but not in the way Annie thought.

"At least you'll get a nice break over Christmas," Annie said kindly, which reminded Ted that he had talked to Pattie that week about going skiing with him after Christmas. She had said she'd have to check with her ex-husband about his taking the kids, and Ted was looking forward to taking a trip with her, if they could stay out of bed long enough to get on skis.

Annie reminded Ted to come home for dinner anytime he wanted and suggested it for the following weekend, but he was vague. She didn't know why, but Annie had the distinct impression that there was something he wasn't telling her, and suddenly she wondered again about a new girl in his life. Annie smiled at the idea and wondered if it was someone at law school with him.

Ted knew only too well, when he thought about it later, that not in a million years would Annie suspect that he was involved with a thirty-six-year-old assistant law professor with two kids. And he knew for sure that he wouldn't be able to tell her for a long time. First he had to get used to the idea himself.

Chapter 6

The days before Christmas were, as always, utterly insane. Annie had five job sites under construction at once, two with completion dates just after the new year. She visited all five of them every day. It snowed twice the week before Christmas, which made it nearly impossible to get around. She had Christmas shopping to do for her nieces and nephew, her assistants, and Whitney and her brood. Two new clients insisted on meetings, and she had to come up with a set of preliminary plans for one of them. It was predictable preholiday chaos, and she was always worried she wouldn't get everything done. And to complicate matters further, her favorite clients, the Ebersohls, had announced that they had decided to get divorced and were planning to sell the new house. It wasn't the first time it had happened, since remodeling or building a house brought out the worst in everyone. It was a painful process, and a perfect setting for endless arguments. Alicia Ebersohl had called her in tears to tell her that Harry was filing for divorce. The house on Sixty-ninth Street was completely torn up, which would make it difficult to sell. Annie was disappointed to hear it, but much more so for them.

And Liz was almost as busy at the magazine. By Christmas, she was finishing up her work for the March issue and already starting on April. She was trying to get everything done before she left for Paris. And she was missing Jean-Louis. He had been especially sweet since his recent trip to New York and was calling her several times a day. He said he could hardly wait for her to come, and she was excited about it too. After spending Christmas with the family, Liz was planning to leave the next day. And Jean-Louis promised that he and his son would be waiting for her. She was bringing the boy a beautiful antique train that had been modernized to run on batteries. And a very handsome watch for Jean-Louis.

Ted spent every moment he could with Pattie before the holidays. The ski trip they'd been planning fell through, since her ex-husband was going away himself and wouldn't take the kids, so they were going to be stuck in New York. Ted was planning to spend time with them, but he had strong feelings about the propriety of staying at her apartment when her children were there, and Pattie agreed, although it was a sacrifice for them.

Ted had final exams and got passing grades, although they were noticably lower than usual. And he was embarrassed when he discovered that Pattie had given him an A in her class that he felt he didn't deserve.

"Is that because I earned it," he asked her honestly, "or because we're having an affair?"

"We're not having an affair," she answered quietly. "I'm in love with you. But yes, you deserved the grade too."

"I'm not sure if I believe that," but he would never know. And Pattie was always adamant about correcting him when he talked about their "affair" or their sexual relationship by saying that they were in love. Ted had not yet said the words, and he knew that when he did, the woman he said them to would be in his life forever. Until then, in his mind, they were having an affair. Lately Pattie cried whenever he said that to her, and she looked deeply wounded by his words. He didn't want to mislead her, and he wasn't sure if he was in lust or in love.

He had hardly talked to Annie and his sisters since Thanksgiving. He just didn't have the time, and he was always with Pattie now, whenever he wasn't asleep or in school. She wanted to know when she was going to meet his family, and Ted had told her gently but firmly that it was too soon. He knew that he cared about Pattie, but he hadn't figured out yet what was happening between them. And he knew without a doubt that his aunt and sisters would be extremely shaken up by her age and the fact that she had kids. Ted wasn't ready to face the hurdle of their opinions yet. And Pattie was hurt by that too. She said she didn't want to be the secret in his life, and she reminded him just before Christmas that that wasn't fair to her. She wanted to be front and center in his life, not hidden in a closet. She said she was better than that, and she was extremely upset that he had told her he wouldn't be able to see her on Christmas. He was going to be at home with Annie and his sisters, and there was no way he could invite Pattie to come by with her kids. Annie would have had a fit, and he wasn't willing to deal with that yet. Annie had no idea she existed, let alone that she was an older woman with two kids.

"So what am I supposed to do?" Pattie asked him plaintively when he stopped by on Christmas Eve. She had been crying for the past hour about him leaving her. "What do you expect me to do? Just sit here alone with my kids?"

"What would you normally do, if we hadn't met? What did you do last year?"

"Hank had the kids, and I cried myself to sleep." Ted looked upset, but there was no way he could spend Christmas with her. And at least her ex wasn't taking the kids this year, so Ted knew she wouldn't be alone.

"I'll try to come over the day after Christmas, or Christmas night."

"And what about later tonight?" Pattie asked, dabbing at her eyes.

"I can't. I told you, we have dinner at home and go to midnight mass."

"How touching, and how un-Christian to leave the woman you love sitting at home alone."

"You'll be with Jessica and Justin," he said gently. "And I can't do anything about it. My aunt wouldn't understand if I went out tonight. It's our tradition." She made him feel like Scrooge.

"You sound like you're twelve years old," Pattie complained, and then she looked disappointed when he gave her a beautiful white cashmere sweater that had cost him a fortune. She didn't say it to him in words, but the message came across clearly that she had hoped for something like a ring, a promise ring of some kind. She had been talking about it for days, giving him strong hints, but Ted felt it was too soon. They had only been dating for four weeks, and as much in love as Pattie said they were, it still seemed very new to Ted. There was plenty of time for a ring of some kind later. He was not thirty-six years old like her, he was only twenty-four, and this was only the second serious relationship he'd ever had.

The compromise they finally came to was that he would try to drop by for a while on Christmas night, but he had already warned her that he couldn't spend the night, whether her kids were there or not. Pattie had been talking about paying Mrs. Pacheco to have them sleep in her apartment if he came by, but he said he would have to go back to Annie's after a few hours. She would be suspicious of what he was up to if he didn't.

"Maybe it's time for you to grow up," Pattie said unkindly. "You fuck like a man, maybe you should act like one too." He was hurt by what she said, and she was looking petulant when he kissed her goodbye and left. She said she'd give him his present when he came back on Christmas night. And there was an edge to her voice as she said it. He took a cab to Annie's, and Kate was already at the apartment when he got there. When she saw him walk in, she looked intently at her brother.

"Wow, what are you so pissed about? You don't exactly look like the spirit of Christmas. What did you get Annie?"

"A cashmere shawl, and a personalized hard hat. It's really cute, I think she'll like it." He hadn't answered his sister's question about why he was angry. He had been upset about Pattie and what she had said when he left her, because he couldn't spend Christmas Eve with her. She refused to understand that he just couldn't, and he hated to leave her on a sour note, but she had still been pouting and gave him the cold shoulder when he left. It had seriously upset him, particularly when she'd told him to act like a man. "I'm not pissed, by the way. I just had an argument with one of my roommates before I came here. He's an asshole."

Kate didn't say anything to him, but she had the odd feeling something else was bothering him. "Annie will love the hard hat, and the shawl sounds cool too." She smiled lovingly at her brother.

"What did you get her?" For a minute it felt like being kids again, while they wrapped their gifts for her together.

"I didn't get her anything," Kate said with a serious expression.

"You didn't?" Ted looked stunned. That wasn't like her. Kate was always generous with them all, despite a limited allowance. But she was always very creative about how she spent it.

"I made her something," she said, and Ted

smiled, thinking back to the old days, when he had made Annie a table in wood shop, and Lizzie had knit Annie a sweater with gigantically long arms. And Annie had worn it on Christmas Day. She had worn their macaroni necklaces too, and everything they gave her.

Kate went to get her portfolio then and carefully took out three large panels with watercolor paintings on them. She turned them around one by one, and Ted caught his breath in amazement. Sometimes he actually forgot how talented his younger sister was, just like their mother. She had done exquisite portraits of each of them to give Annie, and the likenesses were absolutely perfect, even the self-portrait she had done.

"They're gorgeous, Kate," Ted said, studying them at close range. They were flawless, but they also had all the softness of paintings, and didn't look like they'd been done from photographs. She had done them from memory, and each one was a painting he knew their aunt would treasure. "They're really fantastic!"

"I hope she likes them," Katie said modestly, and then put them carefully back in the portfolio. She was going to wrap them that night and offer to frame them afterward for Annie. "So what have you been up to?" Katie asked him casually after she put away the paintings and they both collapsed on the couch. Annie had put up a Christmas tree for them, with all the favorite decorations they loved. She had spent a whole day and night doing it the previous weekend.

"Nothing much. Just papers and exams," he said, and as Kate looked at him, she knew that he was lying. Something was up, and he wasn't telling. Her woman's intuition told her it was a woman. She couldn't wait to tell Liz and Annie. And they had already all agreed that he had hardly called any of them since Thanksgiving.

"What about you?" Ted asked, trying to get the attention off himself. "New pierces, new tattoos, new men?"

"Maybe," Katie said cryptically. She had her own secrets too.

"Oh?" He looked intrigued. "Which one?"

"Maybe all three," she said, and then laughed as Ted flipped on the TV. They were watching **Miracle on 34th Street** when Annie got home, carrying her briefcase and two bags of groceries of things she had forgotten to order that morning. They always had a simple dinner on Christmas Eve, and she prepared a turkey on Christmas Day, just as she did on Thanksgiving. She had tried to make goose one year and it was awful, so they stuck with turkey.

Ted got up and took the two bags into the

kitchen for her, and Katie went to kiss her aunt hello. Annie looked exhausted and breathless. She had been at one of her construction sites an hour before, to resolve a problem between the contractor and her clients. She still had the plans in a roll under her arm and tossed them on her desk before taking off her coat.

"Merry Christmas, everyone!" Annie called out to them both, took off her coat, and turned on some Christmas music. Katie complimented her on the tree, and Ted poured them each a glass of eggnog, which was another family tradition. Annie usually added a drop of bourbon to hers, but Kate and Ted liked it plain, just the way they had drunk it as kids. They were all talking animatedly when Liz walked in, carrying three shopping bags full of presents. She always bought the most extravagant gifts of all, and they loved them. Liz was in high spirits as they all wished each other a merry Christmas, and after admiring the tree, and singing to the music, they all cooked dinner together. It was a perfect Christmas Eve. Liz had promised to stay there until she left for Paris, and Annie loved having them all home.

They sat chatting at the kitchen table until nearly eleven, then got ready to leave for midnight mass. Kate noticed Ted making a call as she walked past his open bedroom door. And she heard him leave someone a message. He sounded upset and looked worried when he joined the others in the front hall. She had made a call herself when she went to get her coat, but it had been friendly and short, and she'd promised to call the next morning. Tonight was a family time that was important to all of them.

They took a cab to St. Patrick's, where they went to midnight mass every year. Only Annie took communion, and as she did every year, they watched her light candles for Bill and Jane. She knelt at one of the smaller altars after she did it, bowed her head, and prayed, and there were tears running down her cheeks when she stood up. It always brought tears to Kate's eyes to watch her. She had never asked, but she knew who the candles were for. Her parents weren't forgotten, and Annie had been wonderful to their children ever since they'd been gone. Ted gave Annie a hug as she slipped back into the pew, and Kate gently held her hand. Liz was looking strikingly chic as usual, in a huge white fox hat and an elegant black coat with tall black leather boots. She reminded Annie so much of Jane at the same age. She was more stylish than her mother had been, but her face was almost the same. It made Annie's heart ache sometimes to see it. She still missed her.

They sang "Silent Night" at the end of the mass,

and afterward they walked out onto Fifth Avenue and took a cab home. Annie made them hot chocolate with marshmallows, and then finally everyone went to bed. And after they did, Annie filled their stockings with little thoughtful presents and wrote them funny notes from Santa, reminding each of them to clean their rooms and wash behind their ears, and on Kate's Santa letter she added a note that she would find coal in her stocking next year if she got any more tattoos. And then Annie went to sleep in the peaceful apartment, grateful that all the people she loved most in the world were home and sound asleep in their rooms. It was her favorite night of the year. It didn't get better than this.

Chapter 7

On Christmas morning Annie got up early to put the turkey in the oven, and she called her friend Whitney, as she had for so many years. They wished each other a merry Christmas, chatted for a few minutes, and Whitney reminded her again to come on New Year's Eve, but Annie still insisted that she didn't want to go to New Jersey if one of the kids would be home alone. She never minded staying home on New Year's Eve, it had never been a night that meant much to her, and she hated to be around people getting drunk, with no one to kiss at midnight, which made her feel more alone than staying home.

"I'll see," Annie promised Whitney. "I have to see what the kids are up to. Lizzie is going to Paris tomorrow, but the other two will be here. And as far as I know, neither of them has any plans."

"Well, come if you can," Whitney said warmly. "We'd love to have you . . . and have a merry Christmas, Annie. Give my love to the kids."

"And mine to Fred and the boys."

Annie lit the Christmas tree then, so it would be festive and bright when the others got up. A little while later Kate emerged from her bedroom, looking sleepy, in a rock star T-shirt, and her spiky hair sticking up straight. Annie noticed then that she was wearing a tiny diamond in her nose, which was new. She didn't say anything to Kate about it, but she would never get used to her pierces and tattoos.

"Santa left me a cool note," Kate commented then with a yawn as she smiled at her aunt.

"Really? What does it say?" Annie feigned innocence, as she always did, and particularly had when they still believed in Santa Claus. She had gone to great lengths to preserve the myth for them. She had wanted them to have all the joy and magic in their lives that they deserved.

"Santa said he loves my new Tinkerbell tattoo, and he just got one himself. He got a huge tattoo of Rudolph on his ass. He promised to leave me a picture of it next year." Katie grinned.

"That is **not** what the note from Santa says!" Annie said with a disapproving look. "I read the note myself when I got up!"

"Yes, it is!" Katie insisted, and ran to get the note. She had written one herself with a funny drawing on it, of Santa with the Rudolph tattoo on his bare behind. Annie burst out laughing when Kate handed it to her, and then taped it up on the fireplace, just as Liz wandered out in a man's pajama top that looked sexy with her beautiful long legs. Annie was wearing an old flannel nightgown and a pink cashmere robe. And Ted emerged a few minutes later wearing boxer shorts and a T-shirt. Comfort was the order of the day on Christmas morning, not elegance. And a few minutes later they all exchanged gifts in front of the brightly lit tree.

Kate's paintings of the three of them were a huge hit, and for her brother and sister she had done a portrait of Annie. She had done portraits of her parents too, from photographs, but she had left them tacked on the wall in her dorm room. She hadn't wanted to upset anyone by bringing them home. Annie loved the three beautiful portraits of the children, and Katie promised to have them framed for her. Annie said she was going to take down a painting and put them up in the living room. There were tears in her eyes as she hugged Kate. And Ted and Liz loved the portrait of Annie.

Ted's gifts to everyone were a big hit too, and Annie put her personalized hard hat on immediately. Liz had given Annie and Kate beautiful gold cuff bracelets, and an elegant Cartier watch for Ted, with a sporty rubber diver's band.

And afterward they all had breakfast in the kitchen. Liz had half a grapefruit as usual and was thinner than ever. Katie had granola, and Ted made eggs sunny side up for Annie and himself. The smell of bacon was delicious, and the turkey in the oven was turning golden brown. It occurred to Annie as she watched them talking and laughing with each other that they had a life of fragments of loaves and fishes. Somehow she had managed to bring up three children, not her own, with no idea of what she was doing, and they had turned out wonderfully, they all loved each other, and they enriched her life in ways she never would have dreamed. She felt very lucky as she put the breakfast dishes in the dishwasher and silently thanked her sister for the three terrific children she had inherited from her. They had filled her life with love and joy ever since.

Everyone went to their rooms for a while after breakfast. All of them had friends they wanted to call. Ted closed the door to his room while he called Pattie, and she finally picked up this time, although she still sounded very upset. He wished her a merry Christmas.

"You should be here with me and the kids," she

said mournfully, and a moment later she was in tears again.

"I have to be with my family today," he explained again. She just didn't seem to get it, or didn't want to. There was no way he would have been anywhere but here today. And after only four weeks it wasn't fair of Pattie to expect him to ditch his family for her. He was upset that she had made such a fuss about it, but he offered to come to see her late that afternoon. He had presents he wanted to give them. He promised to call Pattie as soon as he thought he could get away.

"Have a nice day," she said, still sounding hurt and disappointed, and he didn't apologize to her again. She had to understand that his family was important to him. "I love you, Ted," Pattie said sadly. She sounded as though she had lost her best friend.

"I'll see you later," Ted responded. He still wasn't ready to tell her that he loved her, and surely not as an apology for spending Christmas with his sisters and aunt. He was upset but not feeling guilty, and it bothered him that Pattie was so possessive of him.

Ted looked more relaxed when he came out of his room again. At least this time Pattie had talked to him.

"Love troubles?" Liz asked him with a raised

eyebrow, and he shook his head, surprised that she had guessed and not anxious to open up to her.

"Why would you say that?" Ted commented to his older sister.

"You never close your door when you're on the phone, unless you're fighting with a girl. Someone new?" she asked with interest, and he shook his head.

"No, just someone I've gone out with a few times." He could just imagine the look on her face if he told his older sister she was thirty-six years old and had two kids. "I might go see her this afternoon," he volunteered, and Liz nodded. It didn't sound unusual to her, and she had to go back to her place and pick up a few things for her trip too.

While they were talking, Annie had wandered into Katie's room to thank her for the beautiful portraits again. She truly loved them. She noticed a book on Katie's desk, about Muslim culture and customs. It wasn't the sort of thing that Katie usually read. She had never been much of a reader, and her taste ran more to biographies of contemporary artists and rock stars. And she'd never had an interest in other religions before, or even her own.

"That looks interesting," Annie said, picking it up. "Are you taking a class in Eastern religions? It might actually help us to understand some of the conflicts in the world today."

"I borrowed it from a friend," Katie said, and turned away. Annie went back to the living room to join the others then. They had all dressed nicely for lunch, and Ted was wearing a coat and tie as he always did for family events. She had always insisted that they dress properly for the holidays when they were children.

Liz was wearing a simple little black wool dress, although it barely reached her thighs. Annie was wearing her favorite red Christmas dress, and Katie appeared a moment later in a red leather skirt, Raggedy Ann stockings, red combat boots, a fuzzy white sweater, and Christmas balls hanging from her ears as earrings. She was definitely her own person, but she had just proved to all of them again what a talented artist she was. And Annie was impressed by the book she had seen in her room. She liked to see that Kate was interested in different things and cultures. Kate was a freethinker and never borrowed anyone's ideas without checking them out for herself first. She was a totally independent individual. Annie had tried to open as many doors to them as she could. She had never wanted them to live in a narrow, limited world. And she loved the fact that each of them was so different. Of the three, Ted was the most traditional, and Katie the least. She thought that Jane and Bill would have been proud of them too.

The conversation was lively at their Christmas lunch table, and Annie poured them each champagne. They were all old enough to drink, and rarely did to excess, although Ted had had his occasional sophomoric moments during his first two years in college, but now they were all adults, and reasonable about how much they drank.

Liz said she was excited about going to Paris and spending time with Jean-Louis. The shoot she was doing in the first week of January was an important one and was being done by a famous French photographer, with important jewels from all over Europe. The Queen of England had even lent them a piece, which Lizzie was planning to put on the cover. She talked animatedly about it. Only Ted was a little quieter than usual, and Annie could sense that something was bothering him, but whatever it was, he didn't want to share it with them.

He watched a little football after the meal, and then he stood up and said vaguely that he was going out for a while to see friends. He waited to see if anyone objected, and when they didn't, he went to his room and picked up the wrapped gifts for Pattie's kids. He had bought each of them a game. He wasn't sure what kids liked at that age. He had already given Pattie her gift, in case he hadn't been able to get out on Christmas Day.

He put on his coat and bent to kiss Annie while she chatted with Kate and Liz, and he looked very serious. He had left the gifts for Jessica and Justin at the front door, so as not to draw attention to them.

"I'll be back in a couple of hours," he promised, picked up his keys on the hall table, and the gifts for Pattie's kids, and left.

"What's eating him?" Liz asked the others, and Katie said she had no idea. He hadn't said anything to her, although she had heard him arguing with someone on the phone in his room.

"Sounds like a girl to me," Annie suggested calmly. "He's being very quiet about it."

"He always is," Liz volunteered, and they all agreed that he seemed to be unusually so this time.

"If he keeps seeing her, she'll show up eventually. Maybe she's funny looking or weird or something," Kate suggested.

"Yeah, like with a lot of pierces and tattoos," Liz teased her, and they all laughed. Whatever Ted was up to, they all assumed correctly that he would tell them about it when he was ready to. For now it was a mystery, and he wanted it that way. And Annie respected them all too much to try and pry it out of him.

Ted ran up the stairs in Pattie's building as fast as he could. He had promised her he'd try to be there by five, and it was nearly six. But he hadn't been able to get away before that. He hadn't wanted to run out on Annie and his sisters on Christmas. Their traditions were important to all of them, and to him too.

He rang the doorbell, and for a long moment she didn't answer, and Ted was worried that she might not let him in. She had said she'd be there. He felt suddenly like a very young boy who was in trouble. It was an unfamiliar sensation to him. He had always been responsible and well behaved. Annie had very rarely been angry at him, and when she was, it was hot, clear, and direct. She gave a short blast, and it was over. She had never dragged it out, held a grudge, or been passive-aggressive with any of them. Pattie seemed to be punishing him for spending Christmas with his family. And then finally she opened the door to him with a pained look. It was obvious that she'd been crying, and she burst into tears and threw herself into his arms the moment he walked into the room. Ted was stunned.

"How could you leave me alone today?" she said accusingly, and he looked around and didn't see her kids.

"Where are Jessica and Justin?" he asked, looking baffled.

"I sent them to the movies with Mrs. Pacheco. I wanted to be alone with you when you came."

"I brought some little presents for them," he said, setting the gift-wrapped boxes down on the table. "And I didn't leave you alone, Pattie. You were with your kids, and I was with my family. I couldn't just walk out on them." He sounded calm and reasonable, but her hysteria and demands on him concerned him. It was too soon in the relationship for her to expect so much.

"So you walked out on me instead," she said softly.

"I didn't walk out on you," he corrected firmly. "And we've only been dating for four weeks."

"I'm in love with you, Ted." He would have been more convinced if she hadn't said it to him the first night. For him, love was something that grew slowly over time, not something that burst into full bloom on the first night. He was growing more and more attached to her, but he still wanted to be sure that it was love and not just fabulous sex.

He was pleased to see that she was wearing the

sweater he had given her, although she hadn't seemed excited about his gift and wanted something else from him. She forgot that he was twenty-four years old and a student, and a white cashmere sweater was a big gift for him. Annie had been thrilled with the cashmere shawl he had gotten from the same place. But Pattie had made it clear she wanted a promise ring. The very idea of that had stunned him. It wasn't appropriate after only four weeks. She was going much too fast for him, and it made him uncomfortable. Even a man her own age wouldn't have been ready to move that quickly.

As he looked at her tenderly, she handed him his gift. And as he took off the wrapping, he was ill at ease to see that it was some kind of jewelry box. He gasped when he opened it—it was a beautiful old gold man's watch, and not at all the kind of thing he would wear. He was wearing the Cartier diver's watch from his sister, which was much more age appropriate. And he was even more uncomfortable seeing that Pattie's was an expensive gift.

"Do you like it?" Pattie asked hopefully. "It was my father's."

"It's beautiful," he said quietly, closing the box, without putting it on his wrist. "But I can't accept it. That's a really big gift, and it was your father's. You can't just give that to someone like me."

"Why not? What do you mean?" She looked hurt.

"You hardly know me. What if we break up? You don't want me going off with your father's watch. You should keep that for Justin one day." Just as his own father's watch was waiting for him, but he had never worn it yet. Annie had it in a safe for him.

"Then don't break up with me," Pattie said, sounding pathetic. "I want you to have it, Ted."

"Not now," he said gently, and silenced her with a kiss. And a moment later the predictable happened, their clothes were in a heap on the floor, and the tensions of the past two days had found release. Their passion overwhelmed them both, and they lay breathless, first on the couch and then in her bed, clinging to each other insatiably. He couldn't get enough of her, and she seemed desperate in the way she made love to him, as though she wanted to swallow him whole and become a part of him.

It was ten o'clock when Mrs. Pacheco called her and asked if she could bring the children home. She wanted to go to bed. They had totally forgotten the time, and Ted still hadn't left. They dressed hurriedly, and a few minutes later Jessica and Justin rang the bell, and Ted gave them their gifts as soon as they walked in. They loved the games, and Pattie looked happy and relaxed again. The past few hours had convinced her that Ted was still addicted to her. She had been terrified that she had lost him and had made him miserable as a result, punishing him for going home.

"I have to go," he whispered to her, and she shook her head. She wanted him to stay, but her kids were home, and he didn't want to do something crazy with them there. Instead he wished them all a merry Christmas, kissed her, put on his coat, and hurried down the stairs. He wanted to get home. He didn't know why, but tonight had made him sad. She seemed so desperate, and her father's watch had been too big a gift. It hadn't touched him, it had scared him. He had left the gold watch on the dresser in her bedroom. They weren't married or engaged, he didn't even know if he was in love. He liked her a lot and he wanted to be with her, and their lovemaking was extraordinary, but he didn't want to become her prisoner either, and sometimes there was a hint of that. He took a big gulp of air as he hailed a cab and got in. She had been sexier than ever, but for the first time in a month of making love to her, he was relieved to leave. He wasn't sure why he felt that way, but he suddenly felt as though Pattie were suffocating him.

The others were asleep when he got home. It

had been a long day. When Ted left, they had watched a movie, and after that Kate and Annie had played Scrabble while Liz finished packing for Paris, and then they all went to bed.

Ted tiptoed in when he got home. Annie had left the Christmas tree lit for him, and he sat down on the couch and looked at it, thinking of where he had just been. It was so exciting and intense being with Pattie, but the white heat of her passion seared him at times. And all he could think of now was that it felt good to be home, in the apartment where he'd grown up, with the people he loved. Pattie was like a wild fantasy he couldn't get enough of. But this was real. He sat in the living room, feeling like a kid again, smiling at the Christmas tree, and happy to be home.

Chapter 8

On the day after Christmas, Ted slept till almost noon. Lizzie left the house at ten in the morning for a one P.M. flight to Paris, and Annie was at her desk, working on some plans for Jim Watson's apartment, when Kate wandered in and asked if she could have a friend over for pizza that night. She was always considerate about asking if she could have people in, and Annie was happy to have her entertain her friends. She had always been very welcoming to all of them.

"Of course. You don't have to ask, but thank you anyway." And then she looked at her and smiled. "Is this a new love interest you haven't told me about?"

"No, he's just a friend." But Annie knew better than that after being a surrogate parent for all these years. New boyfriends and girlfriends were always announced as friends. "We might go to a movie, or stay here."

"Do whatever you like. I have some work to do. I can stay in my room."

"You don't have to hide." Kate smiled at her. "I'm not fifteen. I'm not ashamed of you."

"Well, that's nice to know. I was pretty embarrassing there for a while."

"You've improved," Katie said magnanimously with a broad grin.

"What's his name?"

"Paul. He goes to my school. He's really talented. He wants to be a graphic artist one day, but he's really good at fine arts. His parents want him to learn something practical, like design."

"How old is he?"

"Twenty-three." It seemed like a reasonable age to Annie, and she nodded.

"I'll be happy to meet him. I like it when you bring your friends home." Katie nodded and went back to her room and called Paul. He said he'd come over around five. And after she talked to Paul, Ted emerged from his room. He looked exhausted. His sexual adventures with Pattie were wearing him out. Pattie had just called and invited him out to lunch with her kids. There was still snow on the ground in the park, and she had suggested a snowball fight or maybe skating for the afternoon. He liked the idea and had agreed.

He left the house an hour later without telling his aunt or his sister where he was going. He just said he was meeting friends and didn't say when he'd be back. Annie wasn't surprised, and it didn't bother her. She didn't keep track of his every move, and at twenty-four, he had to feel free to come and go when he stayed with her.

Katie went out for a while too. She wanted to check out the sales at her favorite stores, and she came back to the apartment shortly before five. Annie was still working at her desk and had been there all afternoon. The doorbell rang a few minutes after Katie got home, and she went to let him in. Annie could hear them talking and laughing in the living room, and Katie had put some music on. It was the Clash, which Annie actually liked.

They had been there for an hour when Annie walked through the room. She was on her way to make a cup of tea and intended to casually say hello, and she smiled at the handsome young man who stood up and held out his hand to shake hers. He was much more polite and poised than Katie's usual friends. He introduced himself with impeccable manners, and he was wearing a blazer and a tie, which was unheard of among Katie's cohorts. He was a beautiful young man with jet-black hair and deep honey-colored skin and eyes the color of onyx. Annie realized that he was probably from the Middle East, or maybe Indian, and suddenly she remembered the book about Muslim culture that she had seen in Katie's room. She had obviously borrowed it from him. And she hadn't said a word to Annie about him before he came. He was extremely polite as he shook hands with Annie. He seemed very mature for his age, and he was a far cry from Kate's tattooed and pierced friends from art school who wore drooping jeans and torn T-shirts with uncombed hair.

In an effort to make him feel welcome, Annie offered him a glass of wine, and he smiled and said he would prefer a cup of tea. It was a welcome change from the vast quantities of beer Katie's friends always consumed when they came to visit.

The two young people followed Annie into the kitchen while she made the tea. Katie helped herself to a Coke, and Paul chatted easily with Annie. As she served him tea, Paul explained that his parents were Iranian, from Tehran, but they had all been in the States since he was fourteen. He said he still had family there but hadn't been back to his native country for a visit in nine years, since they left, and added that he was an American citizen, as were his parents. He spoke without any trace of an accent and seemed very polished and adult and also very respectful in the way he spoke to Annie. Katie's eyes shone brightly every time she looked at him, and Annie's heart fluttered a little as she watched them.

They were young and very sweet, and Paul was clearly a wonderful young man, but Annie was concerned that their cultures were very different. Katie looked like she was in love, and if so, Annie couldn't help wondering how his parents felt about Katie, with all her pierced earrings and tattoos and her very liberated ways. She was too young to take any romance too seriously, but if in fact she was serious about this, Annie wondered if Paul's parents were concerned. In terms of their origins, Katie and Paul came from two different worlds. And Katie looked a lot wilder than she was. Annie was used to it and knew what a good kid she was. But for strangers who didn't know her, Katie's look could have been quite a shock, particularly for the parents of a boy as polite and conservative-looking as Paul.

All Annie could hope for her was that this was a happy romance but not a lasting relationship that would challenge them too much. But the look in her niece's eyes said something very different. Annie had never seen her look like this at any boy. And Paul was not a boy, he was a man. Annie could easily see everything that Katie loved about him, but that didn't mean that a serious relationship between them at their age would be easy. And Annie knew that relationships were challenging enough without adding extreme contrasts to the mix, and backgrounds that were so culturally different in their traditions. It was hard enough to make a relationship work with someone who had grown up in all the same ways.

Annie was still thinking about it when she went back to her room and sat staring at the plans on her desk. She didn't know what to think—it was the first time she had ever seen her in love, and she was worried for Kate. They were both fine young people, and she didn't want them to get hurt.

Katie and Paul watched a DVD in the living room and ordered pizza. And Annie didn't see Paul again before he left. She had quietly closed her door to give them privacy, but she was worried about it all night and had called Whitney to confide in her.

"What are you so freaked out about? She's not marrying him, for God's sake," Whitney scolded her. Talking to her about the kids was always a reality check for Annie. Whitney was always practical and sensible.

"But what if she does marry him? He's a Muslim. She's a very rebellious, totally liberated American girl. I'm sure his parents must be concerned about it too, if they've met her. Marriage is hard enough without adding cultural and religious differences to it."

"Oh, for heaven's sake, don't be so old-fashioned. People marry into different cultures all the time. And who says they're getting married?" Whitney laughed at her and tried to give her some perspective. Annie was already imagining them married. This was Kate's first serious romance. "First of all, he sounds like he's totally Americanized. And she's not marrying him. They're both kids, and they go to the same school. This is dating, not marriage. She's twenty-one, and he sounds like he's intelligent. You said he's handsome, decently dressed, and has lovely manners. He sounds like a great guy. Don't look a gift horse in the mouth. He sounds terrific. And if you want to have a laugh, think of the heart attack they'll have when his parents see Tweety Bird and Tinkerbell tattooed on her arms, not to mention the ten earrings on her ears. I don't think they'll be calling you tomorrow to arrange a marriage. Why don't you just relax for a while?"

"I'm worried about that too, about his parents, I mean. What if they don't appreciate what a sweet kid she is and judge her by her looks, which I'll admit, even scare me at times? I hate her tattoos. And she **is** serious about this. I can feel it. I know her. I can tell. She's reading books about his culture," Annie said in a subdued voice. "That's fine with me, but not if she's doing it so she can get married." Annie was getting way ahead of herself. All she could think of now was the future and the potential difficulty of integrating their two worlds.

"Okay," Whitney said calmly, "when I was fourteen I wanted to be a nun, and my brother wanted to convert to Judaism so he could have a bar mitzvah, and have a big party to celebrate. None of those things happened, and I don't think Katie is going to move to Iran. Besides, he's an American. He probably doesn't want to live in Iran either, for whatever reason. This is his home now."

"He says he still has relatives there. An uncle and aunt, and a lot of cousins. What if he moves back and she goes with him?" Annie didn't want to lose her to anyone, in any country. Katie was still her baby.

"I have a cousin in Iceland," Whitney added. "I'm not moving there. Annie, you have to let go. You did a fantastic job with them, they're wonderful and your sister would be proud of you, but they're grown up. They have to live their own lives and make their own mistakes. Maybe one of them will marry someone you hate one day, but I don't think any of them are ready to get married yet, not even Lizzie, and she's old enough. And if they really fuck it up and do make a horrible mistake, which can happen to anyone, from any culture, you still have to sit back and watch from the sidelines. It's their life. What you need is a life of your own. You can't hang on to them forever and live theirs or stop them from making mistakes. That's the deal. Once they grow up, they belong to themselves, not to us. It's horrible, and I'm going to hate it with my boys when one of them comes home with some raving bitch, but it's going to be their life, and their turn, not mine. Annie, you've got to get a life. You put in sixteen years for them, you fulfilled your vow to Jane and then some. Now get off the bench and get back in the game yourself. I want you to find a guy."

"I don't want a guy. I'm happy the way I am. I want them to be happy, and I'm not just going to sit here with my mouth shut if they screw up their lives or make some dumb mistake."

"You can't stop them," Whitney said firmly, and Annie hated hearing it and even more knowing she was right.

"Why not?"

"Because we don't have that right. It's not healthy for you, or for them. They're grown up, whether you like it or not. You made your mistakes, let them make theirs."

"What mistakes did I make?" Annie asked, sounding surprised.

"You gave up your life for them," Whitney said gently, and Annie didn't answer. She had, but it had been the right thing to do at the time, and she had no regrets about it. The last sixteen years had been the best years of her life. And the hardest thing for her to adjust to was that it was over now. She had done her job. It was time to open the cage and let them fly, even if Katie wound up living far away or in a different culture. If that was the choice she made, no one could stop her, nor had the right to. Not even Annie.

"I don't know if I can just sit back and watch," Annie said honestly.

"You have no other choice," Whitney said simply. "Your job is over. They're going to lead their own lives no matter what." It was a bitter pill to swallow. It was hard enough living with the empty nest. Watching them make decisions that might cause them unhappiness later was even harder. "You've been lucky so far, and you've done a good job. I don't think they're going to screw it up now. And if they do, you can't stop them. All you can do is help them pick up the pieces later, if they let you. And Katie could be just as unhappy marrying a guy from Paris or London or New Jersey."

"I hate this part," Annie said miserably, "where what they do now impacts their future. The stakes are so much higher as they get older. It was so much easier when they were little."

"No, it wasn't. You were scared shitless you were doing it wrong with someone else's kids. You've just forgotten."

"Maybe I have," Annie said sadly. "He's a nice boy," she said about Paul. "I like him. I just don't want her to wind up halfway around the world, living in Tehran. I don't want to lose her."

"Have a little faith in Katie. She's not going to want that either. She's very close to all of you, and she'll probably wind up living in New York. Besides, Paul lives in New York, and so do his parents. Stop imagining that she's marrying him and moving around the world. You're driving yourself crazy for nothing." Whitney tried to calm her down, and Annie knew that what she had said was true. As agonizing as it was, she was going to have to learn to let go one of these days, and maybe that time had come, whether she liked it or not.

She was sitting on her bed thinking about it when Katie walked into the room. Paul had left. She had a dreamy look on her face and smiled shyly at her aunt. Annie's heart sank when she saw her. She had never seen anyone so in love. And being that much in love put her at serious risk for a broken heart if things didn't work out as she

123

hoped. And at twenty-one, no romance was likely to be forever. The last thing Annie wanted for her was to see her get hurt or even disappointed. She would have liked to keep her in a cocoon and protect her for the rest of her life.

"He's a nice boy," Annie said cautiously, not sure what else to say to someone who looked like she was floating on a cloud. "He has beautiful manners, he's intelligent, and he's very good looking, and he seems like a nice person."

"He's a wonderful person," Katie said, instantly defending him, as though she thought she had to.

"I'm sure he is," Annie said quietly, venturing into dangerous waters. "But he comes from a very different culture. It's something for you to consider." Katie glared at her with instant hostility in answer, ready to go to war, which was what Annie was afraid of. She didn't want to lose her yet to, or over, this boy or any other. Nothing was worth that.

"What difference does it make? He's American. He lives in New York, and he's not going back to Iran, except to visit. His life is here, just like mine."

"That's good. But he may have different ideas than you do. His family isn't American, or his relatives in Iran. I know you don't think so, but that makes a difference. If you married him, how would you raise your children? What would he or his family expect of you? You'd always feel like an outsider or a foreigner. Katie, if you're serious about him, you have to think about that. You come from different backgrounds. It worries me for you." Annie was as honest with her as she could be in voicing her concerns.

"I can't believe how bigoted you are. What bothers you? That his skin is darker than mine? Who fucking cares?"

"Of course not. But I'm concerned that his ideas are different than ours, maybe too different. His parents may think so too, about you."

"You're ridiculous," Katie said with a look of youthful contempt. "You don't even have a man in your life. You never have. You live like some kind of nun, for chrissake. What do you know about loving someone and building a life with them?"

"Not much," Annie admitted with tears in her eyes. Katie had hit hard, and low. "I just want you to understand what you might be headed for. It's true for any relationship. Backgrounds, family customs, and traditions do matter between two people, even if they love each other. I just want what's best for you." She didn't respond to the rest of what Katie had said. She didn't say that she had lived like a nun because she raised three kids at twenty-six, and the man she'd been in love with at the time had dumped her because she had taken on three children who weren't her own, or that she hadn't had time to take anyone seriously since, because she was too busy driving carpool and going to the orthodontist and soccer games. She said none of that and focused the conversation on Katie and Paul, where it belonged.

"I'll do what seems right to me," Katie said, staring at her in fury, and Annie nodded, remembering Whitney's warnings to her an hour before, that it was their lives and they had a right to make their own mistakes and she had to let go. She was trying, but it was hard. And who knew if her relationship with Paul was a mistake? Maybe it wasn't.

"I love you, Katie," Annie said quietly in response, and with that Katie stormed out of her room and slammed the door. All Annie wanted for her was a good life.

Annie lay in her bed that night, thinking about Katie and what they'd said. And she wondered if she was wrong. Maybe she had no right to say anything. Paul seemed like a good person, maybe that was enough. Maybe coming from two different cultures didn't matter and she was wrong. What right did she have to tell Katie who to love and how to live? Maybe Katie would be happy with him. Who was she to judge? And Katie was right about some of it. Annie did live like a nun. For all intents and purposes, her life as a woman had ended at twenty-six. And at forty-two, it seemed too late to get it started again. She had traded a life with a man for them, and she didn't regret the trade. She had no history of relationships to draw from. And all she knew about the Iranian culture was what she'd read. It wasn't the life she would have chosen for Katie, but she had a right to choose it for herself.

And as Annie lay in bed, she thought about Ted too, and wondered about the mystery woman who was distracting him. He had seemed dazed through all of Christmas and had disappeared on Christmas night. She had never seen him like that. And she was convinced that Liz was wasting her time with men like Jean-Louis. Liz was having fun and enjoying her career, but guys like Jean-Louis were never going to take care of her, they were too obsessed with themselves. It was hard watching the three of them grow up.

Annie had a headache when she woke up the next day. Ted and Katie were both already out, and neither had left her a note about their plans. She knew that at their age, they didn't owe her explanations about where they went, and she had no right to ask. Thinking about both of them, Annie made herself a cup of tea and went out for a walk. Whitney called on her cell phone, and she told her about the argument with Katie the night before.

"She's got to defend the relationship, no matter what she really thinks. She can't admit to you that you're right or that she may have questions about it herself. None of us want to admit that we're not sure of what we're doing. It's easier for her to attack you. And saying what you think isn't such a bad thing. Katie knows that your heart is in the right place. Now just back off and see what she does. And have a little fun yourself for a change. Are you coming to New Year's Eve? It might do you good to get out of the house for a night."

"I don't want to ditch them on New Year's Eve."

"Hello? Are you kidding? We've been over this before. They're going to ditch you. They're grown up. They've got their own plans. And I want to introduce you to Fred's friend. He's a terrific guy." As Whitney said it, Annie remembered Katie's comment of the night before, that she lived like a nun. She was forty-two, not ninety-five. Maybe Katie and Whitney were right. At least she had to try. She didn't want to die alone, and if she had another forty or fifty years ahead of her, a little companionship might be nice.

"Okay. I'll come," Annie said, as though she had

just agreed to have her liver pulled out through her nose.

"Great!" Whitney sounded thrilled. "You can spend the night. You shouldn't drive back alone. Think of it, this may be the beginning of a hot romance and a whole new life for you. You're going to love this guy." It had been years since Annie had agreed to a blind date, long enough to forget how disappointing they were. But at least it was something to do on New Year's Eve. And Whitney was right. The kids probably had their own plans.

Annie didn't see Ted or Katie until the following day, and she mentioned to them both that she was going to Whitney and Fred's on New Year's Eve. Had they objected, she would have canceled, but as Whitney had predicted, they both said they had plans with friends. Annie didn't say another word to Katie about Paul. She had said enough, and Katie was still angry at her when Annie left for New Jersey on the afternoon of New Year's Eve.

Chapter 9

Annie arrived at Whitney and Fred's house in Far Hills at six o'clock. There had been very little traffic, and she made good time. She had brought a simple black evening dress and hung it in the backseat. Their three boys were playing basketball in the backyard when she arrived. They were fourteen, sixteen, and seventeen, and all three of them looked like Fred, with freckles and red hair. They were all sports nuts like their father, and their oldest son was currently applying to college. He wanted to go to Duke and do pre-med, like his father. The boys waved to her when she arrived.

Fred was an orthopedic surgeon and had done well. He wasn't a man whom Annie would have chosen, but Whitney was happy and had a good life with him. He had a big ego and had always been impressed with himself, but he was a good father and husband, a good provider, and a responsible person. Annie had always respected him for that.

As she walked into their house after Whitney hugged her, Annie saw that the dining table was beautifully set with gleaming silver and crystal, and there were white flowers and silver streamers everywhere. The evening looked more elaborate than she'd expected.

"How many people are you having?" Annie asked, feeling nervous. She knew that most of their friends were married and were part of a tight circle of people who lived in Far Hills, and many of them were physicians like Fred. She always felt a little strange in their midst, like an outsider or some kind of freak. She tried not to think of it now.

"We're having twenty-four," Whitney said as she helped carry Annie's things to her room. It was a beautiful guest room, and Whitney had thought of every detail. "How was Katie when you left?"

"Still pissed. I've hardly seen her for the past few days. She said she had plans with friends. I didn't ask, but it's probably Paul."

"She'll be fine," Whitney said. "Take a day off. Have some fun yourself tonight. The guests are coming at seven. We'll sit down to dinner at eight or eight-thirty." It didn't give Annie much time to get dressed. And she sank into the tub a few minutes after Whitney left the room. She had promised herself she was going to make an effort and get into the spirit of the evening.

Annie blew her hair dry and did it in a French twist. She put her makeup on carefully and stepped into the black dress. And she wore a pair of high-heeled sandals with feathers on them that Lizzie had bought her in Paris. And she put on diamond earrings that she had bought herself. She checked herself in the mirror before she left her room and decided that her fashionable niece Lizzie would approve. And she carried a small black satin clutch. Annie looked sleek and sophisticated as she left her room, just as the first guests arrived and walked into the living room. They were a couple she had met before. He was an orthopedic surgeon like Fred, and his wife was a friend of Whitney's with kids the same age, and Annie remembered that they always drank a little too much.

The couple looked Annie over as she walked in, and the wife had the smug, condescending look that some married women give single ones, as though they feel sorry for them. Annie wouldn't have traded her own life for hers, but she chatted amiably with them, as other guests continued to arrive. By eight o'clock everyone was there. People arrived promptly in the suburbs, unlike big cities where everyone was late. And she hadn't figured out which one her blind date was yet. All the men in the room had paunches and looked middle-aged, and most of the women were slightly over-weight. Whitney was too, although she was as tall as Annie and carried it well. Annie always suspected that the excess weight was because most of the women drank a little too much wine. Annie had a better figure than anyone in the room. And she was intrigued to discover that the women ignored her, and the men stood in clumps with each other, discussing business or medicine. The men acted as though the women didn't exist, and the women didn't seem to care and talked about shopping, tennis, or their kids.

"Did you see him?" Whitney asked as she stopped to chat with Annie for a minute, then drifted away again. She was busy with her guests. She had introduced Annie to a few people, all of them couples. And Annie had figured out that she and her blind date were probably the only single people in the room. But she hadn't spotted him yet. All she knew from Whitney was that he was fifty-two, a surgeon, drove a Porsche, and was divorced. It would have been hard to identify him from that description unless she'd seen him get out of his car alone.

The women in the room were wearing cocktail dresses or evening gowns, and the men were in black tie, but no one looked really chic, and they seemed a little overdressed. It was five minutes before they sat down to dinner when Whitney brought him over to meet her and introduced her to Bob Graham, the man she was dying for Annie to meet, and as she saw him, Annie's heart sank. He looked like every bad blind date she'd ever had, and he looked her over like a piece of meat. He told her immediately that he was a surgeon and specialized in heart-lung transplants, and he looked as though he expected applause. He looked moderately athletic but still had a paunch and several chins. And he'd had very bad hair plugs done the year before when he got divorced. Annie would have preferred it if he were bald, and she tried to remind herself to be a good sport and give the poor guy a chance. What if he were the nicest man on the planet and had bad hair plugs? It would be worth putting up with his hair if he were a wonderful human being, and maybe he was. Or fascinating. Or funny. Or extremely smart. Anything was possible. She saw him staring at her diamond earrings, and he cut to the chase.

"You're divorced?" Alone at her age, he assumed she was.

"No. I've never been married," she said, smiling

135

at him, wondering if that made her sound racy or like a loser.

"Nice earrings. Your ex-boyfriend must have been a generous guy." She was startled by the comment and had never had a boyfriend who bought her anything other than meals or a scarf.

"I bought them myself," she said, smiling at him, as Whitney herded them into the dining room like sheep, and the heart-lung surgeon sat down next to her. He ignored her completely for the first half of dinner, while he discussed his most recent surgery and hospital politics with two men across the table. And the man on her left had his back turned to her and was in earnest conversation with the woman on his other side. They had reached the dessert course when the heart-lung man turned to her again, as though he had just remembered she was there. She expected him to ask what she did for a living, since she had listened to him discuss his own work all night.

"I'm building a house in the Cayman Islands," he said, totally out of context. "I've got a ranch in Montana, and I needed someplace in a tax haven. I keep my boat there now. Ever been to St. Barts?"

"No, I haven't," she said, smiling at him. "I hear it's lovely."

"I just sold a house there. I made double my money in two years." She wasn't sure what to say to that, and she was fascinated by the fact that he still hadn't asked her what she did or anything about herself. It was all about him. "I just got back from safari in Kenya with my kids. We were there over Christmas. We went to Zimbabwe last year. I liked Kenya a lot better." He made conversation easy, there was none. He asked no questions, didn't care about her opinions, her life experience, her holidays, or her job. "I got some fantastic photographs while we were there." He also wasn't interested in world events, only his own, and Annie listened to him in amazement.

Whitney beamed at her from across the table. She looked as though she had had a lot to drink, and so had everyone else. The dinner had been excellent, provided by the best caterer in Far Hills, but no one seemed to care. All they talked about was the wines. Fred had brought out his best and knew a lot about wine. And so did Bob. He told Annie then about the wine cellars he had at his house and how well stocked they were with the best French wines. Then he told her about his boat and how big it was. He said he had some great art on the boat, and then he commented that he'd given some of it to his ex-wife. By the time they left the table after dinner, Annie had never opened her mouth. The man to her left apologized for not speaking to her as they stood up, and Bob drifted off to talk to Fred and several of their colleagues without a word to her.

She felt like the invisible person in the room. The women were afraid of her because she was thinner, better dressed, and prettier than they were, and the men didn't care. Bob Graham could have talked to himself in the mirror all night and had just as much fun. She suspected he probably normally dated younger women who were impressed by his money, his boat, or his Porsche. She was impressed by none of it, and all she wanted to do was go home. And she was stuck there for the night. She was sorry she had come. Sitting home alone would have been better, but now she had to put a good face on it, for Whitney's sake if nothing else.

"Isn't he great?" Whitney whispered to her as she drifted past her on the way to talk to the women she played tennis with every day. She and Whitney had been friends for years, and Annie loved talking to her, but when she saw her here, she realized how little they had in common, and how different their lives were. Whitney had never worked since she married Fred twenty years before, right out of college. She already had two babies when Annie inherited Jane's family, and Whitney had given her invaluable support and advice. What they shared was history but not much else. And Annie hated their friends. She always forgot how much until she visited her in New Jersey, which she didn't do very often. Most of the time they saw each other in the city when Whitney came in to go shopping, and she was okay one on one. But here, in her natural habitat, with these smug, self-satisfied, pompous people, Annie wanted to scream and run out of the room. The best part of the evening so far had been the food.

Everyone continued drinking until midnight, and Fred counted down, and then everyone screamed and blew little horns that Whitney had produced right before midnight. And then they all kissed, wished each other Happy New Year, and twenty minutes later they all went home. Whitney was totally drunk by then, and Fred went up to bed without saying goodnight to either of them.

"Bob said you were great," Whitney assured her, slurring her words, and Annie hated seeing her like that. She wanted her to be better than this, to be different, but she wasn't. She was one of them. And the fabulous blind date had been another bad joke. Annie had forgotten, since the last one, just how bad blind dates could be. She always swore she wouldn't do it again, but Whitney had pushed her, and after what Katie had said, she thought she should at least try again.

When Whitney went out to the kitchen to pay

the caterers, Annie slipped quietly into her room, took off her clothes and makeup, slid into bed, and turned off the light. And all she wanted was, not a man, but to turn the clock back to when her nieces and nephew were young. They had had such happy times, drinking ginger ale, and staying up till midnight on New Year's Eve, and falling asleep with all three of them in her bed. Those were the New Years she missed. Not dates like Bob Graham. As she drifted off to sleep, she wished she were at home. She was much lonelier here, with Whitney and her friends, than she would have been alone.

Ted's New Year's Eve with Pattie was tender and sweet. They cooked dinner at her apartment, and she had dropped the kids off at their father's, who had just gotten back to town. They toasted each other with champagne, and their lovemaking was alternately wild and gentle, and at midnight they turned on the TV and watched the ball in Times Square come down, and then they made love again. It was a silly, funny evening, full of the passion he had discovered with her in the past month. And she startled him by asking him if he would ever move in with her.

"What would your kids think?" he asked, looking surprised. He had never lived with a woman, just roommates, and his sisters and aunt. He wasn't sure he was ready to move in with a woman, and he felt awkward about her kids.

"They would think we love each other," Pattie said in answer to his question, but he was well aware that it would be a heavy responsibility to bear. What if it didn't work out? What would it do to her kids? They had already been through a divorce. He didn't want to jeopardize them, and he said as much to her, but she wouldn't listen. She was oblivious to his concerns. "Why wouldn't it work out?"

"We need more time," he said sensibly, and she just smiled, as though she knew all the secrets of the world. She told him she loved him a thousand times that night, and he made love to her again and again. It was the most exciting New Year's Eve he'd ever had. They both got drunk on champagne and eventually fell asleep in each other's arms, as the sun came up on a new year.

Paul and Katie spent New Year's Eve at Annie's apartment. She had spent the night at his place before. His roommate had a girlfriend who had her own apartment, and conveniently, he was gone most of the time with her. But this time, Paul stayed with Katie. They made dinner in the comfortable kitchen, watched movies, and kissed at midnight, and they made love in her bed. He was gentle, loving, and respectful, and she knew that everything Annie was concerned about with different cultures didn't apply to him. He was as American as she was, no matter where he'd been born. And he was the kindest man in the world, and Katie was deeply and totally in love for the first time in her life.

Paul was terrified that Annie might come home in the middle of the night, and Katie kept reassuring him that she wouldn't be back till the next day. He made Katie lock her bedroom door anyway. He didn't want anyone to walk in on them. And Katie lay peacefully in his arms as they talked late into the night, about all the things they cared about, their hopes and fears and dreams. He said he wanted to take her to Tehran one day to visit his family there. He wanted to go back to see it again himself. He had so many memories there, and his family, but he wanted to live in the States. He just wanted her to see his country one day, and Katie wanted that too. She wanted to know everything about him and see where he lived as a child.

Paul had introduced her to his parents, who had been extremely polite to her, although a little chilly at first. Paul had explained to her that they always hoped he would eventually marry a Persian girl. But he assured Katie that they would fall in love with her in time, when they got to know her better. It was the same thing that Katie had said about Annie, that she needed to get used to their relationship, and especially the fact that Katie had grown up.

But Katie didn't think about her aunt at all that night. Her heart and mind were full of Paul, and the life they were going to share. It was a new year, a new world, a new life with him. And the differences their families were concerned about didn't exist for them. The only world they cared about was their own.

Chapter 10

Annie could hardly wait to leave Far Hills the next day. She didn't want to be rude and leave before Whitney and Fred woke up. She was up and dressed by nine A.M., and it was ten when Whitney and Fred appeared. She joined them in the kitchen for breakfast, for a recap of the night before. And they both looked painfully hung over. Annie had had very little to drink and felt fine.

"So what did you think of Bob?" Whitney asked hopefully as Fred read the paper. He didn't seem to care about the ill-fated blind date either way. That was Whitney's deal, not his.

"He's a very interesting man," Annie said diplomatically, not wanting to hurt Whitney's feelings by saying what she really thought, that he was an egomaniac and a pompous ass and a crashing bore. "He told me all about his safari in Kenya over Christmas, the ranch in Montana, his boat, the house he's building in the Cayman Islands and the one he just sold in St. Barts. He has a lot to say." But only about himself.

Whitney was getting the picture and looked cautiously at her friend. She realized that there was a lot Annie wasn't saying and she was being polite. Listening to their conversation, Fred got up and walked into the other room. It sounded like girl talk to him. "I'll admit, he's a little full of himself, but he's really a great guy. He gave his wife a fortune in the divorce." Annie wasn't sure that made him such a great guy, unless all you wanted was money and a divorce. If you wanted conversation and a real human being, he wouldn't be an option.

"That's nice for her," Annie said vaguely as she sipped her coffee.

"She left him for the golf pro at the club. It was a terrible blow to his ego, and he's been going out with a lot of young women. They're just after his money. What he needs is a real person."

"Is that his assessment or yours? He's probably having fun with the young women," Annie said sensibly. She really didn't care.

"They're all gold diggers, I've met them. He deserves someone better." Annie wanted to tell her that he didn't. He deserved whatever he got, and wearing his wallet on his sleeve, he was going to find women who were after that. Maybe all he wanted now was to buy one. But he was of no interest whatsoever to her. It was obvious from everything she didn't say. She had found him utterly revolting. "I'm sorry," Whitney said—she could tell what Annie had thought of him from the look on her face. "I guess he's not really your style. I just hoped he would be. He's the only single guy I know. Everyone out here is married." And Annie wouldn't have wanted any of them either, from what she'd seen the night before. She had never seen a more unattractive group of men in her life, and their wives hadn't been much better. All they had talked about all night was money. "Did you tell him you're an architect?" Whitney asked her, and Annie laughed.

"He never asked. He talked about all his houses and possessions. I just let him talk. He wasn't interested in me, and I wasn't interested in him. It's awfully hard to fix people up. I think if it happens, it just has to fall on you. I've never had a blind date that worked," she said to Whitney with a forgiving look. She knew her intentions had been good, even if she was delusional about Bob.

"Maybe you should try Internet dating," Whitney said forlornly. She really wanted to help. She hated knowing that Annie was alone, especially now with the children gone. She knew how hard that was for her and what a void it had left.

"I'm not looking for a date, or a man, or a husband. I'm fine the way I am," Annie said. "And I don't have time anyway. I have ten major jobs backed up right now. Honest, Whit, I'm fine. It's not a high priority for me right now." And Whitney knew it hadn't been, for too long.

"It hasn't been for sixteen years," Whitney reminded her. "You have to think of your future. You're not going to be young and beautiful forever, and you don't want to wind up alone." It didn't sound bad to Annie, if the alternative was Bob Graham.

"Alone isn't so bad." Annie smiled at her. "I'm not unhappy. I just miss the kids. But that's going to happen to you one of these days too. They all grow up and leave sooner or later."

"I'm dreading it," Whitney confessed, as Fred walked back into the kitchen and heard what she said.

"I'm not," he said with a grin. "As soon as the last one leaves, we can start traveling, and doing everything we couldn't do for the last twenty years. We'll be able to go away without worrying if they're totaling the car, or getting alcohol poisoning playing beer pong, or will burn down the house. I can't wait until we're done," he said happily.

"I don't think women see it that way," Annie told him. "It's a huge loss to us when they leave. The kids were my best job for all these years. And suddenly I'm obsolete. Thank God I never gave up my day job, or I'd really be lost now." Whitney understood perfectly, which was why she kept trying to find her a man.

Annie got up from the table then and went to get her things. She said goodbye to Fred and thanked Whitney for a nice time and got into her car with a sigh of relief. She couldn't wait to get home. She felt stupid for having come out at all and for thinking that this blind date would be different. She reminded herself, as she had before, never to do it again. But in a couple of years she knew she'd forget and let someone sucker her into another blind date. She hoped that this time she'd remember just how bad it had been.

As Annie left New Jersey, Katie and Paul were making breakfast in Annie's kitchen. They had gotten up early and dressed. Paul wanted to be gone before Katie's aunt got home. He didn't know how she'd react to his spending the night, and he had sensed her reservations about him, although Katie had been gentle in discussing it with him. Both of them were disappointed by their families' reservations but not surprised.

"She thinks we're from two different worlds," he said sadly. He had seen it in her eyes, although she had been kind to him and he liked her.

"She'll get over it," Katie said quietly. "The real problem with Annie is that she thinks I'm still a child. She worries about me a lot," Katie said fairly. "She was pretty young when my parents died, and she took care of us like a mother. I think it's hard for her to give that up now and realize we're grown up."

"She seems like a good woman," Paul said, and then leaned over and kissed Katie. "I love you. You're a good woman too," he said, smiling at her. He had agreed to come back that afternoon. He just didn't want Annie to know that he'd spent the night. He didn't want to get Katie in trouble either. And his timing was perfect. Paul left the apartment ten minutes before Annie came home. Katie had washed the dishes and put them away, and she was making her bed when Annie walked in and wished her a happy new year.

"What did you do last night?" she asked Katie. She had wondered if Katie would let Paul spend the night, but she could see that that hadn't happened. Her room was in perfect order, and there was no sign of Paul.

"We went out with friends. It was no big deal. I was home pretty early," Katie said as she finished making her bed and they walked into the living room together. "How about you? Did you have fun?" Katie no longer seemed to be angry at her, and Annie laughed and told her about the blind date.

"I think it was the worst one so far. I'd rather be a 'nun' forever than go out with guys like that," Annie said, and Katie looked embarrassed by her comment.

"I'm sorry I said that. I was upset." She hadn't liked Annie expressing her concerns about Paul. He was wonderful to her and such a kind man, and she wanted Annie to be as excited about their relationship as she was and have no hesitations whatsoever, which was a lot to expect, no matter who he was. Annie was always protective of her. Too much so, Katie thought.

"It's fine, you're right. I do live like a nun. Where's Paul, by the way?"

"He's coming over later," Katie said casually, trying to sound as though his being there all the time was a common occurrence.

"That's nice," Annie said sincerely. "He can stay for dinner if you want." Annie liked him and

151

wanted to get to know him better, since he was obviously so important to Kate. But she also knew that traditions ran deep, even in a new generation and another country. "Where's your brother?" she asked Katie.

"I don't know. He vanished. He was probably out with friends last night. And wherever he wound up, I'm sure he's still asleep." Katie went back to her room then and called Paul and told him he could come back anytime he wanted and her aunt had invited him for dinner. He sounded relieved.

"She didn't figure out that I spent the night?" he asked nervously.

"Nope. I put away all the dishes. She got home right after you left."

"I'll come over after I have lunch with my parents," he promised, and then Katie lay down on her bed, listened to music, and thought about him. She was the happiest she'd ever been in her life.

Ted and Pattie woke up at two in the afternoon, when her ex called to say he was dropping off the kids. Ted said he wanted to leave anyway. He didn't think they should see him there too often, and they might suspect he had spent the night. He wanted to keep up an appearance of propriety for them.

"I have to get home," Ted said as he turned on the shower, and Pattie stood in the bathroom doorway, watching him and admiring his body.

"Why?" Pattie questioned him, as she stepped into the shower with him. "Why do you have to go home? Why don't you just stay here with us?"

"I want to spend some time with my sister and my aunt," he said honestly. Sometimes he felt as though she were trying to take over his life. She wanted him there all the time.

"Wouldn't you rather be here?" she asked, pressing her body up against his, as the water ran down their faces, and as she cradled him in her hands, he sprang to life again. She had an instant effect on him, like magic.

"Sometimes I'd rather be here," he said as he kissed her, and fondled her breasts in his hands. She used her own to guide him inside her. "And sometimes I like to be with them too," he whispered into her hair, but Annie and Kate were rapidly fading from his mind. Pattie had a way of pushing everything out of his head but her, and she straddled him as they made love in the shower. The effect was instant and explosive, and he could hardly bear pulling away when it was over. Her diligent applications of soap kept him aroused for even longer. "I'm never going to get out of here if you keep doing that," he warned her, and she laughed.

"That's the idea."

He pulled away from her then and looked down at her, putting words to something he often wondered. "What do you want with a kid like me?"

"I'm crazy about you. I've never been in love like this in my whole life." She looked young and vulnerable as she said it.

"Why? I'm not old enough to be a father to your kids. I'm not ready to be a husband. I still have to finish law school. I feel like I've grown up since I met you, but I still have a long way to go."

"Then take me with you. We'll grow up together."

"You're already grown up," he reminded her. "You're a mom, and you've been a wife . . . I'm just a kid."

"I don't care as long as you're mine." And then she said something that terrified him: "I'm never going to let you go."

"Don't say that," he said softly as he dried himself and stepped into his clothes. He felt trapped when she said things like that, and he didn't want to be her hostage, no matter how exciting she was. He wanted to be with her by choice. Sometimes there was an aura of desperation about Pattie that unnerved him. Their relationship was so much more intense than any he'd been in before.

"It's true," she said as she looked at him sadly. "I'll die if you leave me."

"No, you won't," he said sternly. "You have kids. You can't think like that."

"Then don't leave me."

"I'm not going anywhere," he said softly, "but don't say things like that. It scares me." She nodded and kissed him hard on the mouth.

He left minutes before her kids got home, and hailed a cab to take him to Annie's. And he turned back and waved as Pattie watched him from the window. Her eyes never left the cab until it disappeared.

In Paris, Jean-Louis and Liz were planning to pick up his son Damien to spend the day and night with him. They had had dinner with friends of Jean-Louis the night before. Lizzie had been having a wonderful time since she arrived. He had a beautiful little apartment on the Left Bank on the quais, with a terrace overlooking the Seine. She loved watching the boats drift by and looking across the city. When she came here to work, she stayed at the Four Seasons or the Bristol, but it was much more fun and more romantic staying with him. And she was looking forward to meeting his son. Jean-Louis was planning to take him to the park with her and had promised him a ride on the carousel.

Lizzie was getting ready in his funny old bathroom, with the round **oeil de boeuf** windows, when she opened a drawer looking for a fresh roll of toilet paper, since they were running out. She was startled to see several pairs of women's underwear and a lacy black bra. None of it was hers. She wasn't sure if it was a relic of his past, or something more current, but she took it all out and tossed it on the bed, where Jean-Louis was watching a soccer match on TV between Paris F.C. and Saint-Germain.

"I found these in the bathroom," she said casually as he glanced away from the TV for just a second, and Paris F.C. scored a goal. He heard the crowd cheer and looked back at the TV immediately as he talked to her. He had seen the lacy underwear sitting on the bed. He looked undisturbed.

"You've discovered my secret," he said, smiling at her. "I wear them when you're not here."

"Very funny," she said with a faint tremor in her stomach. She was normally not jealous, but they had agreed to be exclusive, and she wanted to be sure they were still on the same page. "Do these belong to anyone you know?" It was unlikely that a perfect stranger had come to his apartment and left her underpants and a bra in a drawer.

"Probably Françoise. I'm sure they've been here for years and she forgot them when she left. I never look through those drawers. Just throw them away. If she hasn't asked for them in four years, she doesn't need them now." Françoise was his son's mother, and it sounded reasonable to Liz, and she smiled at him as she tossed them in a wastebasket under his desk. It didn't look it, but he had a cleaning woman who came once a week. His apartment was as disorderly as his clothes.

"We're out of toilet paper, by the way," she informed him as she continued to get dressed, relieved by his simple undramatic explanation. She hated jealous scenes, and it was nice to know he wasn't cheating on her. It wasn't the love affair of the century, but it was a comfortable arrangement for both of them.

"There's a roll in my desk. Bottom drawer." The incongruous location for toilet paper was typical of him. His housekeeping skills were nil. "I know that sounds crazy, but I forget where I put it otherwise."

She had put on jeans and a sweater by then, and sexy high-heeled boots, and she looked rail thin. She wound a raspberry-colored pashmina around her neck and put on a black fox coat she had bought in Milan. She looked very stylish for the park and the carousel, and he smiled at her admiringly as he turned off the TV and got up off the bed. He was happy—his team had won. He was taking her to lunch at the Brasserie Lipp before they picked up his son. And Liz was curious to meet the boy and get a look at his mother. She was an extremely successful model Jean-Louis had lived with for two years, and he had remained on good terms with her. They had split up before the boy was a year old, four years before, and she'd had several boyfriends since Jean-Louis.

Liz ate a salad at the famous old brasserie on the Boulevard St. Germain, while Jean-Louis ate a heavy German meal. And at three o'clock they were at the apartment building where Françoise lived on the rue Jacob. She was twenty-five years old, and she looked about fifteen when she opened the door. She was even taller than Liz and stood six feet tall in bare feet, with huge green eyes, flawless skin, and a long mane of red hair. Damien's hair was the same color as his mother's, but otherwise he was the image of Jean-Louis. He smiled up at his father with a delighted look, and then looked quizzically up at Liz, and Jean-Louis introduced her and said she was his friend. Françoise was looking at her with the same curious expression as her son. She shook Lizzie's hand and asked if they wanted to come in.

The decor of her apartment was decidedly Moroccan, with leather poufs on the floor, low tables, and couches that had seen better days and were covered with colorful shawls. Her housekeeping skills were about the same as Jean-Louis's. There were magazines, loose photographs, her modeling portfolio, half-drunk bottles of wine, and shoes everywhere.

Damien seemed like a happy, easygoing child as he ran to hug his father, and then kissed his mother when they left.

The two women had looked each other over with interest, but said very little. Lizzie had the feeling that Françoise wasn't thrilled to see her, but she didn't seem overly upset either. Jean-Louis had said that they had always had a very open arrangement when they lived together and had never been entirely faithful to each other. He had told Liz that she was the only woman he had promised monogamy to, and he considered it an enormous concession and a big commitment from him. Until then, monogamy, his own or his partner's, had never been important to him. He believed in living in the moment, and seizing opportunities when they arose. And he teased Lizzie frequently about how American she was, and what puritans

Americans were. But she stuck by her rules. She didn't want her boyfriend sleeping with anyone else. She had never had any evidence to the contrary, and when she called him at home at night in Paris, when she was in New York, he was always alone. Liz had been intrigued to see him with Damien's mother when they met. They seemed friendly and nothing more. He had told Liz right from the beginning that he and Françoise were good friends, and she trusted him. He had never lied to her yet.

They went to the Bois de Boulogne, and it was cold, but they ran around a lot and played ball with Damien. He was very cute, and Liz made a big effort to speak to him in French, and all three of them rode the carousel. And afterward they went to Ladurée on the Champs Élysées for hot chocolate and pastries. Damien loved it, and even Lizzie succumbed and had **macarons** and a cup of tea. They went back to Jean-Louis's apartment after that, and Liz gave Damien the train she'd brought. He loved it, and once he tired of playing with it, Jean-Louis put on a Disney DVD for him in the bedroom, in French, and the two adults talked quietly in the living room. It had been a perfect day. Lizzie had wanted to meet his son for a long time, but it had never worked out until then. This was the first time she had had leisure time in Paris—she was always so busy when she came, organizing shoots and flying in and out with no time to spare.

"I wish he stayed with me more often," Jean-Louis said wistfully. "He's such a great kid, but I'm never here. Or not for long anyway. Françoise travels a lot too. Her mother comes up from Nice to take care of him but she's been thinking about sending Damien to live with her, now that he's really starting school. It's hard for him to bounce around between the two of us, and her mother takes good care of him. Françoise was really too young when he was born. We thought it was a great idea at the time when she got pregnant, but we probably should have waited." He smiled at Liz then. "But then he would never have been born. I guess destiny makes the right decisions after all." It seemed odd to her to leave something as important as the decision to have a child to "destiny." She had never felt ready to have a baby so far, and she couldn't imagine doing that for many years. She was too involved in her career, and so were Françoise and Jean-Louis, but they didn't seem to care.

"Won't he miss you both terribly if you send him to live with his grandmother?" She felt sorry for the boy, being shuttled between two very independent people who had had him when they were too young, and a grandmother in another city.

"It would be better for him. She has more stability than we do, and Françoise has two sisters, in Aix and Marseille. He would see his aunts and uncles and cousins. We don't have time to get him together with other kids, except at nursery school, or the day care where Françoise takes him. You were brought up by someone other than your parents. It doesn't seem to have hurt you," he said practically, but what he didn't see and had never understood was how marked Lizzie had been by her parents' death, no matter how wonderful Annie had been to them. It wasn't the same as growing up with a mom and dad, and it had been a crushing loss for her. And perhaps it was even worse if your parents chose to send you away. How would you explain that to yourself later on?

"We had no choice. My parents died. But Damien might feel really abandoned by the two of you. I suffered terribly from the loss of my parents all through my teens. I think I blamed them for dying, although I loved my aunt a lot and she was terrific and like a mother to me. But she's not my mother, she's my aunt."

"We'll explain it to him later on." Jean-Louis smiled at her as he lit a Gitane. "Françoise isn't ready to give up her career. And she can only do what she's doing, at this level, for a few more years. It would be a shame for her to stop now. And I can't. I'm sure he'll understand," Jean-Louis said confidently. Liz wasn't so sure how he'd feel later about parents who hadn't been willing to make the necessary adjustments for him and thought only of themselves. In some ways she thought they treated him like a toy. She was still grateful for the sacrifices Annie had made, which she was even more aware of now. She couldn't imagine what her life would be like if she had been raising three children now, of the ages she and her siblings had been when Annie got them at twenty-six. Liz didn't think herself capable of it, now or at any age, which made her admire Annie even more for all she'd done.

"I couldn't do it either," Liz said fairly, "but I wouldn't have a kid. I don't want to screw up someone else's life."

"We're not," Jean-Louis assured her, blind to what they weren't doing for the boy. And with that Damien walked into the room. The movie had finished, and he was hungry. Jean-Louis put some cheese and pâté on a plate for him, and opened a box of the **macaron** cookies they had bought that afternoon at Ladurée. And Damien seemed perfectly content with that. He lived on pizza and sandwiches when he was with his mother. His father always had better things to eat. But he didn't look unhappy or malnourished, and he was easy

163

to be with. He had learned early to adjust to the grown-ups around him and not cause any trouble. If he did, they sent him away. Liz thought it was a hard life for him and not one she would have wanted to give a child, nor the one she had had with her aunt, who had adjusted herself to them and given them a secure, happy childhood. Annie always talked about how lucky she was to have them. Lizzie was more grateful than ever for her now, in the context of her own life, and how hard it was for her to juggle what she had on her own plate. And she was sure it wasn't easy for Françoise and Jean-Louis either. But Damien was paying the price for it. She never had. She had had a perfect childhood, under the circumstances. And even with that, she was shy of long-term commitments now. She had never told a man she loved him, for fear that if she did, he might die or disappear, and she didn't think she had ever been in love. She was still asking herself the question about Jean-Louis. She was attached to him, and she enjoyed him, but to her love was something much deeper than this, from which there was no turning back. She had never given up her option to end a relationship or leave. And this was the extent of the commitment she wanted for now. She couldn't even imagine having a child with him. And surely not at twenty, as Françoise had done. Jean-Louis often said that he'd like to have another one sometime. Liz was not planning to volunteer.

Lizzie played cards with Damien for a little while, and with his new train again, and then Jean-Louis put on another DVD. And eventually the irresistible little boy with the big green eyes and red hair fell asleep on his father's bed, and Jean-Louis scooped him up and put him on the narrow bed he had set up for him in a tiny room, where he stayed when he was here. They were taking him back to Françoise the next day.

Liz and Jean-Louis spent a quiet evening talking and drinking wine after Damien fell asleep. They talked mostly about fashion, and the editors and photographers they knew, the politics at various magazines, particularly hers, and their careers. They were comfortable and compatible, had the same interests, knew many of the same people, and worked in the same milieu. It was an ideal situation for both of them. And a perfect way to spend New Year's Day. She cuddled up next to him when they went to bed that night. She didn't want more than this, and she liked staying with him in the funny little attic apartment in Paris, and the loft in New York. They didn't make love that night because Lizzie didn't want Damien to walk in on them, and there was only one bathroom in the apartment, although Jean-Louis assured her he wouldn't hear anything and never woke up during the night, but she didn't want to risk it and traumatize him. She felt responsible for him while she was there.

They all woke up at the same time the next morning, and Damien appeared in their bedroom doorway in the same clothes he'd worn the day before. Jean-Louis hadn't wanted to wake him by trying to take them off, and he hopped onto the bed with them and asked what they were doing that day. Jean-Louis said they were taking him back to his mother after breakfast, because he and Lizzie had to get ready for work the following morning, and they had a lot to prepare.

"My grandma is coming tonight," Damien said happily. "Maman is going to London tomorrow, to work. She'll be gone for five days." He already knew the plan and seemed happy that his grandmother was coming. "We have ice cream every day when my grandma is here," he explained to Liz, and her heart went out to him. Ice cream didn't seem like enough to make up for parents who were so seldom there, and so self-involved when they were. She hoped that his grandmother made it up to him as best she could.

Liz made toast with jam for all of them and boiled an egg for Damien, while Jean-Louis made café au lait and gave some to the boy too. He served it in bowls, the way they did in the old cafés. It was delicious, and Damien had a milk mustache from the fragrant brew. Liz drank all of hers.

They were back at Françoise's Moroccan lair on the rue Jacob by eleven, and Damien was happy to see his mother, although he looked wistful as he said goodbye to his father. Jean-Louis explained that he would be in Paris for two weeks, and he planned to see his son again soon, and Damien looked happy about it. It was obvious that he loved his father.

There was a man at the apartment when they got there, and he looked very young to Lizzie, no more than nineteen. And she recognized him after a few minutes. He was a young British model **Vogue** had been using a lot recently, and he was very sweet to Damien when they walked in. He talked to him like another kid, and Damien seemed to know him. His name was Matthew Hamish, and Jean-Louis knew him too. He seemed slightly annoyed about it after they left, which surprised Liz. And the comments he made about the young British model almost made her think that he was jealous.

"Are you jealous of him?" she asked as they walked away from Françoise's building.

"Of course not. Who she sleeps with is none of

my business." He didn't know that for sure, but Matthew had been lying on the couch bare chested, in jeans with bare feet, and looked like he had just gotten out of the shower when they arrived. "I just think it's a little foolish to have people come and go in Damien's life, who aren't important to her."

"How do you know he isn't?" Lizzie asked with interest. He definitely sounded jealous to her. Françoise had been more gracious to Liz than Jean-Louis had been to the young male model. He'd barely spoken to him, and Françoise had thanked her for taking care of Damien and been warmer at their second meeting than the first.

"He's not her type," Jean-Louis answered somewhat tersely, and changed the subject. But Liz could see that he was annoyed for a while. He finally relaxed when they went back to his apartment. They both had calls to make for the shoots they were doing the next morning, and Liz was sorry they wouldn't be working together. Hers was a big jewelry story that she had been setting up for months, and he was shooting the cover for the April issue of French **Vogue**.

They went downstairs to a nearby bistro for soup and a salad at dinnertime, and when they went back to his place afterward, they made love. His irritation over Françoise and the British model seemed to have dissipated again, and Lizzie realized that he was just being territorial. No one liked to be faced with their ex-lover's current significant other, no matter how over it was. And she realized that their openness with each other, mostly because of Damien, was very French. But in any case Jean-Louis was in good spirits again when they went to bed that night, and they both fell asleep with their arms around each other. Jean-Louis had set the alarm for five A.M. They both had to be on their sets by six. And as she fell asleep, Liz found herself thinking about Damien. She didn't know why, but she couldn't get him out of her mind. Her heart ached at the life he led. He deserved so much more than he was getting. It almost made her wish that she and Jean-Louis would be together for a long time. And who knew, maybe they would. So far their days in Paris had been perfect.

Chapter 11

Liz was one of those meticulous editors who tried to anticipate every possible problem in advance. She hated surprises, particularly bad ones, and did everything to avoid them. But in spite of all her careful preparation, she had a dozen knotty problems to deal with on the set the next day. They were shooting outdoors on the Place Vendôme, and the first thing that went wrong was that it started to rain. They placed a huge tent over the models and filtered in artificial sunlight. It took them longer to set up, but it was manageable. They had set up heaters against the freezing cold. But one of the models said she was getting sick anyway and didn't want to work.

The clothes in the shoot were secondary, and she and the stylist had chosen several simple black and white dresses by an American designer, two of which had gotten stuck in French customs and couldn't be released, so they had to make do with what they had. And the stylist substituted a great-looking white shirt for one of the dresses, which worked. The whole focus of the shoot was the jewelry Lizzie was featuring, and that was their worst problem. All of the jewelers she had worked with to pull pieces had sent what she had chosen, but one of the more important jewelers had substituted several pieces she didn't like. She called him immediately, and he apologized, but he had sold the pieces she had picked, and never told her. Worse yet, he was a designer in Rome so she couldn't go back and find something else. She raced to two of the jewelers she was working with in Paris, during a break in the shoot, but she didn't find anything there she liked, and she was short three or four pieces for the shoot. It was the kind of stress and aggravation she hated but that just couldn't be avoided sometimes.

"Jesus, I should have read my horoscope for today," Lizzie complained to the head stylist. She had no idea what to do. She reorganized the jewelry for several of the shots, but no matter how she rearranged it, she came up short, and this was a major story. The editor in chief in New York was not going to care that a model had been sick, two dresses were stuck in customs, and four major pieces of jewelry that they had planned to feature had been sold. Lizzie sat quietly in a chair at the edge of the set with her eyes closed, trying to figure it out. She was good at pulling rabbits out of hats, but this time she was coming up dry. One of the assistant stylists approached her after a few minutes, and Lizzie waved her away. She didn't want to be bothered right now. Jean-Louis called her too during his own lunch break, and she told him she was up to her ass in alligators and she'd call him back. He said his shoot was going great, which only irritated her more. She had her own problems right now. As she turned off her cell phone, the young assistant approached her again.

"I'm sorry, Liz. I know you're busy, but Alessandro di Giorgio is here."

"Shit," Lizzie said through clenched teeth. He was one of the important jewelers whose pieces they were using, and the last thing she needed now was a nosy jeweler who wanted to be sure that his work was the most important in the shoot. Some jewelers were like stage mothers, and she didn't need one of them telling her what to do, or trying to sweet-talk her into giving him a better spot. "Can you tell him I'm off the set?" She had never met him personally and had dealt with him by e-mail, and all of his big pieces had been sent with armed guards from Rome.

"I think he knows you're here," the young stylist said apologetically. She was terrified and fresh out of school. This was her first big job. She knew Liz's reputation as a perfectionist, and given everything that had gone wrong that morning, she was scared to death someone would take it out on her. Fashion was a high-tension business, and when things went wrong at a shoot, invariably shit rolled downhill. She was at the bottom of the hill. Liz looked at her in annoyance but was polite.

"I don't have time to talk to him right now. I'm trying to figure out what the fuck to do about the three pieces I don't have. Four, to be exact."

"That's what he wants to talk to you about. He said he had to come to Paris anyway, to see an important client, and he has several other pieces with him you haven't seen. He stopped by the set, and I told him what happened, and he was wondering if you'd like to see what he's got." Lizzie stared at her in amazement and broke into a smile.

"There is a God. Where is he?" The young girl pointed to a tall blond man wearing a tie and a dark blue suit, carrying a large briefcase, and flanked by armed guards. He was looking straight at her with a cautious smile. As he approached her, he looked just like the photographs she had seen of him, and he was impeccably dressed.

"Miss Marshall?" he asked her quietly, as both

guards stood slightly back but close enough to take action if he were attacked. "I understand you have a problem. I will be meeting with a client this afternoon, and I saw the shoot happening here. I thought I'd walk by. My client will be upset if I bring her fewer pieces, but she'll never know what she never saw. And you can send them back to me later. I'll tell her there was a delay in my atelier, if you select some of the pieces she was interested in."

"There must be a patron saint for jewelry editors who are in a jam," Liz said gratefully. She was a great admirer of his designs.

"I'd rather not show you the pieces here," he explained. "I'm sure you understand. If you have a few minutes, I have a suite at the Ritz. We could go there." The hotel was literally twenty yards away, as she looked at him with wide eyes. He spoke perfect English, with a slight Italian accent.

She felt like a bum walking into the Ritz next to him, in his perfectly cut suit. She was wearing leggings, running shoes, a sweatshirt, and a raincoat, and for once she didn't even have high heels in her bag. And she hadn't even bothered to brush her hair at five A.M. She'd just jammed it into a clip, drunk a cup of Jean-Louis's coffee, and run out the door. And now she looked a total mess.

She was impressed to see that Alessandro di Giorgio had an enormous suite on the Vendôme side of the Hotel Ritz. He was using it to see private clients, and without hesitating, he opened the lock on the briefcase and took out a dozen pieces of breathtaking jewelry in diamonds, rubies, emeralds, and sapphires. The pieces were even bigger and more impressive than what she had planned to use from the other jeweler, and it meant that there would be more di Giorgio pieces in the spread, but at this point she had no choice, and it was the most beautiful work she had ever seen.

"Do I dare ask who your client is for pieces like this?" She was fascinated. They were huge.

"The wife of an emir," he said discreetly, but didn't say which one. "Will this help you out?"

"Oh my God, this is a miracle," she said, looking at him with amazement.

"Take whatever you like, whatever you need. I'll make my excuses to the emir's wife." And this was good publicity for him too. He was well known in the States but much more so in Europe. He was the third generation of jewelers under his name. His grandfather had started the business, and his father was still alive and involved. Alessandro was thirty-eight and had been designing for his father for fifteen years. Liz had researched them carefully for the story and liked the fact that many of their pieces were unique and one of a kind, and that their work was so respected in Europe. They had stores in Rome, London, and Milan but none in Paris. He saw clients there himself, and it was just sheer luck that he was there today.

Liz picked four of the biggest pieces, and Alessandro nodded as she chose. He could see the direction she was going, and the look she wanted, and he suggested a fifth piece that he thought could work too. She agreed with him and added it to the others. He packed her choices in boxes and assigned one of his guards to go back to the set with her, and ten minutes after they had walked into the hotel, they walked out again, with Liz carrying an innocuous Ritz shopping bag with everything she needed in it and even an extra piece. She stood looking up at him when they got back to the set and didn't know what to say. He had saved her ass, but saying that to a man as well-bred and polished as he was would have been rude. He was extremely polite.

"You really saved my life." She almost cried as she said it, and he smiled. "I'll get everything back to you tonight, or tomorrow at the latest."

"Take your time," he said calmly. "I'm here for three days. We have a number of clients to see in Paris."

"Do you ever come to New York?" she asked him. She really felt she owed him something for his generous help.

"Not very often. We do most of our business in Europe. But I come once in a while. I like New York very much." He looked younger when he talked to her. He was so serious and well dressed that at first she had thought he was much older. But she remembered now that he was only ten years older than she was.

"Well, the next time you come to New York, I owe you lunch, or dinner, my first born, something."

"I was happy to help you. I hope your shoot goes well, Miss Marshall," he said formally.

"It will now, thanks to you." She beamed at him, and he had no problem looking past the unbrushed hair and the work clothes to see that she was a beautiful girl.

"**Arrivederci,**" he said, and then walked away and got into a chauffeur-driven Mercedes with the single armed guard, leaving the other guard with her since she had some of his most important pieces now.

And half an hour later they got back to work. Her spirits were buoyed, knowing she had what she needed, and the photographer was excited when he saw the pieces. They were much more beautiful than the ones they had been promised by the other jeweler.

At six o'clock they were still working when Jean-

Louis dropped by. Liz was looking tense, still shaken by the calamities of the morning, but it was going well.

"Almost done?" he whispered as he came up behind her, and she turned with a start and then smiled.

"About another hour." She was frozen to the bone but didn't care. The weather had been awful, but the shoot had been great.

"What did you do about the jewelry you didn't get?"

"An angel fell out of the sky, carrying a briefcase, and gave me even better stuff." She grinned at him, still in awe of her good luck.

"What does that mean?" Jean-Louis looked baffled, and he knew what a genius Liz was at problem solving, but that was too much for even her to pull off.

"Just what I said. One of the jewelers we used happened to be in Paris, and walked by. He was taking a briefcase full of incredible pieces to a big Arab client and gave me five of them for the shoot. It's the best jewelry I've ever seen, better than what we had. And bigger."

"You're a magician," he said, giving her a hug, "and you lead a charmed life." She definitely felt blessed that day. "I'm meeting a friend at the Ritz for a drink," he told her. "Come in when you're finished, and we'll go home." He disappeared then into the Ritz, and Lizzie went back to work.

As it turned out, it was another two hours before she was finished, and they had shot all the di Giorgio pieces. She returned them to the armed guard who'd been with her all afternoon and wrote a hasty note to Alessandro di Giorgio, thanking him again. She promised to send him tear sheets of the shoot. And then she met Jean-Louis in the bar. He was happily drinking Kir Royale with an old friend. They had gone to school together, and he looked as disreputable and unkempt as Jean-Louis. They almost looked like twins. Jean-Louis explained that he was an artist and had a studio in Montmartre that once belonged to Toulouse-Lautrec. And she had to admit to herself that for once she looked as disheveled as they did. She couldn't wait to go home, get warm, and take a long hot bath.

They got back to his place at ten o'clock, and Lizzie had to be up at five again for the second day of the shoot. They were using the Place de la Concorde as their location this time, and the Arc de Triomphe the following day. She had a heavy week. Jean-Louis had the following day off and was planning to spend it with friends.

As Liz sank into the tub and closed her eyes, she thought back over the shots they had done, the jewelry they'd used, the models and their clothes. As she ran the film of the day through her head, she was satisfied with the work. And she was still thinking about it, and already worrying about the next day, as she fell asleep in Jean-Louis's bed. He glanced over at her and smiled as he turned off the light. He had never known anyone who worked as hard as Liz, and he certainly didn't want that for himself. Few people did.

Annie's first days back to work after the holidays weren't much smoother than Liz's. It seemed like there was chaos at all her construction sites, her most important contractor had quit, and there were delays on all her projects. After the first of the year, all hell had broken loose. She was so stressed that she didn't have time to stop for lunch all week. It was Thursday afternoon when she got back to her office at a decent hour. She had some plans she needed to change, and she wanted to get her files in order. And she had dozens of calls to return and e-mails to answer. She asked her assistant for a cup of black coffee and got to work. She decided to open the mail on her desk first. The second letter she opened was from Kate's school, and she suddenly panicked, thinking she had forgotten to pay her tuition. Her accountant usually handled it, but the check could have gotten lost in the mail. Instead, her heart stopped when she saw what the letter said. It confirmed the fact that Kate had dropped out of school for a semester. And Annie's week had been so stressful so far that she was furious the minute she read it. What the hell was Kate doing? Annie forgot everything else she had to do as she dialed Katie's cell phone in a fury.

"I want to see you at the apartment tonight," she barked into the phone, which was unlike her. She rarely lost her temper with her nieces and nephew. She preferred to explain things and be reasonable. But what Kate had done was not reasonable. Annie was not willing to let her drop out of school, and she hadn't asked Annie's permission. But at twenty-one, she didn't have to.

"What's wrong?" Katie asked, sounding stunned.

"I'll discuss it with you when I see you," Annie said tersely. "Not over the phone. I'll be home by eight o'clock. Be there." And with that she hung up, without waiting for Katie to answer. Annie was so mad, she was shaking. She hadn't raised them for sixteen years, and taught them everything she could, and given them all the opportunities their parents would have wanted, in order for them to become dropouts. Katie was a talented artist, and Annie wanted her to go to school and get the degree she'd started.

Annie finished everything on her desk in record time and took the plans she had to change with her when she went home. She'd been so distracted for the rest of the afternoon that she couldn't think straight. The lights were on when she got home, and Katie was in her room listening to music. She walked out the minute she heard the front door close and stood looking at her aunt. Annie was obviously livid. She took her coat off, hung it up, and walked into the living room, and Katie followed. Annie sat down and looked at her, with a mixture of disappointment and anger. It was the disappointment that shook Katie, more than the anger.

"What the hell are you thinking?" were Annie's opening words to her. "I got the notice from your school. You didn't even ask me. How disrespectful is that? And what are you planning to do now, without a degree? Work at McDonald's?"

Katie fought to keep her voice calm. She wanted to prove to Annie that she was an adult, not a child. She had a right to make her own decisions. "I got offered a job that I want to do for one semester. I thought maybe I could do it as an art project or an internship, but they wouldn't let me. So I took a semester off to do it. It's not such a big deal. I'll go back to school next term."

"What kind of job is it?" Annie said, still upset

by the way Katie had done it. She had said nothing to her aunt over the holidays about wanting to drop out of school, or do an internship. She could at least have discussed it with her.

"It's a good job," Katie said, balking at the question. "I want to do it."

"What is it?" Annie was fierce as she asked her, as only Annie could be when she was angry, which was infinitely rare. And all she wanted was what was best for Katie.

"I'm going to be doing designs at a tattoo parlor," Katie said quietly, and Annie stared at her in horror.

"Are you crazy? You're giving up a term at Pratt, one of the best design schools in the country, to work in a tattoo parlor? Please tell me you're kidding."

"I'm not kidding. They do some great art. I know I can do some really creative things there. There are some major emerging artists who have gotten their start in tattoo parlors."

"If I didn't love you so much, I'd kill you. Katie, you can't do this. Is it too late to sign up at school for this term?"

"I don't know. I won't do it. I'm going to work at the tattoo parlor. I started on Tuesday, and I love it. I've already given up my room at the dorm, as of this weekend."

"Then I expect you to live at home." Annie's tone was icy. She was so angry and upset, she could hardly speak.

"I was planning to do that anyway," Katie said politely. "I told you, I'll go back to school next semester. I want to do this for a while. It's very creative."

"Will you please tell me what you think is creative about tattooing anchors and eagles on people's asses? This is the craziest thing I've ever heard." Katie had always been different from the others. She was more independent, more artistic, more of an individual, braver, and was never afraid to try out new ideas. But this one was one of the worst she'd ever had, in Annie's opinion. She had always been supportive of her niece's creativity, but this time she had gone too far.

"Did Paul have anything to do with this?" Annie asked suspiciously, and Katie shook her head with tears in her eyes.

"No. He's mad at me too. He thinks it's stupid, and undignified, and not right for a woman."

"He got that right." Annie couldn't even imagine saying that her niece was a tattoo artist, or what her parents would have thought of it. It didn't bear thinking. "I'm very disappointed in you, Katie," Annie said, calming down a little. "I expect you to finish school. Not for me, but for

185

you. You need the degree to do something important with your art, or even to get a good job."

"I know I do," she said reasonably, as tears slid down her cheeks. She hated to disappoint the aunt she loved so much and whose respect was so important to her. "I just wanted to do something different and more creative, and I've always loved tattoos."

"I know," Annie said, as she leaned over and put an arm around her. "But I just want you to finish school, and a tattoo parlor is such an unsavory place to be. The people are awful."

"You don't know that, and I don't care anyway. I just want to do the art. Someone else can do the tattoos." She didn't tell her aunt that they were teaching her to do that too.

"Do Ted and Lizzie know about this?" Annie asked, wondering if it was a conspiracy or just one of Kate's crazy ideas. But Katie shook her head. "They're not going to be happy either." And as Annie said it, Katie stuck out her chin in defiance, just as she had when she was five years old. She had always been the toughest of the kids to manage, never afraid to back up her own ideas or take the consequences for it when she did.

"I have to do what makes me happy, and what's right for me, not just what works for all of you. I want to learn how to do beautiful tattoos. It's a form of graphic art, even if you don't like it. And after that, I'll go back to school." She sounded stubborn and defiant as she said it.

"I'm going to hold you to that," Annie said sternly, and then wiped the tears from Katie's cheeks, and spoke more softly. "I wish you weren't so damn independent and listened to me once in a while."

"I do. But I have to do what I think is right too. I'm twenty-one years old. I'm not a baby."

"You'll always be a baby to me," Annie said honestly. It was the conversation she'd had with Whitney a month before, about letting them go, make their own mistakes, and have their own lives. She couldn't protect them forever.

"Where is this place?" Annie asked, and Katie told her. It was in a horrible neighborhood, and just the idea of her being there filled Annie with terror. What if something happened to her? Or she got AIDS from one of the needles? "I wish you'd give up this idea," Annie pleaded with her. "It really is one of your worst."

"I'm not going to," Katie said fiercely. "I'm an adult, and I have a right to make this decision."

"I guess you do," Annie said sadly. "But not all the decisions we make are good."

"We'll see," Katie said quietly, prepared to defend her independence with whatever it took. She didn't share with her aunt then that she also wanted to do some traveling, and she wanted to go to Tehran with Paul for a visit to his family in the spring. She figured that right now that news could wait. And after they talked quietly for a few more minutes, Kate went back to her room. She was planning to bring home all her things from the dorm that weekend.

In her own room, Annie took two aspirins for the headache she'd had since that afternoon and lay down on her bed. She would have called Lizzie, but she didn't want to bother her in Paris. And it was three in the morning for her by then. Instead she called Ted. He didn't answer, and it went straight to voice mail. Annie left him a message to call her as soon as he could. She couldn't believe that Katie was going to be working in a tattoo parlor. The idea of it made her sick. And all she could hope now was that Katie would come to her senses and do what she had promised and go back to school. And the worst of it was knowing that no matter how much she loved her, there was nothing Annie could do. Overnight she had become obsolete.

Chapter 12

The following day was even more stressful for Annie. She had an argument with two contractors, and a very difficult meeting with one of her more challenging clients. The weather was terrible, which was slowing everything down, and the fact that Katie had dropped out of school, without even discussing it with her first or asking her advice, had Annie on edge all day. The idea of Katie working in a tattoo parlor seemed even worse the more she thought about it. And she hadn't heard from Ted yet. She at least wanted a shoulder to cry on, and maybe he could influence his younger sister, or Liz could when she got back. But for now, Liz was in Paris up to her ears in her own work, and Ted hadn't called.

By the end of the afternoon, Annie couldn't stand it any longer, and after visiting a job site where everything was going wrong, she hailed a cab and gave the driver the address of the tattoo parlor Katie had mentioned the night before. It was on Ninth Avenue, in what had once been called Hell's Kitchen but in recent years had been cleaned up. But it still wasn't where Annie wanted her niece to hang out, let alone go to work every day instead of school. She groaned out loud when they got to the address. The tattoo parlor was lit up in neon, and a cluster of unsavory-looking people were standing around smoking outside. Annie had never seen uglier people in her life.

"Wrong address?" the driver asked her when he heard the sound of despair from the backseat.

"No, unfortunately the right one," she said as she paid him, with a good tip.

"You getting a tattoo?" He seemed surprised. She didn't look the type. She was wearing a black wool coat with black slacks and a black cashmere sweater, and she looked impeccably groomed.

"No, I'm not. Just looking." She didn't want to admit to him that her niece was working there. It was too embarrassing and depressing.

"I wouldn't do it if I were you," he advised her. "You can get AIDS from the needles," he warned.

"I know." She thanked him again and slid out of the cab, and she pushed open the door to the tattoo parlor and looked around. The people working there all had pierces and tattoos, and most of them had full sleeves of colorful tattoos. She didn't care what Katie said, Annie still did not consider it art.

A woman came over to ask if she could help her, and Annie said she was there to see Kate Marshall. Annie looked like a visitor from another planet with her sleek blond hair, fashionable high-heeled boots, and new black coat. She wanted to run right out the door, but she stood her ground as she waited for Kate, and a few minutes later her niece came through a back door where the private rooms were. She was wearing a miniskirt, red turtleneck sweater, and combat boots with her short blue-black dyed hair. But even dressed like that, Annie thought she looked much too good for this place.

"What are you doing here?" Katie asked her in a whisper. She looked nervous that Annie had come.

"I wanted to see where you work." The two women looked deep into each other's eyes, and finally Katie looked away first. She knew she couldn't convince Annie that this was acceptable instead of school, but she thought she shouldn't have to defend it either. She had made a decision that felt right to her. "Are you okay?" Annie asked her gently, and Katie nodded, and then she smiled, and looked happier than she did a minute before.

"I'm having fun. They're teaching me a lot. I want to learn how to do tattoos, just so I know what it takes and how the designs work on skin." Annie refrained from saying "Why?"

Annie only stayed for a few minutes, and Katie didn't tell her co-workers who she was. It made her feel like a child to have her aunt check up on her, and she was no longer a child as far as she was concerned. She was an adult. She looked visibly embarrassed to have Annie there, so once she had looked around, Annie left.

Annie wanted to cry as she drove away in a cab. She couldn't get the image of those people out of her head. They had bolts and pierces everywhere. They looked like a scary lot to her. She had one more job site to visit before she went back to her office, and then home at the end of the day.

The construction site was another one of her trouble spots right now, and she was fiercely upset when she saw that one of the workmen had left a hose on earlier in the day, and in the freezing weather, the water had turned to ice on the ground. It was an invitation to accidents and another headache she didn't need. She pointed it out to the foreman, and the contractor who was there too, and then, still thinking about Katie and her

new job, Annie stepped over the construction de-
bris and hurried out of the site and back toward
the street. It was getting late. Her mind was so full
of Katie that she didn't see the last patch of ice she
had complained about, and suddenly her high-
heeled boots flew into the air, and she came down
hard on one foot with a sharp yelp. One of the
construction workers had seen her fall and rushed
to help her. He picked her up, dusted her off, and
steadied her on her feet. But the moment he did,
she winced, her stomach flipped over, and she
thought she was going to faint from the pain.
Someone got her a folding chair, and the pain in
her ankle was excruciating.

"Are you okay?" the foreman asked her with a
worried look. It was exactly what she had just
warned them about. What she hadn't expected
was that the accident waiting to happen was her.
She had been totally distracted and distraught
since her visit to Katie at the tattoo parlor, and she
hadn't looked where she was going in her rush to
leave and get back to the office. And it was one of
the very rare times she had worn high heels to a
construction site. She hadn't planned to visit any
of them that day and changed her mind once she
got to work.

Several of the men had gathered around her by
then, and she tried standing up again, but she

couldn't. She was seriously annoyed at herself. She had been visiting construction sites for twenty years and had never injured herself. The high-heeled boots that day had been a big mistake.

"I think it may be broken," Annie said, wincing, as she tried to stand up. She could put no weight on it at all.

"You'd better go to the hospital," the foreman advised her. "It may only be a bad sprain. But either way, you should get an X-ray so you know, and you can get a cast on it if you need to." That was all she needed now. With everything she had to do these days, she didn't want to have to hobble around on crutches or in a cast.

"Maybe I'll just go home and put some ice on it," she said as she tried to limp off the site, but in the end it took two men to get her to a cab. And a third one was carrying her briefcase and purse. "Thanks, I'm sorry to be such a pain in the neck."

"You're not. But get yourself to the ER," the foreman insisted. She nodded, pretending to agree with him, but once in the cab, she gave the driver her office address. She was sure she'd be fine when she got home and took her boots off, but for now it hurt like hell. And when she got to her office, she couldn't get out of the cab. The driver turned to look at her as she struggled.

"Looks like you got hurt pretty bad," the driver said sympathetically. "What happened?"

"I fell on some ice," she said, trying to use the door as a prop, but she couldn't put her injured foot on the ground without wanting to scream.

"Lucky you didn't hit your head," the driver commented, and it was obvious she was going nowhere. She couldn't move. "Why don't you let me take you to a hospital? Maybe it's broken." She was beginning to think it was, and was furious over the bad luck that it had happened. She slid back onto the seat and asked him to take her to the NYU Medical Center emergency room. She felt stupid going there, but she couldn't take a single step either. She needed crutches at the very least.

The driver took her to NYU Medical Center, and left her in the cab when he went inside to get an attendant. A woman in blue pajamas came back out with him, pushing a wheelchair, as Annie sat helplessly at the edge of the seat. She couldn't walk.

"What do we have here?" the ER tech asked pleasantly.

"I think I may have broken my ankle. I fell on some ice." Annie was pale and looked like she was in a lot of pain. The nurse helped her into the wheelchair, Annie handed the driver another ten dollars, and he wished her luck. She felt sick from the pain, and she wanted to cry, more about Katie than her hurt foot. She hated her working at a tattoo parlor, and the place looked awful. It was all she could think of as the woman in blue scrubs wheeled her to the registration window in the ER, and Annie handed the clerk her insurance card. She filled out the form, they put a plastic bracelet on her arm with her name and birth date on it, and then they parked her in the wheelchair, handed her an ice pack, and told her to wait.

"How long?" Annie asked, looking around the crowded waiting room. She wasn't sure if it was by triage or order of arrival, but either way it could take hours. There were at least fifty people there, most of them injured or sick.

"Couple of hours," the woman said honestly. "Maybe less, maybe more. It depends how serious the cases ahead of you are."

"Maybe I should just go home," Annie said, looking discouraged. It had been a totally rotten day, two days, and now this.

"You really shouldn't go home if it's broken," the woman advised her. "You don't want to be back here at four in the morning with an ankle like a football, screaming in pain. You might as well get an X-ray now that you're here, and check it out."

It seemed like sensible advice, and Annie decided to wait. She had nothing else to do at home. She hadn't even been able to get to her office and bring plans home. And she couldn't have worked anyway, with the acute pain she was in. She was still feeling sick and hoped she wouldn't throw up. She was amazed by how a small thing could make you feel so awful. The pain was excruciating as she propped up her leg in the wheelchair. She sat there with her eyes closed for a while, trying to tolerate the pain, and then the woman in the chair next to her started to cough. She sounded really sick, so as discreetly as she could, Annie wheeled herself away. She didn't want to catch a disease here on top of it. The ankle was bad enough. She wheeled herself into a quiet corner, where no one was sitting yet, and watched as paramedics brought a man in on a body board with a suspected broken neck. He'd been in a car accident. And a man with a heart attack came in immediately after. If they were using a triage system, she realized she might be there forever, while the more severe cases were treated before her. It was five-thirty by then, and liable to be a long night. She looked around, and it seemed as though they had dumped an entire airport in the waiting room for the ER.

She closed her eyes again, trying to breathe into the pain, and a moment later someone jostled her wheelchair, then apologized profusely as she opened her eyes. It was a tall, dark-haired man with an inflatable splint on his arm. He looked vaguely familiar as she closed her eyes again. One of her boots was tucked into the wheelchair, and her naked foot had swollen to twice its size since she got there, and it was starting to look badly bruised. She didn't know if that meant it was broken or not. She dozed in the chair for a while, but the discomfort in her ankle kept her just this side of consciousness, and she finally opened her eyes. The man in the inflatable splint was sitting in a chair next to her and looked grim. The splint was on his left arm, and he'd been using his cell phone with his right hand and canceling appointments. He sounded like a busy man. He was wearing shorts and a T-shirt and running shoes, and she heard him tell someone on the phone that he had hurt himself playing squash. He was good looking and looked very fit. He seemed like he was in a lot of pain when he talked. They sat next to each other for a long time without speaking. She was in too much pain to be social, and she wanted to cry. She was feeling acutely sorry for herself as she sat there.

The seven o'clock news was coming on the waiting-room TV, and when it began, they announced that their anchor Tom Jefferson wouldn't be on the air that night. He had sustained an injury playing squash and was at the hospital at that very moment. Annie was watching it, not paying much attention, and then realized who he was. She turned to him with a surprised expression, and he looked mildly embarrassed.

"That's you?" He nodded. "Shit luck about your arm," she said, and he smiled.

"Looks like you too. It must really hurt. I've been watching it swell while we sat here." Her ankle got bigger and bluer by the minute.

She nodded agreement, and then sat back in the wheelchair with a sigh. She tried to wiggle her toes once in a while, to see if she could, but now it hurt too much. She had seen Tom Jefferson do the same thing with his fingers, trying to assess the extent of the damage, and if it was sprained or broken.

"I think we may be here all night," Annie said when the news was over. Problems in Korea and the Middle East seemed a lot less important to her right now than her ankle. "What about you? Can't you pull rank?"

"I don't think so. I think the three heart attacks, the broken neck, and the gunshot wound take precedence over air time. I'd be afraid to ask." She nodded. He had a point, and he was certainly discreet. They were both completely focused on their respective injuries, and she felt as though they were shipwrecked together on a desert island. And no one seemed to know they were there, or care.

She texted Katie eventually that she'd be home late, but she didn't say why. She didn't want to worry her. So she was alone at the emergency room, sitting next to a total stranger with a broken arm.

"I got shot in the arm once," he said after a while, "covering a story in Uganda. I know it sounds ridiculous, but this actually hurts more." He was looking sorry for himself too.

"Are you showing off?" she asked with a grin. "I broke a rib falling out of bed once, as a kid, and my ankle hurts more. I've never been shot. So you win." He laughed when she said it, and she noticed that he had a nice smile. It was hardly surprising, since he was something of a star on TV.

"Sorry. I didn't mean to be rude. How'd you do it?" Tom asked her, looking concerned.

"On a patch of ice at a construction site. I'd just told them to clean it up before there was an accident, and then I slipped."

"You're a construction worker?" he asked with a mischievous look. At least talking to him was passing the time. They had nothing else to do as they sat and waited.

"More or less. I have my own hard hat," although she hadn't been wearing it. And the cab driver was right. She was lucky she hadn't hit her head. "I'm an architect," she said, and he looked impressed. He had guessed her to be in fashion or maybe publishing. She was well dressed, well spoken, and seemed bright.

"That must be fun," he commented, trying to distract them both.

"Sometimes. When I'm not breaking my neck on a site."

"Does that happen to you often?" he teased her.

"First time."

"First time I've had a sports injury too. I spent ten years doing dangerous assignments in the Middle East. I was bureau chief in Lebanon for two years. I survived two bombings. And I break my arm playing squash. How pathetic." More than anything he felt stupid. And then he looked at her, as she sat slumped in the wheelchair with her foot out. It was turning bluer by the minute from the bruising, and it was huge. "Are you hungry?" he asked her.

"No. I feel sick," she said honestly. She didn't know him, and would never see him again, she didn't have to put up a good front for him. She felt ghastly. And he had seen her cry once or twice. He thought it was from the pain, but it was about Katie. She couldn't get the vision of the tattoo parlor out of her head. And there was nothing she could do to change Katie's mind.

"I was thinking of ordering a pizza," he confessed, feeling slightly embarrassed for being hungry at a time like this. "I'm starving." He had a healthy appetite, and he was a big man.

"That must be a guy thing. You might as well. We'll probably be here for hours." He smiled sheepishly when she said it, called a number on his cell phone, ordered the pizza, and then sent several texts. She wondered if he had a girlfriend or a wife, and if a woman would show up to be with him. He looked about forty-five, with dark hair, just beginning to gray at the temples.

His pizza arrived an hour later, and they were still waiting. He had ordered everything on it but anchovies, and he offered her a piece, but she couldn't eat. He nearly finished it himself, in spite of the injured arm. When he stood up to throw his pizza box away, she could see that he was even taller than she'd guessed. But she was more impressed by how pleasant and unassuming he was. He wasn't asking for any kind of special attention and was waiting patiently for his turn. He offered to get her a glass of water or some coffee from the machine when he got back, but she declined.

"I realized just now that you know my name, and I don't know yours," he said pleasantly when he sat down again. Their chitchat was something to fill the time.

"Anne Ferguson. Annie. Any relation on your side to the illustrious president?"

He smiled at her question. "No, my mom was a history buff. She was actually a history teacher. Maybe she thought it was funny, although she was pretty impressed by him. I've been teased about it all my life."

Annie smiled as he talked. And after that they both dozed for a while. It was nine o'clock, and she had been there for almost four hours.

Her ankle was throbbing by then and finally at ten o'clock an attendant called her name, came to get her, and they wheeled her in. She said goodbye to Tom Jefferson, thanked him for the company, and wished him luck. "I hope it's not broken," she said to encourage him. It had been nice sitting next to him for four hours. She didn't feel so alone.

"You too. And watch out for the ice on those construction sites!" He waved as she disappeared into the ER. She was there for another two hours, for an X-ray and an MRI to check for torn ligaments. The diagnosis was a bad sprain—it wasn't broken. They put a brace on it, gave her crutches, and told her to keep her weight off it, but putting weight on it wasn't an option anyway. She couldn't have stood the pain. And they told her to see her own orthopedist in a week. They said it would take four to six weeks to heal, and to wear flat shoes in the meantime.

It was midnight when an ER nurse wheeled her to the curb and hailed a cab for her. She had glanced around the waiting room on the way through. Tom Jefferson was gone by then too. She wondered if the arm was broken or just sprained like her ankle. It had been nice talking to him and helped pass the time. But her mind was back on Katie and her own troubles on the drive home. It had been a long, painful night.

Annie hobbled unsteadily into her building on the crutches they'd given her. She hadn't gotten the hang of it yet, and they'd given her a pain-killer at the hospital, so she was a little woozy and felt slightly drunk. She let herself into the apart-ment, and the lights were on. Katie was home, and watching a movie with Paul. The only good news, Annie realized, of her dropping out of school was that she would be living at home again, so Annie could keep an eye on her. And Katie turned with a look of shock as Annie walked into the living room on her crutches with her boot in a plastic bag. Annie's face was sheet white.

"What happened to you?" Kate asked, as she rapidly came to help her into a chair. Annie looked like she'd been through the wars. Katie looked upset, and Paul stood up to help too.

"Really stupid. I fell at a job site. I was wearing those boots, and I slid on a patch of ice. Just dumb."

"Oh, poor thing." Katie ran to get an ice pack for her, and Paul helped her out of the chair and walked next to her into the kitchen. Annie was unsteady on the crutches and looked totally worn out. Both of the young people looked deeply concerned. "I thought you were out for dinner or something. Why didn't you call me? I could have come to the hospital with you. What time did it happen?" Katie asked her as Annie half-fell into a kitchen chair.

"It happened right after I left you. Half an hour later." Annie didn't tell her that in part it had happened because she was so upset about her and had been distracted. "I've been at the hospital since five-thirty. It took forever." She didn't tell her about the TV anchorman she'd met. It seemed irrelevant, although it had helped to pass the time while they waited to be examined.

"Do you want something to eat?" Kate offered, and Annie shook her head.

"I just want to go to bed. I'm stoned from the pain pill. And hopefully it will be better tomorrow." She had to deal with crutches now, and hopping around on one leg. Nothing was going to be easy for the next several weeks.

She hobbled into her bedroom with Kate and Paul right behind her. He went back to the living room, and Katie helped her undress and get into her nightgown. It was complicated standing on one foot and having to use crutches. Kate was afraid she'd fall in the bathroom and told her to call her during the night if she needed help.

"I'll be fine," Annie reassured her. It had been an exhausting night and an upsetting two days, with the news of Kate dropping out of school. She still hadn't heard from Ted, or from Lizzie in Paris, for the past few days. She tried not to think of any of it as she crawled into bed. She took another pain pill, as they had told her to do, and by the time Annie's head hit the pillow, she was out like a light. Katie kissed her, tucked her in, and went back to Paul. They had been making some very important plans that night.

Chapter 13

It was harder than Annie had expected getting dressed the next day. Getting into the shower and not falling had been challenging, as she tried to stand on one foot. And by the time she got to the kitchen on crutches, she was exhausted. But she had too much work to do to stay home. Kate helped her get downstairs and into a taxi, and Annie got to her office at ten o'clock, which was rare for her, and she wouldn't be able to do job site visits for a while, at least a few days, she told herself.

Ted finally called her that morning and apologized for not calling her back sooner. He said he'd been really busy. Katie had texted him to tell him about Annie's ankle the night before, so he knew about it and asked how she was.

"I'm fine. It hurts like hell, but it's nothing. Just a sprain. I've been calling you about your sister.

Are you aware that she dropped out of school and is working in a tattoo parlor?" Annie was upset about it all over again as she told him. The ankle was unimportant compared to that.

"You're kidding, right?"

"I wish I were. I'm dead serious, and so is she. She took a semester off, and she's working at a tattoo parlor on Ninth Avenue, and considers it graphic art."

"That's disgusting. And no, the little shit didn't tell me. Do you want me to talk to her?" He sounded as upset as Annie still was. Dropping out of school was major to them.

"Yes, but I don't think it'll do anything. Maybe she'll listen to you, but I doubt it. She's determined to take some time off from school."

"I think that's a stupid idea, and I'll tell her so." Sometimes Kate listened to her siblings more than to her aunt, so Annie was briefly hopeful, but once Katie made her mind up, it was always hard to sway her, and Ted knew that too. She and Annie had that in common. They were both fiercely stubborn.

"What about you? Are you okay? You're awfully quiet these days. I worry about you," Annie said gently. She worried about them all.

"I'm fine," he said, sounding gruff. He had been with Pattie every moment that the kids weren't there, and he felt like he never had free time now. He was constantly running back and forth to her apartment, or making love to her. He hadn't seen any of his friends for weeks. But he said none of that to Annie. There was no way he could tell her about an affair with a woman twelve years older than he was. He knew that Annie would never understand it, and sometimes he wasn't sure he understood it himself. It had just happened, and now the relationship had a life of its own and was moving ahead at lightning speed, like an express train, with Pattie at the wheel.

"Come and have dinner at the apartment sometime. I miss you," Annie suggested, and Ted sighed. He had no time now for anything, unless it involved Pattie.

"At least Katie will be around to help you now, if she's living at home." He felt guilty for not calling or seeing Annie more often, but Pattie always had something for him to do and wanted him with her all the time.

"I'd rather she were back in school," Annie said sadly.

"Me too. I'll call her. I'll call you soon, Annie," he promised, and after she hung up, she got some work done and was hobbling around her office, trying to carry files and plans, which was nearly impossible with the crutches. Managing them was harder than she'd thought it would be, and she was still in pain.

She had just gotten back into her desk chair when the phone rang. Her assistant was buzzing her to say that a Thomas Jefferson was on the phone. Annie was surprised to hear from him, took the call, and asked him immediately how his arm was.

"It's broken," he said, sounding discouraged. He had hoped for only a sprain. "How's your ankle?"

"Just badly sprained. But getting around on crutches is a bitch." She was exhausted after only an hour in the office, and her ankle was throbbing.

"I know, that happened to me once. Playing basketball at school." And then he shifted gears. "I enjoyed meeting you yesterday, Annie. I was wondering if you'd like to have lunch sometime. Or maybe we could go to Lourdes," he said, and she laughed.

"I'd like that. Lunch, not Lourdes, although that might be nice too. I've always wanted to see it."

"Me too," he said easily. She assumed he wasn't married, but didn't want to ask. She was sure it was just a friendly lunch between invalids, not a date, so asking if he was married felt stupid. There had been nothing romantic about their initial meeting. And it had been a funny way to meet. "How about tomorrow?" he suggested. "Can you get out on the crutches?"

"I'll manage. I have to. I can't let my job sites sit forever without seeing them."

"You might want to give that a day or two." He suggested a small French restaurant that she knew and liked, and he proposed they meet at noon the next day. It sounded like fun, if she could get there.

"I'll cut your meat for you," she offered, and he laughed. "I'll carry you to the cab." It was something to do, and he seemed like he'd be interesting to know. He was intelligent, pleasant, and nice looking.

It was a long day after that, and she had to cancel several meetings. It was too hard to get around, and she sent her assistant to two job sites. Katie called to check on her and was very solicitous. And Annie finally gave up and went home early at four o'clock with two shopping bags full of work. She saw Tom on the news that night, after she took a pain pill and had a nap. And Tom looked back to normal on screen, other than the cast on his arm. His shirt cuff was rolled up, and he couldn't wear a jacket. But he was in good spirits and looked good on the news.

Tom was waiting at the table for her when Annie walked into the restaurant the next day. She was getting more proficient with the crutches, but he walked to the door to help her anyway.

"We look like we've been in a train wreck together," he said as he walked her to the table. "Thanks for meeting me for lunch. I enjoyed talking to you the other day." They sat down, and they both ordered iced tea. She said that if she had wine she'd fall on her crutches, and he said he never drank at lunchtime.

After they ordered lunch, Tom smiled at her and got right to the point. "I never asked you the other night. I assume you're not married," he commented hopefully, and she smiled. No one had come to the hospital for either of them, and they had each guessed that the other was single. But he wanted to confirm it.

"No, I'm not. And you?" Annie smiled at him.

"Divorced. I was married for eight years. I've been divorced for five. My kind of work isn't conducive to happy marriages. I was traveling most of the time and away for a long time sometimes. We finally figured out that it wasn't going to work, and she married someone else. We're on fairly decent terms. She has two kids now. I never had time for that either, and that was a big deal to her. I don't blame her. I just didn't want to have kids when I was never there, and now it's a little late." He didn't seem upset about it. "You're divorced?"

At her age, and with her looks, he presumed she had to be and was surprised when she shook her head.

"I've never been married," she said simply. He was so direct and straightforward that she didn't feel like a loser when she said it to him. It was just a fact.

"So no kids," he said. He wanted to get the details out of the way, but she shook her head and then nodded in answer to his question, and he looked confused.

"No, I don't have kids, and yes, I do. My sister and her husband died sixteen years ago, when their plane crashed. I inherited their three children. They were five, eight, and twelve at the time. They're grown up now, or they tell me they are. Sometimes I'm not so sure. Liz is twenty-eight and an editor at **Vogue**, Ted is in law school at NYU, he's twenty-four, and Kate is an artist, she's twenty-one and she goes to Pratt. Or she did until this week. She's just decided to take a semester off, and I'm seriously pissed about it. So that's my story," she said, smiling at him, as he looked at her, impressed by what she had just told him.

"No, that's their story," he said quietly. "What's yours?"

"They're my story," she said honestly. "Inheriting a ready-made family when you're fresh out of architecture school is a full-time job. I was twenty-six when they came to live with me. It took me a while to figure out how to do it. But I got the hang of it eventually."

"And now?" He was suddenly curious about her. He had suspected none of this the other night. But they had exchanged no personal information. They were too busy hurting.

"Just when I got good at it, they grew up. Katie just moved back in, but she's been living in the dorm for three years. I hate this part. I have to sit back and watch them lead their own lives and do all the crazy stuff that kids do, like drop out of school. I really miss them."

"I'll bet you do after all those years taking care of them. Is that why you never married?"

"Probably . . . I don't know . . . I never really had time. I was too busy with them and fulfilling a promise to my sister, that if anything ever happened to them, I'd take the kids. So I did. It's been wonderful. I never regretted it for a minute. They've been an incredible gift in my life." It had been a fair trade. Her youth for theirs.

"That's quite a story," he said with a look of admiration. "It sounds like you wound up with empty nest syndrome without ever having kids of your own. That's not fair. But I guess it met any need you may have had to have children. Do you still want your own?" He was curious about her. She was full of surprises and seemed content with her life. She wasn't one of those desperate, unhappy women who felt that they'd missed the boat and were scrambling to fix it. And he liked that about her. She wasn't looking for a savior or a rescuer. She seemed very whole to him and at peace with herself.

"I don't know." She shrugged easily. "I never had time to think about having kids of my own. I was too busy. It would have been nice if my life had worked out that way, but it didn't. It went in a different direction. I got three great kids anyway." She smiled at him across the table.

"No serious guys?"

"Not in a long time. I was too busy for that too." She didn't apologize for it or even seem to regret it.

"Wow . . . I feel like I'm having lunch with Mother Teresa," Tom said, grinning at her. And she was a lot prettier than Mother Teresa.

"No, I'm just a woman with a full plate. Three kids and a career. I don't know how most women juggle all that and a husband."

"They don't. That's why most marriages end up in the divorce courts. It sounds like you and I are married to our jobs, and in your case, your sister's kids too."

"That about sums it up. And now I have to learn

to let go of them. That's a lot harder than it looks." And for the first time in sixteen years, her life felt empty as a result.

"So I'm told," he said, totally intrigued by her. They talked about his work then, and his travels, his time in the Middle East, the architecture they both loved. They talked about art and politics. They never stopped talking until the end of lunch, and they had both had a great time with each other. "I'm beginning to think it was a blessing breaking my arm," he said with a broad smile as he looked at her. "If I hadn't, I'd never have met you." It was a nice way to look at it, and she was flattered. "Do you suppose we could do lunch again sometime?" he asked, looking hopeful, and she nodded.

"I'd like that." She said it simply, thinking that he'd be an interesting friend to have.

"I'll call you," he promised, but she didn't think much of it. Lots of men had said that to her over the years and never called her. And maybe he had a girlfriend. She hadn't asked him that. The fact that he wasn't married didn't mean he was free. Anything was possible. She wasn't counting on hearing from him again, although she liked him. But he was a celebrity, and his life could have been fuller or more complicated than he admitted. She knew that about men too. She'd been on lots of first dates in the last twenty years. And never heard from the guys again.

He helped her into a cab after lunch, and she went back to her office. Ted called her and said that he had talked to Kate and she was adamant about not going back to school until next semester. She was determined to work in the tattoo parlor. He was very annoyed at her and had told her so himself. Katie didn't care. She had made up her mind.

Two days later Liz came home from Paris, and she got nowhere with Kate either. She wanted to spend time with her younger sister, but she was too busy. Three days after Liz got back, she had to go out to L.A. for a story. She was doing a piece on the important jewelry of big stars of days gone by. She had tracked down more than a dozen important pieces and their new owners. And they had moved up the shooting date on her while she was in Paris. She hardly had time to unpack and switch bags. Jean-Louis was coming back to New York the day she left. He had stayed in Paris for a couple of days to see Damien, and he was planning to be back in New York when Lizzie returned from California.

Liz told Annie that they had had a wonderful time together in Paris, and his son was the sweetest little boy. He was no trouble at all. Lizzie was still sorry for Damien that they were sending him away to live with his grandmother, which was easier for his parents, but not necessarily best for him. Lizzie had her doubts about it, but she didn't feel comfortable being too emphatic about it to Jean-Louis. It was his son after all, not hers. If Damien had been hers, she would never have parted with him, which was why she didn't want kids yet. She didn't have time for them, and she was smart enough to know it.

Liz stopped by at the apartment before she flew to L.A., and she felt bad to see Annie struggling on crutches, although Annie was better at it than she'd been in the beginning. But she was tired and still hurting and worried about Kate. Liz promised to try and talk to her sister again after L.A.

Paul helped Katie move out of the dorm that weekend. They brought all her stuff back and put it in her room in Annie's apartment, and then they went out to meet friends and go to a movie. Paul was around constantly now, which worried Annie too. No matter how nice he was, Annie was still concerned about their seemingly serious relationship and its potential impact on them.

They were all busy and had their own lives. Annie was busy with her projects, Katie was either at work or with Paul, Ted had become a mystery man, rarely in evidence, and Liz was still in California. And on Sunday, Annie decided she needed a break and went to a farmers' market she liked in Tompkins Square Park in the East Village. There were fresh fruits and vegetables, homemade jams, and canned goods. It was hard to negotiate with her ankle, but she managed with a string bag in each hand as she held her crutches. She was talking to a Mennonite woman in a lace cap about her homemade preserves, when Annie looked up and found herself face-to-face with Ted on the other side of the same stand.

She was startled to see him there. He was with a woman and two children. She was carrying a big basket and filling it with homemade things, and the children were clinging to him as though he were their father. This was no casual acquaintance, Annie realized as she watched them. This was a woman he was deeply involved with, and she was visibly many years older than Ted. In harsh daylight, she looked even older than her thirty-six years.

And as Annie looked straight at him from a few feet away, and their eyes met, Ted looked as though he would burst into tears. There was no escape. He had to introduce them. He introduced Pattie to his aunt, and both her children, and Annie was even more shocked to realize that the woman he was obviously seeing was only a few years younger than she was. And Annie was in better shape and looked younger.

Annie greeted Pattie politely and was nice to the children, and she said very little to Ted. It was obvious that this was the secret he'd been keeping, and he didn't look proud of it. He looked terrified of Annie's reaction. She smiled gently at him and kissed him before she walked away, on her crutches, with her string bags. All she said to Ted as she kissed him goodbye was "Call me this week." He knew exactly what that meant. She wanted an explanation of what he was up to. She wasn't going to let this slip by in silence. He had known that she wouldn't.

And as he turned back to Pattie after Annie left, Pattie stared at him unhappily. He looked sick.

"You look terrified. She can't do anything to you, Ted. You're not a kid." She looked uncomfortable. Annie's shock and disapproval had been apparent, no matter how pleasant she had seemed.

"I am a kid to her," he said, looking nervous.

"You don't owe her any explanations. She's not your mother, and even if she were, you're a grown man. All you have to do is tell her that we're in love with each other, and this is the choice you've made." Pattie was pushing again. He hadn't made that choice. He had fallen into it, like a soft featherbed he enjoyed being in. But he had no idea how long he wanted to be there or what it meant. Pattie was making assumptions that were comfortable for her, but Ted wasn't sure of anything yet except that he liked being with her. And in his own eyes, not just Annie's, he was still a kid. He felt like one. And he didn't want Pattie dictating to him any more than he wanted Annie to.

All he could say to Annie honestly was that he was involved with Pattie and had been since just after Thanksgiving. He didn't know anything more than that. He wasn't sure if that would frighten her or reassure her. But he wasn't ready to tell her that this was a choice he had made, as Pattie wanted him to. Pattie had made that choice. He hadn't yet. He was just having a good time.

He was very quiet on the walk back to Pattie's apartment with the full basket of fruits and vegetables they'd bought. He set it down in the kitchen for her, and she didn't like the way he looked. He had been silent and upset ever since they ran into his aunt.

"What if she doesn't approve, Ted?" she asked him bluntly. They both knew she was asking about Annie. "What if she tells you to give me up?"

"I don't know. She wouldn't do that. She's a reasonable woman and she loves me. But I don't know if she'll understand. Twenty-four and thirty-six is hard to explain." He was realistic about it.

His roommates had met her and thought he was crazy. It was a complicated situation for him to be in, with two kids, no matter how great the sex was.

"It's not hard to explain at all," Pattie corrected him. "We love each other. That's the only explanation anyone needs, including your aunt."

"Maybe I need more of an explanation than that," Ted suddenly said, more harshly than he meant to. But he hated it when she pushed him. "I need to know why this would work, and it's a good idea. I still have to finish law school, and you have two kids. We're at different stages in our lives. Sometimes it's hard to bridge that." He tried to be honest with her, but she didn't want to hear it. She had her own version of the story, which was different from his. To her, this was true love. To Ted, it was great sex, and he didn't know how much more it was than that.

She looked panicked. "This isn't hard to bridge," she insisted.

"You're older than I am," he said bluntly. "Maybe you can handle it better than I can. To be honest with you, sometimes it scares me." He was always honest with her, whether she liked it or not. And she never wanted to hear his side.

"What are you scared of?" she asked plaintively.

"That we've backed ourselves into a corner that we'll never be able to get out of, if we want to."

"Is that what you want?" Pattie asked him with a suddenly evil look. She was whispering so the kids wouldn't hear her. But they had turned on the TV, and they were in the other room. "Is that what you're saying to me," she said, with a malicious glint in her eyes, "you want out, Ted? Let me explain something to you. I waited a whole lifetime for a man like you, and I'm not going to let you cheat me of what we have. If you ever leave me, I'm going to kill myself. Do you understand that? I'd rather die than live without you. And if I die, it will be because of you." Hearing her say that cut through him like a knife, and he closed his eyes and turned away as though to erase from his mind that she'd ever said it.

"Pattie, don't . . . ," he said hoarsely.

"I will, and you'd better know it." It was more of a threat than a plea for him not to leave her. It was a promise to destroy his life, her own, and her children's if he ever left her. They had been together for six weeks, and Pattie had him in a death grip. And worse yet, the life she was threatening was her own. And if she meant anything to him at all, he had to respect it. He couldn't just sleep with her night after night and day after day, and have sex with her, and leave her. Who knew if she really would kill herself? But he didn't want to take the chance. Ted was shaking when she walked out of the kitchen and back into the living room to her kids. Her message to him had been delivered and was even more powerful than his respect for his aunt. Pattie had won this round. Again.

And back in her apartment, after she came home from the farmers' market, Annie was thinking about them. She had no idea who the woman was, or what she meant to Ted. She could see how engaged he was with them, but she hadn't seen love in his eyes when she looked at him, she had seen terror. She wanted to know why, and what he was going to do about it. Everywhere she turned now, the children she loved had put themselves in difficult situations and were at risk. And she was helpless to stop them or even help them. All she could do was watch as they took chances, and they would ultimately have to learn from their own mistakes, just as Whitney had said. She walked back into the living room on her crutches and sat down on the couch. There wasn't even anyone she could talk to about it. All she could do was worry and hope that in the end they made wise choices and everything came out all right. She had never been so sad or felt so useless in her life.

Chapter 14

Annie didn't have to call Ted this time. He called her himself the next morning and asked to have lunch with her that day. He had stayed at Pattie's the night before, so he hadn't called her. He couldn't. The kids had gone to their father's for the night, and Pattie had threatened Ted with suicide again, and then made love to him as never before. The sex just got better and better, but there was something so intense and frantic about it that sometimes it frightened him. The hook she used to keep him close to her was sex. It was addictive, but the threat she had made the night before woke him up. He never wanted to have her suicide on his hands. And she sounded like she meant it. She had said it several times.

Ted looked somber when he met Annie at Bread, which she knew he liked. And when Annie saw him walk toward her, her heart ached for him. He didn't have to say a word to her. She could see that he was in way, way over his head, and he knew it whether he admitted it to her or not. Annie was worried sick about him.

They talked about school and her ankle for a few minutes to break the ice, and then Annie got straight to the point.

"How involved are you with this woman? And what does she want from you? She must be close to forty, and you're just a kid." It was what he had expected her to say.

"She's thirty-six. It happened right after Thanksgiving. She teaches my contracts class, and I got a shit grade on a quiz. She offered to have me come over so she could help me, and the next thing I knew I was in bed with her. I've been there ever since." He was as honest as he always was. He never mentioned love. "But I got straight A's in contracts," he said with a rueful grin. And he tried to make light of the situation he was in. And didn't mention that he was barely passing his other classes. He couldn't cope with Pattie and the demands of law school too.

"Is this serious? Are you in love with her?" Annie looked at him intently. He didn't look in love to her. He looked worried.

"I don't know," he said honestly, and then he

told Annie about Pattie's threat the night before, to kill herself if he ever left her. He hadn't planned to tell Annie, but Pattie had shaken him badly and he trusted his aunt's advice. She was wise, and had always been there for him. Pattie was new to him and seemed a little unstable.

"That's a terrible thing to say to you. She can't hold on to you by terror and guilt. That's black-mail, not love," Annie said, looking outraged.

"She doesn't want to lose me. I think she's al-ready been through too much, with the divorce." Ted tried to be understanding about it.

"Lots of people are divorced, Ted. They don't go around threatening to kill themselves if their new relationships don't work out. That's sick."

"I know." He looked upset, and she didn't want to criticize him for the mess he was in, he was rat-tled enough, and justifiably so.

"What can I do to help?" Annie said quietly. "Maybe you should try getting a little space from her now, before this gets any worse, or she gets more dependent on you than she already is. Are the kids aware of all this?" Ted shook his head.

"They're sweet kids and I like them. They're at their father's whenever I stay over. They have joint custody. And he's a pretty good dad. I want to be with her, Annie. I just don't want it to be this in-tense."

227

"Maybe that's all she knows how to do. People like that worry me too. Try to take a little distance from her, for your own sake. Tell her you need it."

"She goes insane when I do." Annie was at a loss to tell him what to do. She had never dealt with anyone as unbalanced as that, and she was sad that Ted had gotten as deeply into it as he had. She had a strong sense that Pattie had manipulated him into it and knew exactly what she was doing. He was an innocent, and Pattie knew it too.

They talked about the relationship all through lunch, and Ted felt a little better when he went back to his own apartment, instead of Pattie's. Annie had given him good advice. He called and told Pattie he was going to stay at his place that night. He said he had some things to do, and some papers to write. Annie had given him the courage to do that.

"You're cheating on me, aren't you?" Pattie accused him over the phone, and his heart sank.

"Of course not. I just have some stuff to do here."

"Is it your aunt? Is that it? What did she do? Bribe you to stay away from me?" She sounded desperate and on the verge of hysterics. In a short time she had taken possession of his life. He had become her willing slave, and now in the face of her threats and accusations, he felt trapped.

"My aunt wouldn't do something like that," Ted said calmly. "She's a wonderful woman. She's concerned about us, but she respects my right to make my own choices and decisions. She's not crazy, and she wouldn't bribe me."

"Are you suggesting I'm crazy?" she said, sounding very wound up. "Well, I'm not. I'm crazy about you, and I don't want anyone interfering with us."

"No one is. Just give it a rest. I'll come over tomorrow. We can take the kids to the park."

"They're going to be with their father for the weekend." There was a hopeful note in her voice when she said it, and he knew what that meant. Sexual acrobatics worthy of the Olympics for two days. He suddenly felt exhausted thinking about it, and yet he was instantly aroused when she said things like that. It was as though his body were betraying him and wanted her more than he did, and he no longer had a choice in the matter. His penis was addicted to her and taking orders from her.

"I'll call you tomorrow," he promised, and lay down on his bed, staring at the ceiling. He had no idea what he was going to do, or even what he wanted to do. He belonged to her now. He felt possessed. Everything Annie had said to him at lunch made sense. But Pattie was in control, and

229

he wasn't. It felt like there was nothing he or Annie could do. Pattie was running the show.

A week after their first lunch, Tom Jefferson called Annie at her office again. He said he was in the neighborhood for a meeting, and he wondered if she wanted to have an impromptu lunch before he had to go back to the office. It sounded like fun to her, and he met her at the Café Cluny, which was one of her favorite haunts. He was waiting for her out front, and they walked in together. He was in good spirits. She was still on crutches, and his arm was still in a cast, but neither of them was hurting from their injuries anymore. He told her about a big story he was working on, and that he might have to go to California to spend time with the governor. She loved hearing about his work, and his old war stories. And when he talked about his experiences in the Middle East, she told him that Kate was dating a boy from Iran, and was in love with him.

He saw the tenderness in her eyes when she mentioned Katie, and it struck him that her nieces and nephew seemed to add a dimension in her life that was unfamiliar to him since he'd never had children. He could sense how much she loved them, and he had the feeling that her nieces and nephew had lives and opinions of their own.

"He's a very nice boy," she said about Paul. "Polite, kind, intelligent, thoughtful, good values, respectful. He's every mother's dream. But I've been concerned about her going out with someone whose background and culture are so different from her own, even if he's very American and he's lived here since he was fourteen. Ultimately their ideas might be very divergent. She's a **very** liberated young woman. And her ideas can be very extreme at times. He seems a lot more conservative and traditional than she is. That might not work later, if there is a 'later.' And I get the feeling they're very serious about each other."

"What do his parents think?" Tom asked sensibly.

"I don't know. I haven't met them. Kate's pretty New Age, with a dozen pierced earrings and a couple of tattoos. She's working in a tattoo parlor right now. If his parents are surviving that, they must be more liberal than I am. I almost had a heart attack when she told me about her job. She considers it an internship in graphic arts." Tom laughed at the idea and could imagine what she looked like.

"Are Kate and Paul that serious about each

other? Are they talking marriage?" It was a reasonable question, given her concerns.

"No. They're very young," Annie said, smiling at him. "She's only twenty-one, and he's twenty-three. I think it's first love for both of them. They're both pretty naïve. It's hard to take them too seriously, but I still worry. And I think I'd be concerned about any boy, from anywhere. I don't want her to get her heart broken, or get into a situation she'll regret later, that could lead to heartbreak for both of them."

"Don't forget Romeo and Juliet. Kids can get pretty crazy when they're young. But if you say he's a nice kid, I'm sure they'll be fine. She's probably more sensible than you think."

She told him about Ted then and the older woman and how concerned she was about it. "Women like that can be dangerous," Tom said seriously. "She sounds obsessive." She did to Annie too, and she hadn't stopped thinking about it since she'd seen them together and then had lunch with Ted, and he had been candid with Annie about his own concerns. "They keep you busy, don't they?"

"More so now than when they were younger. They took more time then with Little League and soccer games and ballet classes. But now they worry me more. The decisions they have to make are so much bigger, and the risks to them are greater. And they don't always see that and the dangers they're facing." She looked worried as she said it. "And my older niece is commitment phobic and a workaholic. I feel more and more helpless as they get older."

"Yeah, but it's their lives, not yours," Tom reminded her gently.

"That's easy to say and not so easy to live with," Annie said with a wistful expression.

"Maybe if you cultivate more of a life of your own," Tom suggested cautiously, "they'll become more independent. You can't be there for them forever, at the expense of your own life. Sixteen years is a long time." She didn't disagree with him, but she couldn't imagine unhooking from them now. And he surprised her with his next question. "Do you think there's room for a man in your life now, Annie? It sounds like you've waited a long time to have a life of your own." He had figured that out from all that she had told him. "Maybe you don't think you deserve one. It sounds like you've fulfilled your promise to your sister. You can't give up your own life for them forever." She nodded. She knew what he said was true. She just didn't know how to do it, or when.

"I think there's room," she said simply. "I just haven't tried having a life in a long time," or even wanted one. The kids had fulfilled all her emotional needs for so long, and taken up all her time, energy, and attention.

Tom was totally intrigued by her and all that she had accomplished, but he could also see that he had to cross an obstacle course to get to her. He thought she was worth it. "Would you like to have dinner next week?"

"Why don't you come by next Sunday night and meet the kids? We can go out for a grown-up dinner another time." She wanted him to meet her family and see what her life was about. He liked the idea, and also of taking her out alone. There was time for both.

"I'll call you on Sunday and see what your plans are," he promised. She smiled, and they continued chatting until they left the restaurant. And he told her that if he had to leave for California, he'd call her. He still traveled a great deal, although not as much abroad as in the past.

Annie had enjoyed the lunch with Tom, and when she went back to her office, she liked the idea of having him to dinner on Sunday night. She told Katie that evening to be home for dinner on Sunday, and said she could invite Paul. She wanted Tom to meet him. And she left a message for Ted and asked him to come home to dinner on Sunday night. She didn't mention Tom, and she didn't include Pattie in the invitation. And she hoped that Liz would be home from L.A. by then too. She knew it was a short trip, but she hadn't said when she'd be back, and Annie hadn't heard from her since she left. She knew Liz was too busy to call her. She was excited about inviting Tom to meet them.

That night before she went to sleep, she pondered his question to her if there was room in her life for a man now. She liked him and enjoyed talking to him—they never ran out of subjects that interested them both. But the real answer to his question was that she just wasn't sure. After all these years of living "like a nun," as Katie put it, she didn't know if there was room for a man, or even if she wanted one anymore. It had been so long. And life was so much easier like this. It was a hard decision to make at forty-two, whether she wanted to stay alone, or take on the risks of caring about a man again. She didn't know what she wanted, although Tom was very appealing. She wasn't completely sure either if she wanted to close that door and give up on relationships forever. That door stood ajar now, waiting for her to open it wide, or quietly close it and turn the key.

Liz's trip to California went extremely well. She met interesting people, saw fabulous jewelry, and had done great research about the stars the pieces originally belonged to. There wasn't a hitch, and at the end of two days of constant shooting and interviews at people's homes, she was able to pack up and take the red-eye home. It helped that they had no jewelry to return to suppliers—it all stayed with the current owners. She didn't even have time to call Jean-Louis when she left. She ran through the airport to catch the last plane to New York, the red-eye. She was still on Paris time and exhausted. She was hoping to get a breather once she got back to New York, at least for a few days. And she was excited to be going home two days earlier than planned. Paris had been grueling, and L.A. had been fun but a lot of work. She fell asleep before they even took off.

She didn't wake up until the plane landed at JFK in New York. She had only brought carry-on, so she was out of the airport in no time and gave the cab driver her address. And then she thought better of it and decided to go to the loft. It was six in the morning and too early to call Jean-Louis, but she knew where the key was and could let herself in and just slip into his bed. She had done that lots of times in the past year when she got back from trips. She was outside his building by six-thirty in the morning. And she took the key from behind the fire extinguisher in the hallway and let herself in and the room was dark. Jean-Louis had installed shutters when he moved in, like the ones in France. He said he slept better that way, and he was right. Whenever Lizzie slept at his place, she sometimes didn't wake until two in the afternoon, if she was particularly tired or jet-lagged or just back from a trip. The total darkness made her sleep peacefully for hours.

She knew her way around the loft perfectly, and there was a hairline crack of light from the bathroom that helped her find the bed. She dropped her clothes on the floor next to it and slid in next to him and gently put her arms around him, and as she did, there was a sudden scream. She didn't know who it was, but it was not Jean-Louis. She sat bolt upright in the bed, and so did he, as he turned on the light with a rapid gesture. They looked at each other, and then Lizzie looked into the space in the bed between them, and found herself staring at Françoise, his ex-girlfriend and Damien's mother. All three of them looked startled, and Lizzie leaped out of bed. The body she had cuddled up to in the dark was Françoise, not Jean-Louis.

"What the hell is this?" Liz said as she stared at him. She was so shocked that she forgot to get dressed, and all three of them were naked. "I thought you were just friends."

"We have a child together," Jean-Louis explained, looking very Gallic. Françoise just lay there and looked at the ceiling. She looked perfectly comfortable in his bed and made no effort to move, despite the heated discussion between Liz and Jean-Louis. She acted as though it had nothing to do with her.

"What does that have to do with anything?" Liz shouted at him. "What is she doing here?" Françoise propped herself up on one elbow then and looked at them both, taking in the scene, and Liz shot her an angry look. Françoise didn't even look embarrassed.

"She had a job here this week, and she dropped by to say hello," Jean-Louis explained weakly. There was nothing he could say to clean this up.

"This looks like a lot more than hello to me." Liz narrowed her eyes at him then and reached for her clothes on the floor. "You said you were faithful to me, you asshole." She got dressed as she said it. Françoise got up and walked past her to the bathroom.

"I am faithful to you," he insisted to Liz. "I love you. Françoise and I are just good friends."

"Bullshit. Tell that to someone else. This is cheating. That's all it is." And she was sure now that the underwear she had found in the drawer in his Paris apartment was more recent than four years. She wondered how long he'd been sleeping with her, or if he'd ever stopped. Françoise looked totally at ease in the loft and his bed.

"Don't be such a puritan about this," Jean-Louis said, unwinding himself from the sheets and coming to stand next to her. "These things happen. It doesn't mean anything." He tried to put his arms around Liz, and she wouldn't let him.

"It does to me." She felt foolish now for how stupid she'd been and how trusting. Men like Jean-Louis were never faithful to anyone. She realized that he had probably cheated on her for the past year and that his idea of "exclusive" had nothing to do with hers and meant nothing. "I should have known better," Liz said to him, as Françoise wandered into the living room and lit one of Jean-Louis's Gitanes. She was completely passive, and the uncomfortable scene didn't seem to upset her at all, and Lizzie knew she had a boyfriend too. They all screwed anything that moved.

Liz's fatal stupidity was believing that Jean-Louis was different. Men with that much charm were just never faithful. It wasn't in their DNA. She knew it but always tried to tell herself that it would be different this time, but it never was. Jean-Louis was just like all the other men she had dated. They were all clones of each other. She always picked the ones who couldn't be faithful or commit. It fit perfectly with her own fear of commitment and provided an inevitable end. She had been part of scenes like this too often before.

"Don't you have any morality at all?" she said, looking at him with disgust. "I'm better than this, and smarter. I don't know why I believed you." She didn't love him, she was clear on that, but she had liked him a lot, and trusted him, which had been a huge mistake. Men like him were all she ever met in her world, and all she ever wanted. The fashion scene was full of them. Men who wanted to act like boys forever and never played by the rules. There were no rules, there was just fun. And in the end someone always got hurt. She was tired of it. She had her clothes back on by then and looked at him with contempt.

"You're a jerk, Jean-Louis, and a poor excuse for a man. And worse than that, you're a lousy father. You make pathetic excuses for not being there for your son, and for dumping him on someone else. I deserved better than you, but more importantly, so does he. Why don't you and Françoise wake up and grow up, instead of indulging yourselves all the time?" She looked straight at him and at Françoise on the way out. Jean-Louis said not a word as Liz walked out and slammed the door. She was shocked to realize she wasn't even sad as she ran down the stairs, she was relieved. She was finished with guys like him. She was grown up. He never would be.

She made a vow to herself as she hailed a cab. She was never going to settle for a guy like him again. She'd rather be alone than waste her time. She rolled down the window and let the cold air fly in her face as they drove across town. She felt totally free at last. She wasn't angry, she wasn't sad. She was ready to move on.

Chapter 15

Liz called Annie later that morning and told her what had happened. She was sorry to hear it, but she had heard stories like it from Liz before. Something always went wrong in her relationships so she could end them. Annie knew that up to now Lizzie chose men like that so she wouldn't get attached. But Liz sounded different this time. She said she'd rather be alone than get involved with another one like Jean-Louis and she sounded like she meant it. She said she was done with men who behaved that way and were immature, self-indulgent, and dishonest. And Annie hoped that this time it was true.

She wondered if next time she would take the risk of someone real. It was clear from her lack of emotion that she hadn't loved Jean-Louis.

Liz was in her own apartment wrapped in a pink

bathrobe when she called Annie. She had show-
ered when she got home. And Jean-Louis hadn't
called her. She knew he wouldn't. And she was
shocked to realize she didn't care. She was done.

She and Liz talked for about an hour, and then
Annie got up and went to make herself a cup of
tea. Katie was still asleep. Annie invited Liz for
dinner that night, and Liz had said that she'd
come. She liked Sunday-night dinners at Annie's,
and they did them too rarely.

Tom called her late that afternoon, when he got
back from a football game. He was excited that the
Jets had won.

"Are we still on for dinner tonight?" he asked
easily. "I don't want to intrude."

"You won't be. I want you to meet the kids."

"That sounds like fun. You're a fascinating
bunch."

"Wait till you meet us all before you decide that.
We're actually fairly normal."

"Somehow I doubt that. You seem pretty special
to me."

"If that's a compliment, thank you." He seemed
special to her too. He was interesting and intelligent, he seemed to be open minded, and he wasn't
dull. He'd had an exciting life and career. He wasn't
full of himself, and he asked all the right questions.

For now they were just friends, but he was the first man she'd met in years who seemed worthwhile to her, and she liked his looks. He felt the same way about her. She was a rare bird amid flocks of very dull women he had met since his divorce. And unlike most men his age, he had no interest in twenty-two-year-olds. Annie couldn't help wondering, when she invited him to dinner, if he would be taken with Lizzie. She was a beautiful girl. Annie was philosophical about life and perfectly willing to let destiny decide her fate. Tom didn't belong to her, and you couldn't put an option on people. He was just a man she had met at a hospital by sheer happenstance. Nothing more than that.

She forgot to tell the others about him until just before dinner. It was six o'clock, and she had told Tom to come at seven. She had made spaghetti and meatballs and a big green salad. And they were going to have cookies and ice cream for dessert, just the way they had on Sunday nights when they were kids.

Liz was sitting on the couch, talking to Katie, trying to convince her to quit the tattoo parlor and go back to school, and Paul was reading a magazine while the two women talked. Lizzie was saying the same things to Kate that he had said to Kate himself, to no avail. He thought she should go back to school. And all heads turned, including Paul's, when Annie announced casually that there was a man coming to dinner.

"What man?" Liz asked with a look of astonishment.

"Just someone I met recently." Annie looked benign and unaffected as she said it and sat down in the living room with them. Ted hadn't arrived yet. Nor had Tom.

"You mean like a blind date?" Liz persisted.

"No. He broke his arm when I sprained my ankle. We spent four hours in the waiting room at the ER. It's not a big deal. We've had lunch a couple of times." Annie looked like she was telling them she had decided to make hamburgers instead of meatballs, as though it were of no consequence whatsoever, and she didn't think it was. She had been telling herself that since they met.

"Wait a minute." Liz looked at her as if a comet had just landed in their living room. "You had lunch with this guy twice, and spent four hours in the ER with him, and you didn't tell us?"

"Why should I tell you, for heaven's sake? It's not like we're dating. He invited me out to dinner, but I invited him here instead. I wanted him to meet all of you."

"Annie"—Liz stared at her from where she sat—

"you haven't had a date since the Stone Age, and you act like this means nothing."

"It doesn't mean anything. We're just friends," she said casually.

"Who is he?" Kate asked, as surprised as her sister was by Annie's announcement.

"He works in TV. He's divorced, has no kids, and seems like a nice person. It's not a big deal."

"It **is** a big deal," Katie and Liz both insisted, and Paul was interested now too. They were discussing it heatedly when Ted walked in. He had told Pattie he had to go home for dinner and had left even when she had a fit. He wasn't going to let her keep him from his aunt and sisters. Although he knew he would pay for it later, dinner with them was worth it, and he was trying to take Annie's advice and take a little more space from Pattie. And she didn't like it at all.

"What are you all so excited about?" Ted asked as he dropped his coat on the chair in the hall and walked in. He couldn't get the gist of the conversation, but they all sounded animated about something.

"Annie invited a man to dinner tonight. She's had lunch with him twice, and they met when she sprained her ankle." Liz summed it up for him, and he grinned.

"That's interesting." Ted and Paul exchanged a look. This sounded like girl talk to them. "Are you serious about him?" he asked Annie, and she shook her head.

"I hardly know him. I've only seen him three times in my life. He'll probably want to date Liz, although he's too old for her." She tried not to look at Ted as she said it. It wasn't a dig, but it was true. She had told both Liz and Katie about Pattie, and they were worried too. Liz said she sounded like a nutcase. Kate thought it was worth going out with her to get an A in her course. Annie didn't agree.

"How old is he?" Ted asked her.

"A few years older than I am." She had heard him give his age in the hospital. "He's forty-five."

"I'll let you know if I approve after I meet him," Ted said, smiling. But in spite of the questions and teasing, they were all surprised and pleased for her. They couldn't remember the last time Annie had invited a man home for dinner. Maybe never. But Tom Jefferson seemed more like a friend to her than a date. And before they could discuss it any further, the doorbell rang, and Annie went to let him in. He was wearing jeans and a sweater and cowboy boots, and he looked relaxed and pleasant as she introduced him to everyone. She could see the girls looking him over, as he and Ted talked about the football game he'd been to that afternoon. The Jets had scored three touchdowns in a row in the first quarter, which was a miracle for them. Paul joined in, although he wasn't as avid about football as Ted. And both girls said to Annie in the kitchen that he was really good looking and looked very familiar to both of them.

"He's the anchor for the evening news," Annie said simply as she checked on the pasta and tossed the salad. She had set the table in the kitchen, which was just big enough for all of them. It was a homestyle meal, and she hadn't made a fuss. There were only six of them.

"He's the **what**?" Liz said to what she had just told them. "He's **that** Tom Jefferson? You hit the jackpot on this one. He's great."

"I don't know that yet, and neither do you. I just met him. Now let's eat." By the end of dinner, they all acted like old friends. Tom had spent a considerable amount of time talking to Paul about the beauty of Iran, and he knew more about it than Paul even remembered—he hadn't been there since he was in his teens. After that Tom and Ted talked football and law school. And he had a lively conversation with Liz about fashion, and he asked Kate a lot of questions about tattoos, and why she felt it was an important form of graphic art. The only one he hardly talked to was Annie, but he stayed to help clean up the kitchen with her, while she dismissed the others to the living room.

"They're a terrific bunch," he said with a warm look at her. "You've done a great job."

"No, they've always been who they are. I just tried to teach them to be true to themselves."

"They are. And you know, Kate makes a hell of a case for tattoos as graphic art." Annie rolled her eyes at that, and he laughed. And then she turned to him with a warm smile as she loaded the dishwasher.

"Thank you for having dinner with us. I'm very proud of them."

"They're a real tribute to you," he complimented her, as they finished cleaning up, and she thanked him and they went to join the others. The young people insisted on playing charades after that, which they hadn't done for years. Tom was good at it. And it was after eleven when he got up to leave. He said goodbye to everyone, and Annie walked him out, and he thanked her again for a wonderful evening and reminded her of her promise to have dinner with him. "You agreed," he reminded her, and she laughed.

"I'd love to," she said warmly. He fit in perfectly. She didn't know yet if he was a date or a friend, but whatever he was, they had all enjoyed the evening with him, and so had he.

"I'll call you tomorrow and we'll figure out what day." He kissed her lightly on the cheek then, and after that he left. And as she walked back into the room on her crutches, everyone was laughing and talking and smiling at her.

"As the official head of the family," Ted announced, "I approve. He's great. He knows everything there is to know about football."

"And the Middle East," Paul added.

"He actually knows a fair amount about fashion," Liz commented, smiling at her aunt.

"And he totally gets it about the social statement of tattoos," Kate said, smiling.

"I think he snowed all of you," Annie said, smiling, "but I like him too."

"You can marry him anytime you want," Ted added. "I give my consent."

"Relax," Annie reminded him, "he's just a friend."

"That's crap, Annie, and you know it," Kate interrupted. "He looks at you like he wants to kiss you."

"No, he doesn't. He just liked all of you."

"We like him too," Liz agreed. She'd had such a nice time that she had forgotten the hideous scene with Françoise and Jean-Louis that morning. The evening they'd just spent was simple and wholesome and uncomplicated, right down to the charades. They had all laughed a lot.

251

Ted took out their old Monopoly board then, and the four young people played until two A.M., and Annie went to bed long before they were finished. But it was easy to see that the evening had been a success. And Paul had fit in too. Annie liked him. And she liked Tom too. And whatever happened, or didn't, she felt like they could be friends.

Paul and Ted left the apartment after the Monopoly game. Liz decided to spend the night with Kate and Annie, and the two sisters wound up talking in Kate's bedroom until nearly three. Liz told her what had happened with Jean-Louis. Liz wasn't too upset, although she admitted she was disappointed in him, and herself: with Jean-Louis for cheating and lying to her, and with herself for picking another loser. She swore she'd never do it again, and Kate hoped for her sake that it was true.

Ted and Paul shared a cab when they left Annie's, and Paul dropped Ted off at his apartment. It was too late to call Pattie, and he didn't want to stay there anyway. He had enjoyed the evening with his family and their friends. And he liked sleeping in his own bed for a change. He was sound asleep when Pattie called him the next morning, and it took him a few minutes to wake up and make sense.

"Where were you last night?" She sounded frantic and hurt. "I was worried about you all night."

"I was with my aunt and sisters and my sister's boyfriend. We played charades and Monopoly, and it got late," he said sleepily.

"You could have called."

"I didn't want to wake you up." And besides, he had been having fun and didn't want to call her.

"I need to see you right away," she said in a quiet voice.

"Is something wrong?"

She refused to discuss it on the phone, and he said he could be there in about an hour after he got dressed. It wasn't an emergency, and the kids weren't hurt. He had breakfast with one of his roommates before he left, and he got to Pattie's apartment two hours later. He saw that she looked tense and pale. She looked sick.

"What's up?" He was expecting her to give him hell about the night before. She had a chip on her shoulder about his family and didn't want him spending time with them. He expected to hear about that but not what she said. What she said next hit him harder than a punch in the solar plexus.

"I'm pregnant." For a moment he only stared at her, and said not a word. He had no idea what to say. This was a first for him.

"Oh my God," the words came out of him like a small gasp of air. He was going to ask her how that had happened, but he knew. He had tried to use a condom every time, but sometimes she wouldn't let him. She said they irritated her, and it felt so much better without them. He had been such a fool. "Shit, Pattie. What are we going to do?" He knew what they had to do, but he had never been in this situation before. He had always been careful, and his ex-girlfriend had been extremely responsible, and on the pill. Pattie had told him right from the beginning that she wasn't. But he had magically hoped that at her age she wouldn't get pregnant as easily. Apparently that wasn't true.

"What do you mean, what are we going to do? Have the baby, of course. Are you kidding? I'm not going to have an abortion at my age. We might never get another chance. Besides, this is our baby, our flesh and blood, the product of our love." Pattie said it as though it were obvious and she expected him to agree with her.

"No, it's not," he said, sounding angry. "It's a product of our being stupid and sloppy. I was careless, and so were you. That's not love, Pattie, it's lust."

"Are you saying you don't love me?" she said, clinging to him with tears in her eyes. "How can you say something like that to me? I'm carrying our child."

"What about the morning-after pill?" he asked her. "I hear that really works." He had heard about it from one of his roommates. He swore by it; he and his girlfriend had used it several times. You had to take it within seventy-two hours of unprotected sex. "How pregnant are you?" he asked.

"I'm three weeks late." That meant she was five weeks pregnant.

"Why didn't you say something before now?" He was beginning to think she had done it on purpose, and he felt trapped.

"I thought you'd be happy, Ted," she said, bursting into tears. "We'd have wanted it sooner or later. What difference does it make if we do it now?"

"Are you kidding? I'm in law school. I have no money and no job. I live off what's left of an insurance policy my parents left me, and it's almost gone. My aunt helps me out. How do you think I'm going to support a child, or even take care of one? I'm years away from making a decent living, and you can hardly support the kids you have. What's our life going to be like with a baby? What will your kids think? I can't finish law school and support you and a kid. And we're not even married. This is an accident. A mistake. This isn't a baby. It's a disaster. It's a tragedy for both of us, and it would be for the kid. You **have** to have an abortion or give it up for adoption," he said, his face right up against hers. "We have no other choice!"

"Those aren't options," she spat back at him. "We can get married. You can get a job. I'm not giving up our baby, and I'm warning you, if you try to make me, I'll kill the baby and myself!"

"Stop threatening me!" he roared at her with the full measure of his fury and frustration. She was destroying his life. One stupid mistake was going to demolish everything he had struggled for and built. It wasn't fair.

"I'm having this baby," she said quietly, suddenly in total control. "You can do whatever you want, but I'm having our child." He nodded at her. He had gotten the message loud and clear.

"I need to think," he said just as quietly, and walked out. He slammed the door behind him and ran down the stairs into the cold air.

Upstairs, in the apartment, after he left, Pattie sat on the couch and smiled.

Chapter 16

Nobody heard from Ted for the next few days. He didn't call Pattie or show up at her place. He didn't take her calls or answer her texts. He never thanked Annie for dinner, which was unusual for him, and it worried her. She knew that he was in a delicate situation with an unstable woman, although she knew nothing of the pregnancy. But Annie didn't want to hound him, so she waited to hear from him. And finally after three days of total silence, he called his sister Liz. She was surprised to hear his voice, and he sounded terrible. She knew instantly that something was seriously wrong.

"Can I see you for lunch?" he asked her in a hoarse croak. He had been hiding out in his apartment for three days and drinking too much.

"Sure," Lizzie answered immediately.

He picked her up at her office at noon, and they

went to a salad bar nearby. She picked at her lettuce without dressing, and Ted ate nothing at all. He told her about Pattie, that she was pregnant, and he didn't know what to do.

"She won't have an abortion, or give it up for adoption, and she says if I do anything other than congratulate her, she'll kill herself and the baby. I don't want a baby, Lizzie. I'm a child myself. Or I feel like one anyway. I'm not old enough to have kids. I was such a fucking fool," he said, and his sister smiled ruefully.

"That seems to be the operative word. Can you reason with her at all?" He shook his head and looked dismal.

"She was threatening suicide even before she got pregnant. She said that if I ever leave her, she'd kill herself. Now she'll kill herself and the baby."

"She needs therapy. Badly. Teddy, she's blackmailing you. That's what this is. You can't force her not to have the baby. And I guess you'd have to pay her some support for the baby. But she can't force you to be with her and participate if that's not what you want too."

"I can't just walk out on her. It's my kid too. If she won't get rid of it, then I have to be there and carry the load with her."

"That's not fair to you," Liz said firmly. She hated what this woman was doing to her brother.

"I have a responsibility here. To both of them. Whether I like it or not."

"Are you in love with her?" Liz was watching him closely, wondering what he'd say.

"I don't know. She drives me insane. I get near her and my body goes nuts. She's like a drug. I don't know if that's love."

"It sounds like sex addiction to me. She probably did that to you on purpose to keep you hooked."

"Well, I'm paying a hell of a price for it. A kid is forever. I can't let her kill herself, Liz."

"I don't think she will. People who threaten usually don't. She wants you to stick around."

"I have no other choice." He looked so innocent as he said it, and so sad.

"What are you going to tell Annie?" Lizzie wondered aloud.

"Nothing right now. She'd go crazy."

"Maybe not. She has a cool head in a crisis. And she'll figure it out sooner or later. You can't hide a kid forever."

"I'll have to drop out of law school after this semester." Liz hated to see him do that, and she knew how much it meant to him. It was his dream, and he had worked so hard for it till now.

"Don't do anything yet. Besides, you never know, she could have a miscarriage. At her age, that's a higher risk."

Danielle Steel

"I hope I get that lucky." He felt guilty as he said it, but he didn't want a child. He was totally clear on that. "I haven't talked to her since she told me."

"She knows she's got you by the throat." It was an age-old way to catch a man, and she had. Lizzie hated her for it and wished there was something she could do to help her brother. But there was nothing anyone could do right now. Except give him moral support. The rest was in Pattie's hands. And God's.

Ted called Pattie that night. It was the first time he had spoken to her in three days. And all she did was sob when he called. He felt terrible and tried to comfort her on the phone, and she begged him to come over. He felt as though he had to, so he dressed and went over to her apartment. She was calm when he got there and very loving. She begged him to go to bed with her and just hold her, and then she started to arouse him. He didn't want to make love to her, it seemed so wrong right now, given everything he was feeling. But as she held him and caressed him, she overcame his objections, and he wound up making love to her anyway. It was tender and sweet and passionate, and she clung to him afterward and talked about their baby. It made him want to cry.

They made love again, as they always did, and when Ted left the next morning, he felt beaten.

260

Pattie had won. The baby had won. And he was the loser in all this. And that morning before he left, she asked him about getting married. He said he didn't want to. She said it wasn't fair to the baby to have it out of wedlock. She was a decent woman, and she'd been married when she had the others. All he could do was say he would think about it. He didn't want her threatening suicide again. He didn't have the strength to deal with it. And he was starting classes again that day. He could hardly think straight as he walked to the law school with his head down. He wanted a bolt of lightning to come down and kill him. It would have been so much simpler. The last thing he wanted was a baby. And Pattie called him incessantly between classes. She wanted constant reassurance. All he could think of, as he went to the library to work on his computer, was that it felt like someone had ripped his guts out and flushed his life down the toilet. She sent him an e-mail while he was at the library, and he promised to be there for dinner.

By the end of the week, Annie hadn't heard from Ted or Tom Jefferson, either. Tom had promised to call her about dinner, and she never heard from him after his Sunday-night dinner with her family at the apartment. She wondered if it had unnerved him. His silence spoke volumes, and she didn't want to pursue him.

It was another week later when he called her from Hong Kong and apologized for not calling sooner.

"I'm so sorry. I had no phone service or e-mail. I've been in a southern province of China for ten days. I just got to Hong Kong. They sent me on a story. It's been a wild-goose chase." She was so relieved to hear from him that she sounded ebullient on the phone.

"I thought we'd scared you off."

"Don't be silly. They sent me off the next morning, and I didn't have time to call you. Sometimes my life gets a little crazy." It was what had cost him his marriage. His ex-wife had wanted a full-time husband at home, and he was never going to be that person. He wanted Annie to know that now, right from the beginning, or even before anything started.

"Don't worry, my life gets pretty crazy too. Although I don't wind up in China or Hong Kong. When are you coming back?"

"Hopefully tomorrow or the next day. How about dinner on Saturday night?"

"I'd love it." She told him then that she hadn't heard from Ted since that dinner either, and she was worried about him.

"Maybe he's having love troubles."

"I suspect you're right. And I think he just started classes. I just worry about that woman he's involved with." It was comforting to share her concerns with Tom.

"There's nothing you can do about it," Tom reminded her. "He has to work it out for himself."

"I know. He's such an innocent though. And I don't trust that woman. She's almost as old as I am."

"It'll be a good lesson for him," Tom said calmly.

"If he survives it."

"He will. We all do. We pay a price for our mistakes, and we learn the lessons. Sometimes at a high price. I knew I was marrying the wrong woman when I got married. I went through with it anyway, and it just got worse over time. At least you were spared that."

"I've made my share of mistakes too," Annie admitted. Maybe living like a nun was one of them. But she couldn't have handled more than she had on her plate. Dealing with three kids at her age had been enough. And now she was comfortable with her monastic life.

"You look like you've done okay to me. That's a great family you raised. Your sister would be proud of you." It brought tears to her eyes when he said it.

He told her about China then, and the story he was covering. There was a new prime minister, and he had gone over to do an interview with him, about his foreign policies and a trade commission he was setting up. It struck her that Tom led a very grown-up life and was at the hub of world events. She was trying to get contractors to come in on time, and moving walls around to keep her clients happy. Her world was a lot smaller than his. But she loved what she did. It had given her great satisfaction for years. She had always secretly hoped that Kate would get interested in architecture too, and she could have formed a partnership with her in later years, but her artistic talents had found other avenues.

Tom promised to call her as soon as he got back to New York, and he confirmed their dinner date on Saturday night. He said he'd figure out where on the way home and make the reservation. She liked the way he took charge of things and made plans on his own. She didn't have to do it for him. It was a relief not to be the one carrying the whole load. That was new for her.

Annie was in much better spirits after she heard from Tom. And she finally reached Ted. He said he was just busy with classes, but he sounded terrible and she didn't believe him when he said he was fine. He didn't sound it. She called Liz then, who insisted she knew nothing. She hated lying to Annie, but it was up to Ted to tell her that Pattie was pregnant, and he didn't have the courage, and there was plenty of time. Pattie was barely more than a month pregnant. She had told him the baby was due in September. He didn't even want to think about it now. And she was talking marriage now a lot of the time. He had never been so miserable in his life, except when he lost his parents.

Liz called him every day to see how he was, and she hated the way he sounded. He admitted to her that he was in despair and felt trapped. The fetus growing in Pattie's belly had ruined his life, or was going to the instant it was born. It already had. And Pattie was on top of the world now. She was having his baby, and she owned him for life. All she did was thank him for making her so happy, and she wanted to have sex with him all the time. He no longer called it making love. It wasn't. It was just raw sex, and Pattie got her way every time. He didn't want to upset her, so he did whatever she asked. He tried to be gentle with her so as not to hurt the baby, but she insisted that everything they did was fine. He had begun to wish that he had never met her. And he was having very dark thoughts. He was drinking a lot, and he told Lizzie several times that he wished he were dead. She didn't think that Pattie would ever kill herself, but she was worried about Ted. Liz had said nothing to Annie, but she was beginning to think she should. If he didn't feel better soon, she would have no other choice.

Liz was startled a few days later when Annie called her. She sounded serious, and she said she wanted Liz's advice. Liz was desperately afraid that she was going to ask about Ted. But instead she admitted to Liz that Tom had invited her on a real date. He was taking her to dinner, and she had nothing to wear. Liz smiled when she heard the nervous, girlish tone in her aunt's voice. It was sweet.

They discussed where she might be going to dinner, and what kind of impression she wanted to make on Tom. She said that all her good clothes were appropriate for client meetings, but she didn't own anything sexy that might appeal to a man.

"How sexy? Plunging neckline? Short skirt?" Liz asked practically, and Annie laughed.

"I didn't say I want to get arrested. I said I want to look attractive on a date."

"Okay. Pretty ruffled blouse. Maybe Chanel. Short but decent skirt. Pretty fur jacket. I can lend you one of mine. Your hair down framing your face. Nothing hard. Everything soft, feminine, pretty." She brought over several garment bags of things to choose from that night. She had six bags stuffed to the gills, and Annie picked a beautiful organdy blouse and a black lace skirt. Both were elegant but sexy. And she was still on crutches and had to wear flat shoes, so Liz had brought her a pair of satin flats with rhinestone buckles in the right size. She'd had her assistant pick them up. And she lent her a short black mink jacket that Annie had admired for years. She was all set!

Annie looked lovely on Saturday night when Tom picked her up. Katie had helped her dress and did her makeup for her and told her to wear her hair down. She felt like a high school kid going to her first prom when Tom rang the doorbell. He was wearing a black cashmere jacket and slacks, with an open, beautifully tailored shirt. He said he was jet-lagged but he didn't look it, and he admired everything Annie had on. He loved her looks and the way she was dressed. He noticed it all.

"Where is everyone, by the way?" Tom asked, looking around. The apartment was deserted and silent.

"Out. Katie and Paul are at a movie. Lizzie is away for the weekend, and Ted's busy with school.

I hardly hear from him anymore. I don't know what's going on. I hope he's okay and getting a little space from that woman."

"He'll figure it out," Tom reassured her, as they left the apartment and took a cab to the restaurant. It was uptown and very chic. Everyone knew Tom, and he introduced her to half a dozen people who stopped at their table. And the headwaiter made a big fuss over them both. It was fun being out with him. With his face on the news every night, he was universally known, respected, and greatly admired.

Over dinner, Annie told him about the houses she was currently working on, and he told her all about China. For the first time, Annie talked about something other than the kids. She felt like she was out on a real date with him. And when he took her home, he walked her to her door, and she invited him in for a drink. He looked at her ruefully and stifled a yawn. He said he'd had a great time, but the time change was catching up with him, and he was afraid he'd fall asleep.

"Let's do it again soon," he said. It sounded like a good idea to her too.

"I had a wonderful time," she said, as she thanked him, and he smiled and kissed her on the cheek.

"So did I. I'll call you next week, unless they

send me halfway around the world again." He had mentioned that he had to go to London soon. It sounded like fun to her.

Tom left her at the door to the apartment and watched her as she went in. As she walked into the living room, Paul and Katie were sitting on the couch, watching a DVD. And Annie noticed that they looked secretive when she came in. She wondered what they were up to and assumed they'd had sex in Katie's room while she was out. Katie had never asked Annie if Paul could spend the night, because Paul said he felt awkward about it, and neither of them was sure how Annie would react. None of Katie's boyfriends had ever stayed there before. Liz and Ted had never brought anyone home for the night either. And Paul was very circumspect.

Annie was still floating from the evening with Tom when she went to her own room and carefully took off her new clothes. They had been a big success. It was a whole different look for her. And Liz had promised to find some other things for her to wear on future dates with Tom.

Annie was still smiling the next morning as she read the Sunday paper. She was thinking about Tom when Katie walked in. She bustled around the kitchen for a while, and then she sat down at the kitchen table and faced her aunt.

"I have something to tell you," Kate said quietly, and Annie looked at her in shock.

"Oh my God, you're pregnant . . . ," Annie said as Kate looked at her and shook her head.

"No, I'm not."

"Thank God," Annie said, looking relieved. She wasn't ready for that.

"I'm going to take a trip with Paul," Katie said firmly, bracing herself for what would come next. "We've been talking about it for a while."

"To where?" Annie asked with interest. She wasn't shocked that they wanted to go away with each other. They were old enough.

"We're going to Tehran," Katie said, looking Annie in the eye. There was a deafening silence in the kitchen.

"No, you're not," Annie said, without hesitating for a second.

"Yes, I am."

"That's out of the question. I won't allow it. It could be dangerous for you, and it's too far away. That's not going to happen," Annie said firmly. "I don't mind your traveling with him, but not to someplace that could be awkward for you."

"We're going. We can stay with his uncle and aunt. I've already looked into getting a visa. I can get one in a few weeks, and I've already applied. And I'm going to pay for the trip with what I make at the tattoo parlor." They had already checked it out and made their plans. Annie was shocked at Katie's blunt announcement of the trip as a fait accompli. She was not asking for her aunt's permission. And Annie looked panicked at the idea.

"This is a completely crazy thing to do," Annie said, looking worried.

"No, it's not," Katie said stubbornly. "He hasn't been back in years. It'll be interesting for both of us."

"It's not 'interesting' to go to a country that can be problematic for Americans to travel in. It's foolish, if you don't have to go there. That's just not smart. Why don't you go someplace easy for both of you that you'd both enjoy?" Annie was desperate to convince her.

"Paul won't let anything happen to me. And his family will take care of us. He wants to see his cousins, and I want to meet them." Annie sat shaking her head as she looked at her, and then dropped her head in her hands.

"Katie, this is a terrible idea."

"No, it's not. We love each other, and I want to see the country where he was born and meet his family there." She had some strange romantic idea about visiting his roots with him, and Annie was frightened for her. Out of pure ignorance, Katie could offend someone, and wind up with a problem while she was there.

"Go somewhere else. Go to Europe and have some fun. You can get a railway pass and go all over the place."

"He wants to go home, and I want to go with him. We're only going for two weeks." Katie wasn't budging an inch.

"You are not going at all!" Annie shouted at her, frustrated that Katie wouldn't give in. This wasn't one of her harebrained ideas like dropping out of school, which had been stupid too. This was just plain insane. And as usual, Kate was defying her and determined to do what she wanted and convinced that she knew best.

"I'm an adult, and I can do what I want," Katie shouted back at her. It turned into a screaming match in their kitchen, until Katie ran to her room and slammed the door. Annie was shaking from head to foot.

And when Paul came by later that afternoon, Annie said the same to him. But he was as confident as Kate and insisted they'd be fine. He said that staying with his uncle would be fun, and they would be well taken care of. And he said that Tehran was a modern city, and there would be no risk to Katie there. Annie didn't believe him. She called Tom about it that night and told him their plan. She asked him what he thought of it, and he hesitated for a moment before he answered and considered the plan.

"I wouldn't be crazy about the idea in your shoes either. Theoretically, they should be fine, and it's a fascinating place. It is a beautiful city, and an interesting culture, but not for two kids who don't know what they're doing. The very fact that she's American and he's Iranian could cause them a problem, if someone in the street doesn't like it. I think it's potentially sensitive. Tell them to go somewhere else."

"I did," Annie said miserably. "She insists that they're going no matter what, and she says I can't stop her."

"That's true. But she needs to listen to common sense and people who know better."

"Katie does whatever she wants. She's paying for the trip from her earnings. And they're staying with Paul's uncle."

"I hope you can talk her out of it," he said kindly. He was worried about her too. "But having said that, I'm sure they'll be fine."

"I hope I can talk her out of it too. I'm going to be a nervous wreck if she goes there." It was one thing to let them do what they wanted and make their own mistakes, but this one was just too high risk if they did something foolish or something went wrong. "Will you talk to her?" Annie asked Tom. She didn't know what else to do.

"I'll try. I'm not sure she'll listen to me either. Did you call his parents?"

"I was planning to call them tomorrow," she said unhappily.

"I think you should," Tom agreed. "They may not like the idea either. For Paul to go to Tehran with an American girl could be awkward for him, as an Iranian. Maybe together, you and Paul's parents can convince them to reconsider. I'll talk to her too, but Katie is a headstrong girl." He didn't know her well, but he deduced it from what Annie had said.

Annie followed his advice and called Paul's parents the next day. His mother wasn't enthused about the trip either. She wasn't convinced that they would be sensible once they got there, and she thought they were too young to travel together so far away. She said it was the first trip Paul had ever taken with a girl. She told Annie that she had tried to talk Paul out of it, to no avail. And she wasn't keen on his being responsible for a young girl. What if Katie had an accident or got sick? Annie was worried about that too, although it was comforting to know that Paul had family there who would help.

His mother said that Paul was planning to use

the money he had saved from summer jobs to pay for the trip himself, and Katie was paying her own way as well. Paul's mother also expressed, as delicately as possible, that she felt it was not wise for an American girl to travel to Tehran with an Iranian man, even if they claimed to be only friends. And she pointed out that while in Iran, Paul would be considered Iranian, and his dual citizenship and American passport wouldn't be recognized there. She made it very clear that she didn't want Katie causing him problems there. Annie could hear in her voice that she was as uneasy about the trip as Annie was herself. It was reassuring, but their common disapproval didn't seem to hold much sway with the kids, both of whom thought they were being silly and were determined to go anyway.

"What about Paul's father? Can't he forbid him to go?"

"He has," Paul's mother said unhappily. "But Paul wants to see his aunt and uncle and cousins, and his grandfather who is getting very old. I don't think either of our children realize that they could run into problems there." Annie wasn't comforted by what she said.

"What do we do now?" Annie said, realizing that neither she nor Paul's parents were able to control their kids. Technically, they were adults.

Annie was reminded of Whitney telling her that she had to let them make their own mistakes, but it was easier said than done.

"Maybe all we can do is wish them a safe trip," Paul's mother said with a sigh. "And my brother-in-law and sister-in-law will take good care of them." She sounded resigned, and she wasn't hopeful about getting Paul to change his mind, nor was Annie about Kate. The two young people were willing to listen to no one's opinion but their own. They were in control of their own destiny, and their families had no choice in the matter, except to let them try their wings and hope that all went well. Annie knew when she hung up that there was no stopping them from going to Iran.

Tom took Annie to dinner the following week, and they talked about it again. Katie hadn't budged an inch. And he sat down and spoke with her before they went out. He said that it might be difficult for her to travel to Tehran with a male Iranian citizen. Katie once again insisted that it would be fine. There was nothing more that Tom could say, or that Kate was willing to hear from him or anyone else. She said that she appreciated his concern, but she and Paul had decided to go. Tom could see why Annie was so upset. Katie had made up her mind, and nothing either of them had said swayed her. And Paul seemed to have some kind of romantic notion of what it would be like going to Iran with her and showing her all the things he remembered from his childhood. But he had no idea what it would be like going there with an American girl, particularly one as modern and liberated and independent as Katie, or if it might cause either of them a problem, even if they were just friends. Paul also insisted everything would be fine. And Tom felt sorry for Annie, who would be worrying about them at home.

Tom tried to reassure her over dinner, but he was concerned about it too. Katie was determined to go, no matter what they said to her. He didn't envy the ongoing battle Annie was having with her. And he knew that she was worried about Ted and the older woman he was involved with too. These were the times when Tom was glad he didn't have kids. Dealing with these issues seemed frightening to him. And he admired Annie more than ever for how she handled her sister's kids. She was smart, loving, fair, and respectful of their opinions. But despite that, Katie refused to listen to her. She was going to Tehran and that was that. Tom admitted that in Annie's shoes, he would have wanted to strangle her on the spot for being too independent, headstrong, and listening to no one's advice.

"Strangling her is not an option," Annie said,

smiling at him, "although I have to admit it's tempting at times." In spite of her concerns about Katie, their dinner date was as enjoyable as the first one. They were getting to know each other better, and they laughed, talked endlessly, and seemed to enjoy many of the same things. He was a kindred spirit in many ways. And this time when he brought her home, he kissed her. It was a gentle lingering kiss that aroused feelings in her that she hadn't felt in years. It was like being kissed awake by the handsome prince in **Sleeping Beauty**. She was beginning to feel like a woman again. Tom made her happy, and they had a great time together.

He invited her to the TV studio later that week and showed her around. It was fascinating. And she got to watch him do his show. She took him to one of her job sites with her on another day and explained what she was doing and showed him the plans. He was very impressed by the caliber of her work and how talented she was. And they cooked dinner together at her apartment the following weekend. Katie was out, and they had the place to themselves. This time they made out like kids on the living-room couch. Their desire for each other was mounting, but they both thought it was still too soon to give in. They were in no rush, and wanted to get to know each other better. They felt that if this was right, and meant for them, it could wait. They were waiting for their feelings for each other to ripen before they plucked them off the tree. They were in complete agreement about that.

The only thing that still concerned him was if she had room for him in her life. She was still so busy and preoccupied with her sister's kids. And Katie wasn't making life any easier these days, with her stubborn insistence on going to Iran. Annie talked about it all the time and was worried sick. At least half their time together was spent talking about the kids. And Annie hardly saw Ted these days. She was worried about that too. She could tell that he was hiding something. He had gone underground again.

The scene in Pattie's apartment was now one of constant battles. When she wasn't talking about the baby, she was pressuring Ted about marrying her before it was born. She accused him of thinking she wasn't good enough for him, and of being castrated by his sisters and aunt. She had gotten abusive and insulting. She wheedled, she begged, she seduced, and then she accused. And Ted told her honestly that it wasn't that he thought she wasn't good enough for him to marry. It was that he felt too young.

"It's too late for that!" Pattie shouted at him. "We're having a kid!" They fought all the time now. And when they weren't fighting, she wanted to make love. Sex was the only form of communication she knew. She used it for everything, reward, punishment, manipulation, bribery, emotional blackmail. Ted was feeling defeated and used and was seriously depressed about the situation. He knew he was trapped, whether he was married to her or not, and he realized that sooner or later he would marry her, probably right before the baby was born. But he was in no rush to tie that noose around his neck.

He was trying to call Annie more often, so she wouldn't worry about him, but he hadn't seen her. He was too afraid that if he did, she would guess what was going on. He had dark circles under his eyes and had lost weight. Pattie was keeping him up all night, either fighting with him or seducing him, and he was utterly exhausted. He felt like a zombie most of the time, and he was flunking nearly every class but hers. He was behind on his papers, and only Pattie was giving him straight A's. He no longer cared. With a baby to support, and a wife, he had to drop out anyway—it no longer mattered to him if he failed. Pattie was winning on every front. If what she wanted was to destroy his life, she was doing a great job.

Her big battle with him now was getting him to marry her right away. She didn't want to wait. She was afraid he would change his mind. And she argued with him about it now every night. He was holding out. He had agreed to marry her in August, but not before. The baby wasn't due till September. She called him a bastard and a sadist for making her wait. And now she wanted him to tell his aunt about their child. She wanted victory on all fronts. Ted was trying to hold his ground. But Pattie had all the ammo. She had the baby on her side.

Tom and Annie were having dinner at La Grenouille one night, when her cell phone rang. She had forgotten to turn it off. And the people at the tables on either side of them looked at her in disapproval when it rang. She glanced down at her phone and saw that it was Ted. She ducked her head down close to her purse, and with a rapid apology to Tom, she took the call. She heard from Ted so seldom now that she didn't want to miss it. She didn't know when he'd call her again.

"Hi, baby, everything okay? I'm at dinner with Tom," she whispered, nearly hiding under the table, as Tom watched. He wondered if she would ever do that for a call from him. He knew now that there was nothing she wouldn't do for those kids. "Can I call you back?"

"I . . . uh . . . I'm in the hospital," he said, sounding dazed, and suddenly Annie's eyes were filled with fear, and she glanced at Tom.

"Where are you?"

"I'm at NYU Hospital . . . I had a little problem with Pattie," he said, and Annie thought he sounded half asleep.

"What happened?"

"She stabbed me in the hand with a steak knife. I'm okay. They just stitched it up. I thought maybe I'd come home."

"I'll come and get you right away," she said, and snapped her phone shut, as she sat up and looked at Tom. "That lunatic stabbed him in the hand with a steak knife. He says he's okay." Annie looked shocked.

"Oh my God, that's insane." He looked as horrified as she was and signaled immediately for the check. They had only gotten their first course, but there was no way Annie could have eaten dinner now.

"No, **she's** insane," Annie corrected him, grateful that he was willing to leave with her. They talked about it all the way downtown in the cab. "I don't know what happened, but she's obviously gone nuts."

"I had no idea she was this crazy," Tom said, looking worried. "Next time she might kill him."

They both thought Ted looked terrible when they got to the hospital. He was shaking and deathly pale. The doctor said he had lost very little blood, and he had ten stitches in his hand. It was heavily bandaged, and she had narrowly missed cutting a ligament and a nerve.

"What happened?" Annie asked him as the three of them rode back to her apartment.

Ted couldn't hide it from her any longer. He had to tell her the truth. "She's pregnant. She wants me to marry her. I said I would in August. She wants me to do it now. I don't want to. The baby's not due till September." Annie looked grim as she listened. This was hardly the way to start a marriage, with a baby on the way, and a woman who was willing to stab him if he didn't do what she said. "We were arguing about it tonight while we were eating dinner, and she just lost it."

"You can't marry someone like that," Annie said with a dark look at Tom, and he nodded. He totally agreed, and he was just as worried about Ted. He looked emotionally abused, and he had been. And now she had injured him physically too, not just his heart and his mind. It was frightening.

"She says she'll commit suicide if I don't," Ted said grimly.

"Let her," Annie said harshly, as Tom paid for the cab, and they took him upstairs. He looked like he was in shock. And Annie put a blanket around him as he lay down on his old bed in his room. The room was intact and always ready for him, although he seldom used it. But this was still their home. "She's not going to kill herself, Ted," Annie reassured him. "She's just trying to control you," but she already had.

"I don't know what to do," Ted said, as tears rolled down his cheeks. "I want to do the right thing. But I never wanted a kid. Not yet. And I don't want to marry her. But I have no other choice." Tom was standing in the doorway, devasted by the look on Annie's face, and he felt desperately sorry for the boy.

"All you have to do is support the baby," Annie said quietly, sitting on his bed. "You don't have to marry Pattie if you don't want to."

"I don't. She freaks me out." There was good reason for that, as the episode that night had proved.

"I want to tell you something, Ted. That woman is psychotic," Annie said, looking straight at him. "She's an abuser, and she's going to make what happened tonight your fault. That's what abusers do. She's going to tell you that you made her angry, and that you hurt her terribly by what you said, so it justifies her stabbing you. By tomorrow, she'll paint herself as the victim, and you'll be the bad guy. Mark my words, she won't even apologize for what she did to you tonight. She'll blame you. And nothing about this is your fault. You got her pregnant, which was stupid and careless of you, but you're not the one abusing her. And she's going to do everything she can to convince you it's your fault. I want you to stay away from her. I think she's dangerous for you."

The enormous bandage on his hand illustrated her point. Ted thanked her then for her support, and he glanced at Tom with an embarrassed look. Annie lowered the lights, and put another blanket over him, and they left him alone for a while to rest, while she and Tom went out to the kitchen to get something to eat. They were both starving since they had never finished dinner, and she offered to make him an omelette or a sandwich. Tom thanked her but said he was too upset to even want food. They settled for ice cream instead, while they discussed what had happened. These were the things that terrified Annie now. The foolish things they did, believing that they were grown up. Katie's trip to Tehran with Paul, and Ted involved with this lunatic who had stabbed him. It didn't get much worse or more dangerous than that.

"You just can't protect them forever though,"

Tom reminded her, and she shook her head, dis-
agreeing with him.

"Maybe not. But I have to at least try."

"You still can't stop them, and they still do what
they want. Look at Katie, and Ted. My guess is
that he'll go back to this woman, out of guilt."
Annie was afraid that he was right. She could see
that happening too.

They sat and talked for a long time after they
finished their ice cream, and Tom finally stood up
to go home. He kissed her before he left and told
her to call him if she needed anything. She
promised that she would and thanked him for his
help. He looked profoundly upset. And so did she.

Annie heard Ted's cell phone ring just after midnight, and she tiptoed into his room to turn it off.
It had awakened him by then, and as she left the
room, Annie could tell it was Pattie on the phone.
She didn't want to eavesdrop on him, but she
could sense that the conversation had started just
as she thought. Pattie was blaming him for pushing her over the edge. She was saying that the stab
wound in his hand was his fault. Annie could hear
him apologizing to her. Pattie had him completely
spun around. And she suspected that Pattie was
furious he had called his aunt. She would blame
him for that too. Ted looked exhausted when
Annie kissed him goodnight.

"Just get some sleep. Don't think about any of it tonight. Why don't you stay here for a while?" Annie suggested to him as she turned off the light.

"She wants me to come back," he said in a beaten voice. She had said everything Annie had predicted she would. She was blaming him.

"We'll talk about it tomorrow. Don't worry about it tonight." He nodded and closed his eyes, grateful to be home. His eyes fluttered open for a moment, and he thanked her again. She kissed him on the forehead then and walked out of the room. It had been a long night, and she was sorry that Tom had gotten dragged into it too. He had been incredibly understanding about the whole thing and their disrupted dinner at La Grenouille.

In the morning, Ted was still asleep when Annie got up. She had an early meeting and had to leave. Kate was in her room, and Annie left the apartment quietly. She had left Ted a note telling him to take it easy and stay at the apartment all day. The last thing she wanted was for him to go back to Pattie. Who knew what she would do this time? Annie had asked him in the note to call her when he woke up.

He was in the kitchen, looking ghastly, when Kate walked in to get something to eat. She had no idea he had slept there, and she looked stunned when she saw the huge bandage on his hand. It was throbbing miserably by then. The pain medication had worn off.

"What happened to you?" she asked, staring at his hand with a worried look. "Did you get in a fight?" It was hard to imagine. He never had, even as a kid. She wondered if he'd been jumped by a mugger or something.

He nodded and looked at his sister with tired eyes. "Yeah, I did. With Pattie. I upset her, and she did something stupid. She didn't mean to, but I pissed her off. It was really my fault." She had convinced him of it the night before. Annie would have shuddered if she'd been there to hear what he just said. He had been the perfect abuse victim at Pattie's hands. And he had no idea what had hit him. It was a classic case of abuse, and it was now all his fault, according to Pattie. And Ted believed her.

"What happened to your hand?" Katie asked as she sat down and looked at him. His eyes looked dead, and the circles under them were almost black.

"She stabbed me with a steak knife. I shouldn't have made her mad."

"Are you kidding?" Katie looked at him, shocked. "People piss me off all the time. I don't stab them with a steak knife. Is she nuts?" Hers was the right reaction to have.

"She's a very emotional person," he explained, "and I upset her."

"She sounds crazy to me. And dangerous. If I were you, I wouldn't stick around."

"We're having a baby," he said as Kate's eyes opened wide. "In September. She wants to get married."

"I'll bet she does," Kate commented. "You aren't going to, I hope. She's twelve years older than you are."

"It's a little late to think of that now," he said, looking unhappy. And then he heard his cell phone ring and hurried back to his bedroom.

The next time Katie saw him, he was dressed and his hair was combed haphazardly, as best he could with his left hand, and he told her he was going back to his place for a while to get some things. She knew he was lying and he was going to see Pattie. She wanted to stop him but didn't know how. She had the feeling that nothing would have. He was a man on a mission, a robot being controlled by someone else. He turned as he got to the front door and looked at his sister, as she stared at him.

"If Annie calls, tell her I'm asleep. I'll be back soon."

"I'm going to work," Katie said to him in a voice full of pity. "Be careful," she warned him, looking worried, and he nodded, and then left.

Once Ted got to Pattie's, everything was all

right. She held him and crooned to him. She treated him like a baby and cradled his injured hand. She told him that she forgave him for everything he had done the night before, and he thanked her and then burst into tears. He was still crying when she started to fondle him, and then he made love to her to make up for what he'd done. He missed all his classes and never went back to Annie's that night. Pattie had won another round.

Chapter 17

Tom called Annie at her office two days after Pattie's attack on Ted with the steak knife. He'd been working on a breaking story the day before, about a political scandal in Washington that had just been revealed, involving two senators, and he hadn't had time to call her. Annie had learned by then that when Tom didn't call her, it was for an important reason. He wasn't dealing with domestic crises or unreliable contractors, he was reporting on major events in the news, or international crises, or being sent halfway around the world on short notice.

"How's Ted doing?" he asked in a quiet moment, which he said was usually the calm before the storm in his line of work. But it was obvious that despite the stressful moments, challenging demands, and network politics, he loved what he

291

did, and Annie was fascinated by it. He existed in such a broad world, and he knew everything that went on behind the scenes in world events. She loved hearing about it from him. But she sounded discouraged when she answered. Her life was so much smaller than his, and her focus now was on Ted and the dilemma he was in.

"I don't know. He was with her yesterday, the minute I left for work. Katie says she called him, and he said he had to see her. He never came back last night. I'm sure she wouldn't let him. And now every time I don't hear from him, I'm scared to death she's going to hurt him." In Annie's eyes, the incident with the steak knife was no small thing, and Tom agreed with her. Pattie had crossed the line, and having done that once, there was no way to predict how far she would go, or where she would stop. Ted had fallen into the clutches of an unbalanced, dangerous woman, possibly a sociopath. She sounded psychotic to Annie, and Ted had ten stitches to prove it.

"I was afraid he'd go back," Tom said quietly, sorry for him and for Annie. He knew how worried about him she was. "I was in a situation like that once, at his age. A gorgeous lunatic of a girl who was on hard drugs. Situations like that are so abusive, and it's hard to get out once you're in them. You keep waiting for things to calm down, and they never do. People like her thrive on chaos."

"And he's so naïve," Annie said mournfully. "He's way out of his league. And now with a baby on the way."

"He's a bright kid. He'll get out of it eventually," Tom reassured her. "But it may take a while, and I know it's hard on you."

"It's a lot harder on him." She and Katie had talked about it the night before until the wee hours, hoping he would come home, but he didn't, and he wasn't answering his phone. He had answered a text from Kate at one point, saying he was okay, but that was all they had heard. At least they knew he was alive.

"I was actually calling to ask you if you'd like to have dinner. There's a new restaurant I want to try. It might be fun." She didn't feel very lighthearted, but she appreciated his calls, and she liked spending time with him.

"I'm sorry my life is such a mess right now," she said apologetically. "We were all sane a few weeks ago, or a couple of months anyway. Now Ted is being held hostage by a psychopath and having a baby, and Katie is threatening to go to Iran. The only sane one at the moment is Liz," despite the breakup with her boyfriend, which she seemed to have weathered well. She had been very sensible about it and said she was taking a break from dating for a while, until she felt ready to make a commitment herself. "And I'm not feeling so sane myself with all this going on." She was worried sick about Katie's prospective trip, but at least they hadn't set any dates yet. For now it was just an idea, which Annie viewed as a threat. She was hoping they'd change their minds. But none of it was an atmosphere conducive to her being happy and relaxed, or enjoying a new man in her life. And it couldn't be easy for him, Annie knew, trying to get to know her and figure out who was on first. But so far Tom had rolled with the punches pretty well.

"Don't worry about it," Tom said calmly, "it happens. It's called real life. No one's life can be smooth all the time. And usually when things go wrong, they come in bunches. It happens to me too. My mother died unexpectedly while I was getting divorced, and my father had Alzheimer's and I had to put him in a home, while trying to unwind my life with my ex-wife. It wasn't fun for me then either." He'd also had a brief romance then that had gone right down the tubes because of it. He couldn't concentrate on that many things at once. He had broken it off with her, and when he called her again a few months later, she had met someone else. It was just the way life worked, and he knew Annie was under a lot of stress at the moment.

"How about dinner tonight?" he suggested. "I know it's short notice, but it might do you good."

"I'd love it," she said, determined to make it a pleasant evening and not tell him all her problems. She wanted time to enjoy him too. And for the rest of the afternoon, she tried to concentrate on lightening her mood. She almost succeeded—until a burst pipe in one of the houses she was designing caused a hundred thousand dollars' worth of damage and destroyed an important piece of art. And she had to deliver the news to the client, who went through the roof. She was still upset about it when she got dressed for their date that night and there was no news from Ted. She tried to release that from her mind too, for now, since there was nothing she could do about it. However naïve he was, Ted was an adult and had gotten himself into this mess in the first place. Now it was Annie's turn to enjoy a quiet evening and a good dinner with a man she liked. It didn't seem like too much to ask.

She put on one of the new outfits Liz had picked for her, and she was starting to feel better, when Kate walked into her room with a serious expression.

"Can I talk to you?" she asked as Annie hesitated and looked at her.

"Why does that sound ominous to me?" Annie asked her as she put on lipstick. Tom was due any minute. She wondered too why kids always broached important subjects just as you were walking out the door, or the phone rang with the crucial call you'd been waiting for for weeks. Murphy's Law. "If it's something pleasant, you just say it, you don't ask for my permission to talk to me." Katie smiled at what she said. "Which tells me that this might be something I won't like hearing." Katie didn't deny it.

"Yeah, maybe that's true," Katie conceded with a rueful look.

"Is it important?" Annie asked as she put her lipstick in her purse.

"Sort of," Kate admitted.

"Then let's talk about it later or tomorrow. I'm just about to walk out the door. I want to pay attention to whatever this is. And right now I have a date with Tom, and I want to focus on that and enjoy him."

"Okay," Katie said glumly. She didn't look pleased to be put off, but she could see that Annie was going out. "You look pretty, by the way."

"Thank you. I'm hoping to have a decent evening with Tom, without anyone getting stabbed, announcing that they're pregnant, or scaring the hell out of me. I think he's beginning to think we're all crazy."

Tom appeared on schedule, looking handsome and relaxed. And he smiled broadly when he saw Annie. The new additions to her wardrobe were working well for her. The contractor at the flooded construction site called her just as they were walking out the door and told her that they had discovered a second painting that had been damaged. This one was a Picasso. And Annie said calmly that she would call him about it tomorrow. There was nothing she could do about it now. It was her time with Tom.

"Something wrong?" He had sensed her tension when she took the call.

"We had a flood at a construction site this afternoon, and two very valuable paintings got damaged. The client was upset, to say the least. That was the contractor. I'll deal with it tomorrow."

"I never realized how stressful architecture can be," he said as they got in the elevator.

"It's always stressful when you're dealing with deadlines and high-powered clients. And building a house or remodeling one brings out the worst in people. About one in five of my clients, or even one in four, get divorced. If you have a shaky marriage, the last thing you want to do is build a house together."

"Actually, that's true," he said pensively. "I'd forgotten about it, but the last straw for us was a remodel we decided to do on our apartment. It cost a fortune, which pissed me off, and she was mad that I was never there to talk to the contractor. When we decided to break up, we sold it, and I was thrilled."

"See what I mean? I feel like a marriage counselor sometimes. Perfectly sane people turn into monsters when they redo houses, and if they have a good marriage, they take it out on me. In the bad marriages, I get caught in the crossfire."

"Have you considered retiring?" he teased her. He knew she couldn't do that.

"I'd be too bored," she said honestly, "and I worked too hard to get here. Besides, the insurance money for the kids started to run out a few years ago, and I want to help them." She was paying for Ted's law school.

"They're lucky they have you," he said as they got into a chauffeur-driven town car he had hired for the evening since it was so cold. He didn't want Annie freezing while they waited for cabs. And she couldn't walk long distances with her crutches. He tried to make things easy for her. No one else ever had before.

The new restaurant he took her to was beautiful, and the food was delicious. Annie wasn't hungry after all the crises she'd been dealing with, but she was happy to be there. She picked at her food, and

Tom noticed it and asked her if she didn't like it. He looked disappointed. He had wanted to take her out for a special evening, and he could see that she was tired, although she made an effort to keep up the conversation with him.

"I'm just not used to having a social life," she admitted. "I usually get home late from work and fall into bed. I can manage kid problems and work and all that goes with it, but I'm not used to getting dressed up and going out too." He had the same trouble socializing at the end of a long day, but he hadn't wanted to wait until the weekend to see her.

"I have an idea," he said to her as they shared a dessert. It had been a beautiful meal, and the chef had sent them several treats and surprises to impress them. Restaurants often did that when he dined out. "I know it's a little soon, and we wanted to be sensible and move slowly. But we've been going out for nearly a month now, and I don't think we're going to get any peace and quiet around here. What do you say we go away for a weekend? If you prefer, we can get separate rooms. But I'd like to take you away somewhere. How does that sound to you?" It sounded both wonderful and a little nerve-racking to Annie. It was a step she hadn't been ready to take yet, but she could see that he was discouraged by the chaos in her life and by having to fight for her time and attention. She was lucky he was even willing to hang in. She wasn't sure she would have in his shoes.

"It sounds fantastic," she said softly. "Where were you thinking?" With Ted in such a volatile situation, she wasn't sure if she should go far away, but he wasn't five years old either, and she didn't want to say it to Tom. He was trying so hard to please her and give them the best chance he could for success. She couldn't have asked for more from any man. And he genuinely liked her and wanted to give their relationship a decent shot. For a moment she thought it was more than she deserved.

"Why don't you leave it to me? I'll see if I can find someplace fun for us to go, where we'll have peace." He smiled at her and put a hand on hers on the table. So far their physical explorations with each other had involved only kisses. "What would you prefer? Two bedrooms or one?" She wanted to say two but didn't have the courage. And she knew she would be nervous about it whenever they took the plunge.

"One," she said so softly he could barely hear her, and he smiled and put an arm around her.

"How about two, and we can play it by ear."

"How did I get so lucky?" she asked, looking at him in amazement. "You could just tell me to go to hell."

"Yes, but think of what I'd miss. Love can be messy, and at our age it takes a little organizing and adjusting. My life isn't always such smooth sailing either."

"Thank you," she said gratefully, and he leaned over and kissed her.

"Don't ask me why, but I knew the minute I saw you in the waiting room at the ER that you were a very special person, and I wanted to get to know you better." And so far he didn't regret it, and neither did she. "We just have to figure out how to make room in our lives for each other." They both knew by then that it was no small feat. But she had waited a long time for this. Sixteen years. She had lost Seth because of her commitment to her sister's children, and she had had no choice then. But sixteen years later it wouldn't be right to give Tom up for them. She just had to figure out how to be available to them, do her work, and be there for him too. She knew she owed it to herself to try. Whitney had been telling her that for years. And she had finally met someone who was worth it. She hadn't told Whitney about him yet. She and Fred had gone on a cruise for two weeks, and ever since they got back, Annie had been too busy to tell her what was going on in her life. It was strange to realize that she had been seeing him for nearly a month and her best friend had no idea.

But she hadn't taken it seriously at first and thought they were just friends. With his invitation for the weekend, it confirmed to her again that that was not the case.

Tom took her home after dinner and brought her upstairs. He asked her what weekends she was free so he could plan their trip, and he kissed her lightly on the lips. She thanked him for dinner, and he left. As she let herself into the apartment, she saw that Kate was waiting up for her. She had an expectant look on her face, and Annie could sense that if she had come home at two in the morning, Katie would still have been sitting there.

"Whatever it is must be important," Annie said as she hung up her coat with a sigh. It would have been nice to have one evening without drama. She was looking forward to going away with Tom now. And she didn't want Katie to spoil it, but she was beginning to realize that anything was possible at the ages they were now. And Katie and Paul were deeply in love. Annie walked into the living room and sat down on the couch and looked at Katie. "Okay. What is it?"

"I just want to give you a heads-up," Katie said with a serious expression, and Annie could see that she was prepared to put up a fight. Annie waited to hear what it was about. "I'm going to

Iran for two weeks with Paul. I got my visa, and we paid for our tickets. I just want you to know. You can't stop me, and I didn't want to lie to you. So I'm telling you. We leave two weeks from to-morrow." There was dead silence in the room after she spoke. And the reaction she got from Annie was not the one she had expected. Her aunt spoke to her in a low, calm, controlled voice. Maybe the evening with Tom had helped. The time she spent with him gave her perspective.

"I'm going to be totally honest with you," Annie said calmly. She was unhappy about it but not crazed. "I think it's an incredibly stupid idea, to the point of being dangerous. Not only will you be in danger there, but you're going as a mixed couple to a country where you'll both be ostra-cized severely for being together. I think what you're doing is foolhardy, and I'm going to worry like crazy about you while you're there, and Tom told you the same thing and you don't want to lis-ten to him either. He knows a lot more about Iran than I do, or even Paul. But you're right, you're an adult. I can't stop you. You have a right to make your own choices, decisions, or mistakes." Annie's eyes filled with tears then as she spoke to her. "The bottom line for me here is not some kind of power trip. I'm not trying to control you. I buried my sis-ter. I don't ever want to bury one of her kids. I just hope you'll be okay," Annie said as she stood up, picked up her crutches, and walked to her room.

Katie sat staring at her and didn't say a word. She had expected a pitched battle, and hours of screaming and threats. Instead, Annie had done what she knew she had to do—she had respected her niece's right to make her own decisions and let go. She thought Katie was wrong, but she didn't even try to stop her. Now they both had to live with it: Annie with the worry, and Kate with the full responsibility for being an adult. What Annie had just done was much more impressive, Kate realized, than if she had yelled and forbidden her to go. And now suddenly Kate was worried too. But she had promised Paul she would go. He wanted her to know everything about his world. The hardest part for Katie was if Annie and Tom were right. And as she walked to her own bedroom, two tears of terror slid down Kate's face. In this case, for the first time, the victory of adulthood was not so sweet.

Chapter 18

Annie's weekend with Tom was a dream come true. She didn't even know that people did things like that and indulged themselves with such luxury. For all of her adult life, she had worked and taken care of kids and never even thought of spoiling herself. Her trips had been to Disneyland when they were young, flying around the country to meet with clients, and to Europe twice with the kids and planning their trips around them. She had never taken a vacation by herself and wouldn't have known what to do with herself if she did. She had filled all the spare time she had in recent years with work. Tom opened up a whole new world for her. He said he had never been there either, but he had put some serious research into the ideal place to take her. And this was it. He took her to the Turks and Caicos in the Caribbean.

They flew directly from Kennedy Airport to Providenciales, and the flight took three and a half hours. They were picked up at the airport by a limousine and taken to the hotel, where he had reserved a villa for them, with its own beach and a private pool. The sand was the color of ivory and as fine as sugar, and the water was completely transparent and turquoise in color. And true to his word, there were two bedrooms in the villa. She had never seen anything so luxurious, and there was a butler to serve their every need. A huge basket of fruit was sitting on the table, and a bottle of champagne. She felt as though she had died and gone to heaven. This was as far as you could get from the stresses and anxieties of daily life. They were planning to be there for three days, and she just prayed that no emergency would come up for either of them that would interfere. In her case, her nieces and nephew, and in his, some kind of news crisis in the world. He was vulnerable to that at any time.

"I don't believe this," she said with a look of childlike disbelief. It was like finding out that Santa Claus really did exist, and Tom was it, minus the red suit and white beard. He had planned the perfect vacation for them. They could go to nearby restaurants or eat at the villa, lie in the pool, walk on the beach, swim in the translucent water, and see no other human for three days if they chose. It was like being dropped off in paradise, and he put his arms around her as she looked at everything with delight and amazement. It was the nicest gift anyone had ever given her. The gift of time and peace, to share with him. It was like a honeymoon. "I have to be the luckiest woman in the world," she said, smiling at him, and he kissed her.

"It's a reward for the sprained ankle and being a very brave girl about everything you do." What he said brought tears to her eyes. "I've never known anyone who handled so much and does so much and does it well. I'd just love to get you to handle a little less, so we have time for us," he said gently. This was a great place to learn. She felt completely removed from real life, even the kids, although they knew how to reach her and where they were. And she had promised herself not to talk about them constantly for the next three days.

They walked on the beach that night before they went to bed and swam in their private pool. They both wore bathing suits since they hadn't crossed that bridge yet, and they talked for hours in the moonlight, and when they finally went to bed, it seemed like the most natural thing in the world to share a bedroom. She lay in Tom's arms, totally at ease with him. She was shivering a little, but it was anticipation, not terror, and neither of them was disappointed. It was exactly what they had hoped it would be, two halves coming together as one whole. They both felt as though it was meant to be.

They sat on their terrace naked afterward, holding hands and kissing, and swam in the pool again, naked this time, and then they went back to the bed where they had discovered each other and lay cuddled close all night. They slept like children and woke up early and made love again. It was noon when they ordered breakfast on their terrace, and they went for a walk on the beach afterward. They were in and out of the ocean all day and had dinner on their terrace that night. They made love in the pool. They laughed at silly things. And Annie told him about losing her sister while Tom held her. They talked about their childhoods, their hopes, their disappointments, their dreams. They learned each other's bodies and it really was a honeymoon. It was the foundation they had needed, the time away from everything.

By the end of three days their bodies had meshed together, their hearts, and their souls. Annie had never been as comfortable with anyone in her life, and Tom felt more married to her than he had to his wife. They had been so different and had had so little in common. That had been all about passion and it burned out very quickly. This was about something so much deeper. Annie felt as though they shared one soul. What they shared defined **kindred spirit** or **soul mate.** She never wanted to leave, and they had to tear themselves away on Sunday. Annie told him she would never be able to thank him enough for what he'd done by giving them this vacation.

They sat on the terrace on Sunday morning, trying to figure out where to go from here. The children she had raised were adults now and certainly old enough to understand his spending a night or weekend with her, although they both suspected it would be more peaceful at his place. They talked about living together at some point, and he asked her how she felt about marriage. She wasn't sure she cared. That had stopped being a goal or even a possibility for her a long time ago, although it was an option again now. In the end, they decided to play it by ear and see how things went. And they made a vow to each other to at least try not to let everyone intrude on them, and to make their relationship a priority. She didn't care about how much he had to travel for work. And he said he was fine with her work and the kids, as long as there was room in all of it for him too. Their relationship would start in earnest when they left the Turks and Caicos, and they left the villa hand in hand. They both looked back at it and smiled, knowing that they would never forget it. It was the place where their love was born.

On the day Annie and Tom had left for the Turks and Caicos, Lizzie was in her office at **Vogue**, doing research for a story for the June issue. She had a temporary assistant who buzzed her on the intercom to tell her that she had a call from someone named George. Mr. George, she corrected herself. It sounded like a hairdresser, and Liz had no idea who it was. She started to tell her to take a message, then picked up the call herself. It was faster than explaining it.

"Yes? Liz Marshall," she said in her official voice. The voice that answered her had a heavy Italian accent but spoke English fluently. She didn't know who it was at first, and then he introduced himself again. Alessandro di Giorgio, the Roman jeweler who had saved her hide at the shoot in the Place Vendôme. That had been more than a month before.

"Oh, hello!" she said, embarrassed not to have recognized him. "What can I do for you? Are you calling from Rome?" She had promised him advance copies of the piece, but they weren't ready yet.

"No, I'm in New York," he explained. "I'm just calling to say hello." A lot of jewelers kept in touch to keep themselves foremost in her mind, so she wasn't surprised to hear from him, although she had never had direct contact with him until she met him in Paris. And she hadn't heard from him since.

"What happened with the emir's wife? Did she buy any of the other pieces?" She remembered that he had brought the pieces to Paris for her.

"She bought all five pieces that you photographed. She's very excited that they're going to be in **Vogue**." Liz recalled that it represented five or six million dollars' worth of jewelry, which was very impressive. But di Giorgio was an important name.

"What are you doing in New York?" Liz asked politely. He was a pleasant man, and he had certainly helped her out.

"I'm looking at a store, but I can't decide if we should open one here. It's always been a debate between my father and myself. He thinks yes, I say no. I prefer to stay more exclusive and in Europe. He wants to open in New York, Tokyo, and Dubai." He laughed then. "In this case the elder is the more modern in his thinking, and I am more conservative. I don't know. Perhaps we should open here. I am here to look at some stores that are available. And I called to see if you would like to have lunch, if you have time. Will you be in the city this weekend?" Liz liked to get away on weekends when she could, but most of the time she was working, on research or shoots. Sometimes she worked a seven-day week. And she had hoped to go skiing that weekend, but her plan had fallen through.

"Actually, I'll be here," she said pleasantly.

"Are you free for lunch on Saturday? I'm staying at the Sherry-Netherland, and Harry Cipriani downstairs is very nice." It was one of her favorite restaurants, and one of the most fashionable in New York. She smiled. He made it sound like a little bistro that happened to be in his hotel.

"I'd like that. I'll meet you there."

"I can pick you up if you like," he suggested.

"I live downtown, it's too far away. I'll just meet you at the restaurant." He was very gentlemanly and had courtly old-fashioned manners that were rare in the States, but she liked it. It gave her the feeling that he was protecting her. She'd had the same feeling about him in Paris.

Liz met him the next day at Harry Cipriani, in black pants, a black sweater, and towering Balenciaga heels. He was a lot taller than she was, and they made a striking couple as they walked into the restaurant together. He had been waiting for her outside. She wore her long blond hair down, and she was wearing a vintage lynx coat that she had bought in Paris. They looked very glamorous together, and Alessandro spoke to the headwaiter in Italian, in a deep rumbling voice that sounded like most of the men Liz had met in Rome and Milan.

He was fun to talk to and told her endless stories about their stores and the business, some of their famous clients who had done outrageous things over the years. None of it was mean-spirited, and he made her laugh all through lunch. They had a great time together, and it was four o'clock when they left the restaurant.

"Would you like to see the stores I'm considering?" he asked her. They were all on Madison Avenue and not far away. They walked a block over to Madison, and there were three of them, all with huge spaces and enormous rents. He didn't fall in love with any of them, and she didn't either. There was something very cold about them.

"My aunt is an architect. You should have her design something for you," Liz suggested offhandedly. It was more in jest than a serious suggestion, but he looked as though he liked the idea. And then as a casual aside, Liz said that she had grown up with her and she was like a mother to her.

"Your parents left you with her?" He seemed

surprised. She hadn't mentioned it over lunch, but they hadn't shared any personal details. She knew he was single and had a sister who was in the business too. She handled publicity, not design.

"My parents died when I was twelve," Liz said simply. "My aunt brought up my brother, my sister, and me. I'm the oldest." He looked deeply touched as she said it.

"That must have been terrible for you," he said sympathetically, "to lose your parents at such a young age. I can't imagine it. I'm very close to my parents and my sister, my grandparents. Italian families are like that."

"So are we. I'm very close to my aunt and siblings."

"She must be a very nice woman to have taken care of you. Does she have children too? Your cousins?"

"No. She's single. She never married. She was too busy with us. She was twenty-six when it happened. She's been great to us." He looked enormously impressed and very touched by what she'd told him. They walked back down Madison Avenue, and it was five o'clock by then. She thanked him for lunch, and he offered to take her home.

"It's fine." She smiled at him. "I live in the Village."

He looked hesitant, but he clearly didn't want

her to go. "Would you like to have dinner with me tonight?" He had nothing else to do in New York, except see the three stores and a client on Monday. He was free for the weekend.

"That would be fun. Why don't you come to my apartment for a drink at eight? There's a nice Italian restaurant near me, Da Silvano. I'll make a reservation for nine or nine-thirty. It's livelier downtown, there are more young people who live there. It's more trendy," she explained. "You can wear jeans, if you brought any." He had but didn't dare wear them uptown. He looked happy to be seeing her again so soon.

She wrote down her address to give him, and he hailed a cab for her. As it drove away, she waved at him. He was nice to be with, kind, polite, intelligent, funny, creative, and she enjoyed talking to him. It was fun to have someone to spend time with on the weekend. He was an unexpected blessing. She bought an armload of flowers on the way home to put in her apartment and put a bottle of white wine in the fridge.

Da Silvano gave them a reservation for nine-thirty. And when Alessandro arrived at her apartment at eight o'clock, the flowers looked beautiful, the music was on, and she was wearing black leather leggings and a long white Balenciaga sweater. And Alessandro was wearing a black sweater and jeans. He looked casual and a lot younger than he had over lunch.

He looked over her music and discovered that they liked most of the same things. And he liked her apartment. He had brought her a bottle of champagne and a scented candle. They talked so much that they almost missed the reservation at Da Silvano at nine-thirty. Liz ran into a number of friends there, all from her business, and she introduced them to Alessandro. She could see that they were impressed by how good looking he was. She was much more impressed by how nice he was, and how much fun to talk to. He was the consummate well-educated, sophisticated European.

They didn't get back to her apartment till midnight, and he was extremely polite as he left her downstairs and kissed her on both cheeks. They had already made a date to have brunch at the Mercer Hotel in SoHo the next day, and go for a walk in Central Park afterward. Just as he had in Paris, Alessandro had fallen from the sky, like an angel from heaven.

Chapter 19

In spite of everything Annie and Tom had said to dissuade her, and Paul's parents had done the same, Katie and Paul left for London two weeks later, to connect with the flight to Tehran. They were excited about the trip, and Paul was thrilled at the prospect of seeing his relatives again, especially the grandfather he had worshipped as a child. They were planning to stay with Paul's family for two weeks. And Annie and Paul's parents went to the airport with them to see them off. The adults chatted amiably with each other, and Paul's parents were very pleasant to Annie and Kate. Paul's father helped them check in their bags, and his mother discreetly handed Katie a neatly folded head scarf and a thin, loose gray cotton coat. She explained that Katie would have to wear the head scarf when she got off the plane in Tehran and possibly on the flight. Katie would have to keep her hair covered at all times, and she might need the cotton coat on some occasions. Paul's family would tell her when. Annie had convinced her to leave her most radical miniskirts at home, so as not to draw attention to herself, or offend anyone when she was there, and Katie had very sensibly agreed. She didn't want to offend Paul's family or anyone else. Annie was at least comforted by that.

Paul and Katie hugged all three of them and waved as they went through security. And once they were gone, Paul's father reassured Annie and told her they would be fine. He said that Tehran was as sophisticated as New York, and he promised that his sister-in-law would take Katie under her wing, and Paul was a responsible young man. To Annie, they seemed too young to be going anywhere, especially so far away. It was the farthest distance Katie had ever traveled, and she had looked like a child when she picked up her backpack and went through security with Paul. Annie already missed her all the way home. The house was going to seem very empty without her. Katie was a huge presence in her daily life, and her absence would be sorely felt. And she told herself that the trip to Iran would be fine, and they'd be home in two weeks.

She had invited Tom to stay with her while

Katie was gone, and they were both looking forward to it. The two weeks since their magical trip to the Turks and Caicos had been miraculously peaceful. None of her contractors had quit, her clients had behaved, Liz was busy at the magazine, they weren't hearing much from Ted as he wrestled with his difficult situation, and Katie had been preoccupied with her preparations for her trip. And other than Annie's worries about it, things had been pretty calm. She and Tom had managed several quiet dinners in good restaurants, and even the world news scene was uneventful at the moment.

The only thing on Annie's stress agenda for now was Katie's trip, and she was trying to be philosophical about it. She had almost convinced herself by then that she'd be all right, and Paul had solemnly promised to take care of her. They had looked like two innocents to Annie when they left. And she said a little prayer for them on her way home in the cab.

Annie called and talked to Whitney later that afternoon. She had told her about Tom by then, and Whitney was wildly excited about it and wanted her to bring him out to meet them. But her visit to them on New Year's Eve had brought into sharp focus for Annie how different their lives were. She and Whitney shared history and a lot of years, but for an outsider, and even her, their quiet suburban life in Far Hills was incredibly boring. Their friends all drank too much and talked about their children. Most of them were doctors, and their conversations were about medicine, their latest trip, or their kids. She didn't want to subject Tom to a painfully dull evening, and Whitney and Fred never came into town for dinner. So they hadn't met. Whitney was enormously impressed that Annie was dating a well-known TV anchor. Annie didn't want her making an issue of that if they came out to see her either, and she knew they would. His celebrity was too hard to resist. She could see it whenever they met new people or went to restaurants. He was a star in his own right, and some people reacted to it strangely, by showing off or trying to compete or being passive-aggressive and making rude comments. Tom was always polite about it, but she couldn't see him enjoying an evening with Whitney and Fred and their friends in New Jersey. The truth was, she didn't enjoy their circle of friends either, and the New Year's Eve she had recently spent with them had been one of her worst ever, not to mention the appalling blind date. Tom had saved her from a lifetime of those evenings and men like Bob Graham, and Annie was forever grateful.

Whitney congratulated her on her new-found

maturity that she had let Katie go to Tehran with Paul. She said it was going to be a fabulous experience for her, a whole new culture to discover, and she was impressed that Annie was being so reasonable about it.

"I had no other choice. I'm not calm about it. But I realize that you're right, and I have to let them make their own mistakes. But don't think for a second that this is easy." She had had nightmares about it for weeks. But Katie had her Black-Berry, plenty of money, a credit card, and her return ticket home, and Annie had told her to call immediately or send a text if she had a problem. Katie had laughed at her when she said it.

"So what are you and Tom going to do while she's gone?" Whitney asked. She knew that Katie living at home and not in the dorm this semester had cramped their style a little, but Annie had spent several nights with Tom at his apartment. And Annie suspected correctly that when she wasn't around, Paul spent the night. They were dating, but if they decided to get married and have kids, it could get extremely complicated. But Kate was only twenty-one, and they weren't discussing marriage, just a trip. Annie was trying to calm down about it and not get too worked up.

"Tom and I are going to run around the apartment naked while they're gone," Annie said with a grin in answer to Whitney's question. "I have to admit, there comes a point when it's a little challenging living with your adult kids. It's awkward with Tom, but I love having her here. I just hope she goes back to school next term." Annie was still upset about her job at the tattoo parlor, but she was trying to be less vocal about it. Tom had tempered her a little. She felt more relaxed about everything now that she was sharing life with him. She had another adult to talk to, and his perspective on most subjects was sensible, although he'd never had children and didn't fully understand her bond to them and how close it was. But on the more practical issues, he was a big help. And with Katie gone for two weeks, they'd have the place to themselves.

Ted hadn't come home for the night since the stabbing incident, although Annie had met him for lunch. He seemed to be doing all right, given the circumstances, although Annie thought he seemed nervous and very stressed. He was still upset about the baby. And despite Pattie's constant pressure, he hadn't agreed to marry her before August. She said it would be humiliating to get married when she was so pregnant, but Ted wouldn't relent on that. August was the best he was willing to do, no matter how much she cried and whined about it. He felt pressured enough as it was, and he still thought it was wrong for them to have the baby. He wasn't prepared to take that on, but he had agreed to step up to the plate. He was being very good to her and had taken over all the household chores for her. And he was honest with Annie that he was behind in his studying and was worried about his midterms. Even an unmerited gift of Pattie's A couldn't pull up his GPA.

And Liz had said something to Annie about a new man in her life, but she hadn't said who. She was being mysterious about it, and Annie didn't push. She assumed it was one of her typical guys, a photographer or model or someone she had met through work.

"I thought you said you were taking a break," Annie reminded her, and Liz laughed.

"I am . . . I was . . . I don't know . . . this is very new. It's nothing yet. He lives in Rome, and I've only seen him a few times. I met him in Paris over New Year's, and he was here on business a few weeks ago. We had lunch and dinner, but it probably can't go anywhere. He hardly ever comes to New York, and I only go to Rome a couple of times a year." A relationship with Alessandro wasn't a very realistic hope, but he was calling her several times a day, and Liz had wonderful conversations with him, about serious subjects. He had promised to come to see her in Paris the next time she was there.

"Geography isn't insurmountable, you know," Annie reminded her, "for the right guy. If it ever got serious, maybe you could get a job at Italian **Vogue**."

"That's what he says," Liz said thoughtfully, "but we're a long way from there. I haven't even slept with him yet. I didn't want to get carried away with a guy I might never see again." But she had to admit to herself, if not to Annie, that it had been hard to resist. He had kissed her when they walked through Central Park, and she nearly melted in his arms, and there had been a serious makeout session on her couch that night, but they had both managed to restrain themselves, and Liz was glad she had.

"It doesn't sound very likely that you won't see him again," Annie commented with a smile. She'd never heard Liz sound like this about any man. But the men she had always gone out with were boys. Alessandro was a man. And she didn't sound frightened this time. For the first time in her life, Liz was willing to risk her heart. Annie was happy for her, and relieved. Liz deserved a good man, and not the flakes she'd been going out with for years. And she wished Ted would find a nice girl too. That certainly wasn't the case for the moment.

Ted had gone to a basketball game at NYU with one of his roommates on a Friday night, on a weekend when Pattie's kids were with their father, and she had complained that she wanted Ted home with her. She said she had a headache, but he'd been gently insistent that he needed a break. He never saw his friends anymore, and she had insisted he be with her constantly ever since she told him she was pregnant. But for once he told her he was going out, and said he'd stay at his own apartment afterward, since he'd probably have too much to drink, and she didn't like that either. He needed a little room to spread his wings.

But he didn't drink as much as he thought he would at the game, their team lost, and he felt guilty on his way home, so he left his roommate and went back to Pattie's apartment to surprise her. She was lying on the couch with a bowl of popcorn, watching a romantic comedy, and she was thrilled to see him when he walked through the door with his key.

"What are you doing here?" she asked with pleasure. She still looked the same. She hadn't started to gain weight yet, but she was only two and a half months pregnant, and she was a tall, full-bodied woman and carried it well.

"I missed you," he said simply, and smiled at her. In part it was true. He was used to her now. But he also knew that she'd find some way to punish him the next day for going to the game with his friends. She had none of her own. She was completely dependent on Ted for all her entertainment, emotional sustenance, and distraction. She never wanted to spend five minutes away from him, so it was easier to just go back to her apartment than listen to her complain about it later.

"Did you eat dinner?" she asked him as she lay on the couch. She wasn't much of a cook, but she kept him fed. They lived mostly on pizza and Chinese takeout, which he paid for, and once in a blue moon she cooked. There was a bucket of KFC in the kitchen, and he helped himself to a piece.

"I had a hot dog and nachos at the game," he said, and then finished a piece of chicken, cracked open a beer, and decided to go to the bathroom first. He closed the door and turned on the light and then stared at what he saw in the bowl. He didn't understand it. It didn't belong there, and there was no one in the apartment but her. It looked like an injured mouse, but it was a bloody tampon, and there was blood in the bowl. She had forgotten to flush. And she clearly wasn't having a miscarriage or distressed about it. She was laughing loudly at the film she had seen a dozen times before, and she smiled as he came out of the bathroom.

His head was reeling, but he said nothing to her. He walked into the kitchen and stared out the window, trying to understand what he'd seen and what it meant. It didn't seem possible that she would do that to him. But what if she had? What if it was all a lie and a hoax? His whole body was trembling as he stood there, and he had to know. He grabbed his coat, strode to the door, and said something vague to Pattie about being back in a few minutes.

"Where are you going?" She looked surprised that he was leaving.

"I'll be back in five minutes," he said, looking distressed, without further explanation, and then he was gone. She wasn't worried. She knew he'd be back. He acted like a kid sometimes.

There was a Duane Reade two blocks away that stayed open all night. He bought a pregnancy kit with two tests in it, put it in his pocket, ran back to the apartment, and sprinted up the stairs. He was still shaking, and there was a look in his eyes she had never seen before. She reached out and touched his crotch, and he took her hand, and then pulled her firmly up from the couch. He still had his coat on, and there was a frightening look in his eyes.

"What are you doing?" She looked puzzled and confused, as he led her into the bathroom, and she followed. "What is this, Ted?" She had no idea what he had in mind or why he had gone out.

"You tell me," he said in a shattered voice. She reached for him, thinking he wanted to have sex with her, but it was clear he didn't, and he wouldn't let her touch him. He reached into his pocket and handed her the pregnancy kit, and Pattie looked startled. "I don't need that," she said, laughing at him. "Don't be silly." She tried to make a game of it and stroked him through his jeans. He didn't move an inch and opened the box for her and handed her the test, as her face went pale.

"Do it," he said in a voice that sounded like someone else's. He looked cold, and he was shaking. She had tried to destroy his life and had almost blackmailed him into marrying her over a baby he now suspected didn't exist. He left the bathroom and waited just outside the door. She took a long time, and he could hear her crying. The game was over. And then she finally came out, without the test, and looked at him in despair.

"I'm sorry," she whispered, as tears poured down her cheeks. She looked panicked. They both knew that if she'd done it, the test would have shown she wasn't pregnant. Now he understood why she had told him she had a headache that afternoon. For once, she was willing to forgo sex, because she didn't want him to discover that she had her period. But the game was up now. He saw all the life go out of her as they both stood there.

"I love you, Ted," she whispered through a sob. "I'm sorry."

"How could you do that to me? Threaten me and tell me you would kill yourself and the baby, that I had to marry you **now** and not later? What were you going to do when you never got big— tell me you lost it? What a fucking fool I was, and what a bitch you are!" he said, still shaking with rage and relief. "Don't ever come near me again. Never!" he said as he walked past her to the door, and she ran to him, sank to the floor, and clung to him.

"Don't leave me," she said, clutching at his legs. "I love you, Ted." She was begging him not to go.

"You don't know the meaning of the word," he said as he opened the door and pulled away from her. He still had his coat on from when he'd gone to the store. There was nothing he wanted from the apartment. Whatever he had there, he never wanted to see again, and especially her. She had lied to him about being pregnant and tried to destroy his life. He looked down at her with disgust, left, and slammed the door behind him. He ran down the stairs, threw open the door that led to the street, and took big gulps of the cold air.

And then he ran all the way home. He felt like

he had escaped from prison. He had broken out. He had gotten one lucky break with the bloody tampon she'd forgotten to flush down the toilet. He wanted to shout as he ran down the street. He didn't love her. He hated her. She had tried to ruin his life, and he had tried to do the right thing. He had almost given up law school for her, and his life, and she had lied to him and manipulated him. She had used sex to control him and threats of suicide to hold him prisoner. His cell phone was ringing as he ran down the street, and he didn't answer it. She had lied to him totally. There had never been a baby. Just Pattie with her hooks into him.

He let himself into his apartment and poured himself two stiff shots of tequila and downed them at one gulp as one of his roommates walked in.

"Are we having a party?" he said with a broad grin.

"I am," Ted said. He already felt better than he had in weeks, even months. He was free.

He poured himself a third shot, and his roommate cautioned him. "Take it easy, buddy. You'll feel like shit tomorrow." But he felt incredible tonight. It was strange, suddenly hating someone he was supposed to love and had even promised to marry. But she was never the person she pretended to be. He sat on the couch, watched TV with the tequila bottle between his legs, poured himself shots, and stared into space, trying to absorb what had happened to him.

It was two in the morning when the emergency room at Downtown Hospital called his apartment. One of his roommates answered it and told Ted it was for him. He listened to what they said and made no comment.

"Will she be okay?" he finally asked in a dead voice. He was very drunk but not totally incoherent. He understood what the man had said. Pattie was in the emergency room and had had her stomach pumped. They said she had taken six sleeping pills, which wouldn't have been enough to kill her, and had called 911 herself. They said she'd be fine tomorrow, although she was on a psychiatric hold for evaluation, since she admitted it was a suicide attempt, and she had told them to call him. It had been a feeble attempt.

"She'd like you to come in to see her," the attendant told him.

"Tell her I'm too drunk. I'll come by in the morning." And with that, he hung up, took a last shot of tequila, and went to bed. He didn't care about her suicide attempt. It was as fake as their baby that had never existed, and just another manipulation. He understood that now.

331

He woke up with a huge headache the next morning, but at nine-thirty he was at the hospital as he'd said he would be. He found her room easily, and she was lying on the bed looking sick. A nurse's aide was sitting in the chair next to her, on suicide watch, and she offered to leave when Ted walked into the room, but he declined. He looked young and handsome and very hung over. But in spite of the excesses of the night before, he felt better than he had in months. Pattie looked considerably worse. They had decided to keep her for another day, until the psych resident saw her. And she didn't look pleased to be there. She started to cry the minute she saw Ted, and held out her arms to him. Ted didn't move toward her. He stood just inside the doorway where she couldn't reach him, and he didn't approach the bed.

"I'm done, Pattie. It's over. Don't threaten me anymore, don't bother to kill yourself over me, or pretend to. Don't tell me you love me or anything about our 'baby.' I'm done. Finished. I don't care what you do. You never should have done this, any of it, or pretended you were pregnant." The nurse's aide was watching them with interest and Pattie lay facedown on the bed, sobbing. "Get out of my life. You **are** out of my life. And don't call me. I'll send you my papers for the contracts class, and I don't give a flying fuck if you flunk me. Do

whatever you want. What you did is disgusting."
And with that, he walked out of the room, and the
door whooshed slowly closed behind him. He
could hear her sobbing, but he didn't care.

It was the icing on the cake when one of the
nurses spoke to him on the way out and said how
sorry she was that Pattie was back again. She said
that after four such attempts, she would probably
benefit from in-patient treatment this time. And
she guessed correctly that Ted was one of her students. She said that her last two boyfriends had
been too. It was indiscreet of her, and Ted's stomach turned over as he listened. He wondered how
many of his fellow students she had done this to,
how many times she had pretended to be pregnant
and faked suicide to keep them. The thought of
what she'd done to him made him feel sick. Pattie
was a desperate woman.

Ted called Annie as soon as he got home and
told her what had happened.

"It was all a lie," he told Annie in a dead voice.
"She was never pregnant."

"How did you find out?" she asked. She and
Tom were at the breakfast table reading the paper.
They had plans for the weekend.

"I just did. She was lying the whole time." His
voice choked as he said it, thinking of all the times
she had cried and berated him and threatened to

kill herself if he didn't do what she wanted. He wasn't even afraid of that now. He couldn't imagine ever being afraid of anything again, or believing anyone. It was going to take him a long time to trust someone again. "It's over," he said quietly. And then he called Liz and told her.

He lay on his bed after that with a pounding head and a light heart, thinking about what had happened. He realized now that he had been addicted to her, she had wanted it that way, and she had used his addiction to control him. It was terrifying to think about it now. All he could think about was how lucky he was that he had found out, and how grateful he was to be free.

"What happened?" Tom asked Annie when she hung up. He could tell that it was something important.

"I don't know. Ted discovered that Pattie wasn't really pregnant. He said it was all a lie, a hoax. Apparently, he discovered it last night. He said it's over. Thank God." She heaved a sigh of relief and smiled at Tom.

"Well, you can take that off your worry list," he said as he leaned over and kissed her. "Sounds like he got a lucky break." She smiled broadly and poured him a second cup of coffee. By then Ted was already sound asleep on his bed, with a smile on his face, sleeping off the tequila.

Chapter 20

When Katie and Paul got through the security line at JFK Airport, they turned and waved to her aunt and his parents, and then disappeared in the activity of the airport, and Katie felt a wave of excitement wash over her. They stopped and bought cappuccinos at Starbucks and knew that they were the last ones they'd have for a while. After this they would be swept into his family life in Tehran.

Paul hadn't been back in nine years, since they moved to New York. His parents talked about going back, but they never had. They had settled into their American life, and after adjusting to new ways, they had never gone back to Iran. And time had drifted by. Paul's father had originally come to work for a few years, became more successful than he expected, and stayed. Paul's father's family had always begged them to move back, but he had a successful business in New York and worked hard, and Paul's mother enjoyed the emancipated life she had adapted to in the States. She no longer covered her head or followed many of the old traditions, and that would have been a problem if they moved back to Tehran. They loved being Americans now, and integrated into their new life. It was Paul who most wanted to return to visit their family in Iran, and he had fond memories of his boyhood there. He longed to see his homeland again, and all the places he had known and loved as a child, and to share his history and heritage with Kate. She was thrilled to be taking the trip with him.

Paul had described Persepolis to her, the countryside outside Tehran, and the exotic look and smells of the bazaar. He wanted to show it all to her now and was proud to be returning as a man, not a boy. His mother also hadn't wanted him to go back until his exemption from military service had been resolved, which had finally been settled the year before. Otherwise, as an Iranian, he would have been expected to serve. He had had a minor heart murmur as a child, and they had acknowledged his exemption at last. Now he was free to visit without concern.

Despite his American citizenship, Paul still had his Iranian passport and was considered Iranian once back in Iran. Katie was carrying Xerox copies of both their American passports, in case they lost them or had a problem on the trip. She had obtained her visa from the Pakistani embassy, since there was no Iranian embassy in the States, and no American embassy in Iran. The U.S. State Department had told her to go to the Swiss embassy if she had any problem once in Tehran. It seemed highly unlikely to her and to Paul that she would ever need their help, but it was good to know. And sensibly, they had been told to stay away from political demonstrations and protests of all kinds, which would have been good advice in any country in the world. Especially since they were young. They didn't want to get arrested by mistake for being in the wrong place at the wrong time. And Paul would be treated as an Iranian citizen if that was the case, and she could wind up in jail if she was mistaken for a dissident. But there was no reason for either of them to have a problem with the law in Tehran. Paul's father had said as much to Annie as well. And his brother's home was in a wealthy residential neighborhood in the city.

Katie was anxious to see the museums, the university, and the bazaar. Two of Paul's male cousins attended the university, and his uncle taught there. And his oldest female cousin would be enrolled at the university the following year.

Paul and Katie had bought tickets on a flight to London, and from there they were flying Iran Airlines into Imam Khomeini International Airport in Tehran. His mother had given her the head scarf she would have to wear when she got off the plane, and the long gray billowing cotton overcoat that women wore if it was required. Katie already knew from what she'd read and Paul had told her, that Iranian women were fairly liberated, went to universities, were highly educated, and were allowed to vote and drive and hold public office.

They both watched movies on the flight to London and eventually fell asleep. They wandered around the shops in Heathrow Airport, then boarded the plane for the six-hour flight to Tehran. They took their seats in coach, and were offered tea, water, and fruit juices before takeoff. No alcohol was served on the flight or anywhere in Iran. As one of the smiling flight attendants handed her a glass of fruit juice, Katie smiled at Paul and already felt as though she had entered a different world.

Paul had written to his aunt and uncle, explaining that he was bringing a friend with him. He said she was a young woman he went to school with, who was interested in visiting Iran to further her studies. They had both decided that it was best for now to say that they were friends, and not that they were in love. Paul had mentioned no hint of romance between them in his letters, and he had warned Katie that they would have to behave themselves, even in his uncle's home. He didn't want to offend his family, and neither did Katie. And it was likely to be a surprise for them that Paul was involved with an American girl and not a Persian, so they had agreed to be discreet. And Katie also knew that public displays of affection were discouraged and were not acceptable between a Muslim man and Western woman, and Katie had assured Paul that she would follow the rules. She had no desire to upset anyone while she was there. They just wanted to see his family and enjoy the trip.

The meal that was served on the flight was traditional and according to Muslim dietary laws and restrictions. The food was plentiful, and they both fell asleep after they ate. There were films on the flight, but they slept most of the way. With the two flights, the trip from New York to Tehran took thirteen hours, and they were due to land in Tehran after another brief meal. And as she looked happily at Paul before they landed, she felt closer to him than ever. She was excited to be making the trip with him.

The neat, orderly airport was teeming with activity when they arrived. There was only one terminal, and all the international flights from everywhere, within and without the Arab world, came through there. It took them nearly an hour to get their luggage, as Katie looked around, her head scarf neatly in place. She had brought very little with her, some longer skirts, a few pairs of jeans, sweaters, and two dresses, all in sober colors. She had brought nothing low cut, too short or revealing, or too punky, since she didn't want to offend his family with outrageous clothes. And for the first time since she was thirteen, she had taken all the earrings out of her ears. She didn't want to shock his aunt and uncle, and she was planning to wear long-sleeved shirts and sweaters to cover her tattoos. Annie had noticed the absence of her earrings the night before she left and realized how much she loved Paul, to make so many adjustments for him. Katie was wise enough not to want to attract attention or censure and to remain appropriately discreet. Meeting Paul's family was important to her.

He had told her about his family before the trip and on the flight. She knew that his two female cousins, Shirin and Soudabeh, were fourteen and eighteen, and that his male cousins were twenty-one and twenty-three. The cousin his age was studying to be a doctor at Tehran University, and the cousin her age was studying art history and wanted to work in a museum as a curator one day. She knew that the museum in Tehran was exceptionally good.

Once they got their luggage, they had to go through immigration. Katie presented her passport and was fingerprinted as part of the routine for all foreigners. They looked at her visa, stamped her passport, and she went through. Paul had to present his passport and his military exemption card, which were in good order. He was no longer considered American here. While still on the flight, he had put his American passport in a pocket in his backpack, and he would be unable to use it anywhere in Iran. He was an Iranian citizen for life, and if he one day had children born in the States, they would be considered Iranian too. And so would Katie, if they ever married.

Everyone was extremely helpful and polite to them as they came through customs and immigration, and Katie was careful not to stand too close to Paul. She didn't touch him or smile at him too warmly. For these two weeks they were just friends and nothing more, even in his uncle's home. Her head scarf was in place, and she had put the thin cotton coat in her backpack, and as they scanned the faces outside the gate at the airport, Katie recognized Paul's family immediately.

His uncle looked exactly like his father, only shorter and older, and his aunt Jelveh was a small, warm, friendly-looking woman. And both of Paul's male cousins bore a strong family resemblance to him—they looked like they could have been his brothers and were close to his age. Their sisters hadn't come to the airport, and Paul instantly threw his arms around his cousins whom he hadn't seen for so long, and then their parents embraced him and welcomed him home. There were tears of joy in their eyes as they hugged him, and Paul introduced Katie to them as his school friend from New York, as she shyly said hello.

And then she noticed that there was an older man standing just behind them, quietly observing the scene with a serious expression, and he looked at his son, as though confused about who Paul was. And then Paul's aunt gently explained it to him, and he burst into tears and came to hug Paul. It was a touching moment, and Paul was crying too. He had changed so much in the last nine years that his grandfather didn't recognize him. And as they walked outside to their van, his grandfather kept an arm around Paul's shoulders. He acted as though Paul were the prodigal son returned. Once his grandfather got in the van, Paul explained to Kate that he had aged enormously in the last decade, and he seemed very frail to her too. He seemed somewhat disoriented, and Jelveh explained to Paul that his grandfather thought he had returned to Tehran for good. Hearing that tugged at his heart, and he was happier than ever to be back, even if only for two weeks. As soon as they landed, he was instantly reminded of how much he loved it there, and in many ways it was still home. He wondered if that was why his parents didn't go back, because it would be too hard to leave again.

Everyone was very friendly to Katie as they got into the van, and one of Paul's cousins carried her bag, as she got into the back row with Paul's aunt, so the three cousins could sit together. She asked Katie if she was very tired from the long trip and promised her a good meal when they got home. She said that her daughters had stayed home to prepare it. Paul had told her that his aunt was a great cook.

As they drove toward the city, with Paul's uncle at the wheel of the van, Jelveh admitted to Katie that she had never been out of Iran, and New York seemed so far away. And even to Katie it certainly did right now. And Jelveh complimented her on her interest in Iran to complete her studies. Katie didn't explain to her that the genesis of her interest was not academic but romantic, and that she was in love with her nephew. The charade of their friendship had begun, and would have to last for the entire two weeks they were there. It seemed too soon to tell them that theirs was a serious romance, or that they were involved at all. Paul wanted them to get to know Katie first.

The traffic around the airport was heavy, and the roads into the city were choked with cars. It took them an hour and a half to get there, and their house was in the Pasdaran district of the opulent northern part of the city. Katie looked around in fascination as they drove into town, and she spoke very little. She was too busy watching everything and trying to absorb it all, as the whole family chatted animatedly in Farsi around her. But all of them spoke excellent English whenever they talked to Kate.

Tehran looked like a modern city, with mosques dotting the landscape; there were tall buildings, and short ones. There was a financial district, and she was dying to see the bazaar that Paul had described to her so vividly. She wanted to buy something for Annie there. Paul pointed out the university to her, and the Azadi Tower as they drove home. And Paul realized as he looked around that the city had grown since he left. It was even busier and more crowded than it had been then, with fifteen million people living there now. Katie realized with amazement that it was busier and seemed even more crowded than New York. But even in a city as metropolitan as this, Katie had a sense of being in an exotic place. She loved being there with him and felt comfortable with his family, who all seemed like nice people to her and treated her with kindness and respect.

She noticed too that his grandfather in the front seat spoke very little and seemed lost in thought as he looked out the window. And every now and then he would turn to look at Paul, seated in the row behind him, and as soon as he did, tears of emotion sprang to his eyes again, and once or twice he leaned back and patted Paul's hand, as though to be sure that he was real and not simply an illusion. And then he would say something quietly to his son in Farsi. Paul and his cousins were chatting and laughing, and Jelveh continued to point out important landmarks to Katie as they drove home.

And when they finally pulled up in front of their home, it looked like a sprawling family house, no different than the ones she had seen in the suburbs of New York. This one was only a little larger and had beautiful arches over the doors and windows. Both of Paul's female cousins were waiting for

345

them on the front lawn, and they threw their arms around Paul as soon as he emerged from the van. It was a shock for him to see them since they had been five and nine years old when he last saw them. And now they were beautiful young women, with velvety brown eyes, the same honey-colored skin as his own, and Katie suspected they had dark, almost jet-black hair like their brothers, under their head scarves. They had stayed home to prepare an enormous lunch for Paul and Katie. The two girls and their mother had been hustling around the kitchen since dawn.

They all left their shoes at the front door, and the moment they walked into the house, with all the young people chattering loudly, Jelveh hurried into the kitchen to finish cooking the lavish meal. The house was filled with the delicious smell of cinnamon and oranges and lamb, which sparked familiar memories for Paul, as Kate wandered into the kitchen and offered to help Jelveh. She introduced Kate to Shirin and Soudabeh and commented proudly that Soudabeh was going to be getting married later that year. The four women worked together with the help of three young girls who worked for them.

"She has been betrothed to her future husband since she was thirteen," Jelveh said happily as Soudabeh beamed. "We arranged a marriage for

Shirin last year. Once her older sister is married, Shirin can get married too, next year." Kate realized it meant that the younger one would be getting married at fifteen, which wasn't uncommon here, and Paul had told her that in traditional families, marriages were often arranged. Both girls spoke excellent English and giggled when they talked about getting married.

Once the meal was properly organized, Jelveh offered to take Katie to her room. The men went outside to talk and catch up. They were thrilled to have Paul home. What Katie had seen so far was no different than any family scene in the States.

Shirin and Soudabeh led Katie upstairs, to a room on the second floor, near their own. It was a small cubicle with a narrow bed and a dresser for her things, and a small window high up on the wall that she couldn't see out of, but it shed sunlight into the room. The room was sparsely decorated, and Katie saw as she walked by them that the two girls had similar rooms. Shirin commented that the boys had larger bedrooms, on the upper floor, and Soudabeh said that their parents' bedroom was at the opposite side of the house, and their grandfather had a suite of rooms downstairs. He had come to live with them after Paul had left, and they said he had been sick.

Katie put her bag down in her room and left her

passport in her backpack, with her credit card and traveler's checks. She had the money in rials that she had exchanged in her pocket, with some dollars. She had been told not to bring her computer to Iran, when she got her visa. They had told her that there were Internet cafés everywhere where she could get Internet access. And she had a BlackBerry in her pocket.

As soon as she had put her things down, the girls beckoned her back down the stairs to the kitchen, where Jelveh and the girls put the lavish meal on platters, and the three servants helped take the food to the dining room.

The family was not fabulously rich, but it was obvious that this was a wealthy household. Jelveh was wearing a sober-looking black dress and a very nice diamond watch, and Kate noticed that the two girls were wearing gold bracelets, and the men in the family wore large gold watches, even Paul's cousins.

And just as Jelveh was preparing the meal, Katie heard the **adhan** for the first time. It was the midday call to prayer, announced on loudspeakers all over the city, as the muezzin made the same haunting sound that they heard five times a day. And everything instantly stopped. There was no sound in the household as each member of the family listened to the seven verses in the call to prayer. Katie was mesmerized by the sound. Paul had told her she would hear it at dawn, midday, midafternoon, just after sunset, and for the last time two hours after sunset. It was the reminder to the faithful to stop and pray five times a day.

When the muezzin's call ended, the house sprang to life again.

The food that Jelveh had prepared with the girls' help was delicately scented with saffron, fruit, and cinnamon blended in. There were chicken and lamb and fish, and it all smelled delicious to Katie as the men came in from outside and Katie realized how hungry she was after the long trip, although she had eaten two meals on each flight. She had no idea what time it was in New York, but she felt as though it was in another world, on another planet, a million miles from here. She had only been in Tehran for two hours, but Paul's family was making her feel completely at home.

Everyone took their places at the table, and Katie sat down between Shirin and Soudabeh, while the three serving girls passed the platters and the whole family chattered excitedly at once. Paul's homecoming was a major celebration for them all. The men were speaking animatedly to each other in Farsi and laughed a lot. Paul seemed completely at ease with them, as though he had never left, and Shirin and Soudabeh were busy asking Katie questions about fashions in New York, just like girls their age anywhere in the world. And every now and then Paul smiled at Kate reassuringly, and she realized it was going to be a long two weeks without physical contact, or being affectionate with each other. But it was a small price to pay in exchange for the experience of coming to Tehran. She was glad that she had come.

"Are you all right?" Paul asked her across the table at one point, and she smiled at him and answered, "Fine." He knew this was very different for her, especially not speaking the language, and he wanted her to feel at home. His aunt, uncle, and cousins had done a great job so far of welcoming her. And Katie loved the food as well. She helped herself from several platters and enjoyed the pungent food and delicate spices.

The boys talked to her about going to visit the university the next day, and Katie said she wanted to see it and the bazaar most of all. They promised to show her all the sights while she was there. And Katie couldn't help thinking that they were making every effort to make her feel at ease with them. Paul's grandfather spoke up then in Farsi, with a puzzled look. He asked Paul a question, to which Paul said no.

"What did he ask you?" Katie asked with interest. She had the feeling that his grandfather had asked about her, since he had glanced at her several times.

"He asked if you were my girlfriend," Paul said quietly. "I said no." It was the agreement Paul and Katie had made before they came, and Katie nodded. It was best if they didn't know. If they did, it would only complicate things for Paul.

After lunch Jelveh suggested that all three girls go upstairs and rest. Katie followed them to the floor above, and both of Paul's girl cousins joined her in her room, where she unpacked her bags, and they admired her clothes. Shirin held all of it up in front of her and would have loved to try it on, but didn't dare ask, as Katie put her belongings in the chest and closet and rapidly unpacked.

She then decided to put her money and Black-Berry away—it seemed silly to carry them in the house. She reached in to tuck them in the pocket of her backpack, with her passport, but as soon as she unzipped the pocket, she saw that her credit card, traveler's checks, and passport were gone. The pocket was empty. Someone had removed them during lunch, since she had checked her backpack just before. Katie felt a wave of panic rush over her. It was a strange feeling being without them. She wondered if maybe Paul or one of his cousins was playing a trick on her and hoped that was the case.

But when Paul showed up a few minutes later and she mentioned it to him in an undervoice with a look of concern, he looked surprised too. He went to tell his uncle about it immediately. All he said in response was that Kate did not need any of it during her stay with them, and he thought it was safer to keep them locked up. They didn't intend to let her pay for anything so she didn't need her credit card or traveler's checks, and he pointed out that Katie didn't need her passport until she left. Paul had no idea who had gone through the backpack and didn't want to ask. His uncle was the authority here, and when he explained it to Katie a short time later, she still looked upset. Paul had gone to check his own room by then and found that both of his passports and money were gone too. Kate was grateful that she'd had her money and phone on her at lunch when Paul told her what his uncle had said about her passport and credit card being safer if locked up.

"Can you ask him to give them back? I'd feel better hanging on to them myself," Kate asked Paul as they conferred about it in whispers in the upstairs hall. "I'm really not comfortable without my passport." And she was glad she had made Xerox copies of his and her own, which were still in the bottom of the backpack.

"Neither am I," he assured her. It was the first

hiccup of the trip. "I'll talk to my uncle about it again." But when he did, his uncle told him that neither of them needed to have their passports. Paul didn't want to argue with him and be disrespectful, and his uncle was very firm about keeping them in his possession for safekeeping. Kate looked like she was going to cry when Paul told her.

"That really makes me nervous," she said, wishing she could hug him then. She needed the reassurance. Losing control of her passport was frightening for her. It made Kate feel completely helpless. She realized then that she hadn't texted Annie when they arrived, and she wasn't sure if it would work here. She decided to try, and sent a short text that said only, "Safely arrived. I love you," and then she decided to turn it off to save her battery, in case they wouldn't let her have that either.

She was sure they meant well in keeping her passport, but it still made her uncomfortable to have lost possession of it. She put the BlackBerry in a sock and hid it far under her mattress, where she knew it was safe. It was her only means of communication with the outside world, and she didn't want it running down, or taken. She didn't like being without her passport at all, nor the traveler's checks and credit card, all of which were tangible signs of her freedom and independence. It was a shock to have them taken away, however benevolent their motives. It made her feel like a child instead of an adult. And Paul was unhappy as well. His uncle had pointed out to him that only his Iranian passport mattered here, and his American one was useless to him in Tehran anyway. But Paul didn't want to lose possession of his passports, and Katie only had one. But there was nothing they could do about it. Paul's uncle was the head of the family, and he made the decisions for all of them, even for Katie while she stayed with them.

After that, Paul and his male cousins went out to drive around old familiar places. The women stayed home, and Shirin and Soudabeh played cards with Kate. She would have liked to go out with Paul and the boys too, and see more of the city, but she didn't want to be rude to the girls, who were so excited to have her there.

The boys came back three hours later in high spirits. Paul said he had seen his old school and visited one of his boyhood friends. He had been surprised to discover that his friend was the man betrothed to Soudabeh and would be marrying her that summer. It felt strange to think of his own friends getting married, but he knew that people got married younger here. As much as he loved

Katie, he didn't feel ready for that himself. He loved being back in Tehran, seeing family and friends and all the familiar sights and places, and enjoying the sounds and smells that he had missed for so long.

He went out with the men again that night. This time Paul's uncle went with them, and they were meeting other friends on the way. Paul looked apologetically at Kate as they left. His uncle wanted her to stay home with Jelveh and the girls. The men wanted to go out on their own, which was customary here.

That evening, Kate, Shirin, and Soudabeh lay on her bed and talked about fashion again, and movie stars. They didn't know them all, although they knew some, and were fascinated by everything Kate had to say. They treated her like a visiting dignitary in their midst. And Katie knew that Annie would have been relieved to see what a close-knit, wholesome family they were, and how well taken care of she was. And she didn't mind Paul's boys' night out. She was understanding about it and wanted him to enjoy the company of his male relatives too after so long away.

The three girls laughed and giggled a lot that night, and Soudabeh asked Katie if she had a boyfriend. She gasped with excitement when Kate said she did. And Kate laughed out loud at the irony that it was their cousin, which she couldn't tell them. The fact that she was not Muslim, at least not yet, made it unwise for her and Paul to admit to their relationship here.

The girls went to bed long before the boys came home, and Kate wondered what they were doing. In spite of herself and her good intentions, as it got late, she felt left out. And she didn't see Paul again until breakfast the next morning, and he was very solicitous over breakfast. He apologized again for not taking her out the night before.

"Did you sleep okay?" Paul asked her, wishing he could put his arms around her, but certainly not here.

"Fine." She smiled at him. "What time did you come in?"

"Around two," he said, and a little while later his cousins all came downstairs, and they discussed their visit that day to the university. All three boys were going and Soudabeh and Kate. They were all in high spirits when they left in the van right after breakfast.

Kate was impressed by how enormous the university was, and they were there all day, while the boys showed them around. They stopped several times to chat with friends, and Paul's cousins introduced him to several young women students.

The university was even bigger than NYU,

where Ted went to law school, and way, way bigger than Pratt, where she and Paul studied design.

Excited by their visit to the university, Kate tried to suggest they go to a museum afterward, but no one wanted to go with her, and Paul promised he'd try to arrange it. And she was also anxious to see the bazaar that she had heard so much about.

She turned her BlackBerry on briefly when she went to bed that night and saw that she had a text from Annie. "Take care, I love you" was all it said, and after reading the message, she turned it off. It still had plenty of power, and she was glad it did, because the power cord and transformer she'd bought had both disappeared from her backpack. Neither Soudabeh nor Shirin had cell phones and said their father didn't like them, but both had iPods they listened to constantly.

At breakfast with Kate the next day, both girls talked about their weddings. They were excited about them, and Shirin didn't mind at all being betrothed to a man five years older than she was. She thought he was very good looking. And both girls wanted to have babies soon. It was a culture where everyone started young. Jelveh had told Kate that she had gotten married at fourteen and had her first son at fifteen, and her husband was considerably older than she was. Kate realized when she said it that Jelveh was three or four years younger than Annie, which seemed amazing to her, and had a twenty-three-year-old son. She explained to her then about her aunt raising them, and her parents dying when she was five. Jelveh was shocked to learn that Annie wasn't married and didn't have children of her own. "How sad," she said, looking sympathetic, and Kate realized that maybe it was, but Annie didn't seem to mind. She had them.

True to his promise, Paul organized a visit to the Museum of Contemporary Art that day. And this time both girls went with them. It had one of the finest collections of modern and contemporary art Kate had ever seen, and much to her delight, they stayed for hours and explored the sculpture garden afterward.

At the end of the week, Kate, Paul and the others went to the enormous bazaar, and she bought a beautiful silver necklace for Annie. The sights and sounds and smells of the bazaar seemed dizzying to Katie. There were miles of stalls, selling every kind of wares. People crowded around, and serious negotiations were being engaged in. The bazaar was far bigger than she had imagined, it was full of people, and Kate had a terrific time.

Their first week in Tehran had been wonderful, but at the end of it, Paul and Kate admitted to each other that they were getting homesick for

New York and their lives there. The time had been so full that they felt like they'd been gone for longer. And Kate missed Annie. She was enjoying Paul's family but she suddenly felt far away and missed her own.

Kate decided that day to send Annie an e-mail. Instead of using up the dwindling power in her BlackBerry, she asked one of Paul's cousins to take her to an Internet café after school, and he was nice enough to do it. In the e-mail she told Annie what they'd been doing, that it was very interesting, and that she missed her. And she assured her she was fine. She sent short ones to Ted and Lizzie too. And after writing to them, she missed home even more. Despite the wonders she was discovering in Tehran, she was beginning to get seriously homesick, and when she got back to the house, she looked a little glum. Paul felt sorry for her when he saw it and admired her for being a good sport about everything so far. She had fit into everything they were doing. It had been an action-packed week, and Paul had the feeling at times that his family were subtly trying to convince him to move back to Tehran, and to remind him of how much happier he'd be here, where he belonged. He loved being back in Tehran, but he also realized that it was no longer home for him, and he missed his parents, friends, and familiar life in New York. His grandfather reminded him at every opportunity that he was Iranian, not American, and his uncle and cousins had echoed the same thought. He still felt totally at ease in Tehran, but he was ready to go back to New York. A week had been enough. Two was beginning to seem too long.

Katie felt that way too, and was tired of the charade that they were only friends. She missed cuddling with him and kissing him whenever she wanted. And sometimes she found it exhausting trying to absorb a whole new culture, and to understand all their customs. Paul was glad they had come, and particularly to have shared the experience with Katie. Contrary to all of Annie's dire warnings, there was nothing either of them regretted about the trip so far. On the contrary they had both loved it. And they were hoping to take a trip to Persepolis before they left. Paul had shown her everything he wanted to and that Kate had been hoping to see before they arrived.

It was the day of their second visit to the bazaar to buy a bracelet for Liz and a belt for Ted that Katie began to feel strange at dinner. She got very pale, said she was a little dizzy, and then broke out in a sweat. Jelveh looked instantly worried, felt her head, and said she had a fever. And looking embarrassed, Kate left the table, went upstairs, and got violently sick two minutes later. She looked considerably worse when Paul went upstairs to check on her after dinner. He helped Katie into bed and went downstairs to tell his aunt that he thought Katie needed a doctor. She went upstairs to see for herself, and by then Katie was shaking violently with chills and had a raging fever. Katie was crying, said she had terrible stomach pains, and Paul was worried sick about her. She insisted she hadn't eaten or drunk anything at the bazaar, and Jelveh said it looked like a very bad flu they'd all had earlier that winter. Katie said she'd never felt so sick in her life, and Paul bent down to kiss her forehead, just as Jelveh came back into the room to check on Kate again, and saw him do it. She looked at Paul with strong disapproval.

"You can't do that here, Paul, and you know it. And if you kiss Kate in public, it will cause you both a great deal of trouble. It's not proper behavior, and even more so since she's not a Muslim. If your grandfather saw you do that, it would break his heart." And then she looked searchingly at both of them. "Is she your girlfriend?" she asked her nephew in a whisper, so no one else would hear her. Kate watched him with wide eyes as he paused before he answered, then nodded. He didn't want to lie to his aunt, and he trusted her to be discreet about it. He knew she liked Kate a lot although not necessarily for him, since she was Christian.

"Yes, she is," he answered simply.

"Do your parents know?" She looked shocked, as he nodded again.

"Yes, they do. They like Kate, although they're worried about how it would work out in the future. But it's different for us. We live in New York, not Tehran." Jelveh didn't say anything for a long moment as she thought about it.

"It's not different for you," Jelveh said quietly. "You're still a Muslim, even in New York. And Kate isn't. I think you've been away from home for too long. It's time for you to come back here and remember who and what you are." She was very clear on that.

"I can't do that," he said quietly. "I have a life in New York, and my parents are there."

"Your parents were wrong to take you away when you were so young." And then she took his breath away with what she said next. "We want you to stay here now. You can study here with your cousins. You can live with us." Her heart was in her eyes as she said it. She meant well, but Paul didn't want to stay. He was ready to go back. Kate was listening with wide eyes.

"I can't do that, Jelveh," Paul said, with a sound of panic in his voice. "My parents would be upset if I didn't come back. And so would I. I love it here, but it's not my home anymore."

"Tehran will always be your home," she said firmly. And as she said it, Kate ran to the bathroom again, and they could hear her retching through the door. "I'll call the doctor," Jelveh said calmly. "We can talk about this later." But the way she said it made him nervous. They had both his passports, and he couldn't leave Tehran without at least one of them. And Jelveh made it sound like they were determined to keep him in Tehran.

He didn't have time to discuss it with her further. The doctor came half an hour later, and by then Katie had a 103-degree fever and was even sicker than before. The doctor examined Katie and thought she had a virus of some kind, or a bacterial infection. He thought about putting her in the hospital, but after discussing it with Jelveh, he decided to leave her at their home.

The fever raged on for three days, while Jelveh nursed her, and Paul visited her every chance he got. And he was grateful that Jelveh hadn't told anyone in the family that Katie was his girlfriend, but the sicker she got, the more obvious it was. He was out of his head with worry for her. And Katie looked like a skeleton when the fever broke after four days, two days before they were due to go home. She was deathly pale and had dark circles under her eyes, and she hadn't contacted Annie because she didn't want to upset her. They were going home soon anyway. When the fever broke finally, Paul told Katie she had been very brave. He patted her hand as he said it but made no move to kiss her again. He knew full well from Jelveh what a scandal that would cause.

The doctor declared that she would be well enough to return to New York on schedule, and Katie looked relieved. She didn't want to get stuck here. She was still feeling sick and wanted to go home to Annie and her own bed. She had felt like a five-year-old when she was sick. But Jelveh had taken good care of her, almost as good as Annie, although with different remedies. But she had been an excellent nurse, and very motherly to her.

Paul reconfirmed their airplane tickets that day and went to see his uncle about reclaiming their passports. His uncle listened to him, nodded, unlocked a drawer in his desk, and handed him Kate's, but neither of Paul's. He handed him Katie's credit card and traveler's checks too, but nothing of Paul's.

"I need mine too," Paul said quietly, as his uncle shook his head.

"I don't think you do. Your aunt and I would like you to stay here. This is where you belong," he said firmly.

"No, it isn't," Paul said hoarsely, as a shiver of fear ran down his spine. "You can't keep me here, uncle. Sooner or later, I'll find a way to leave. My home is in New York."

"You don't belong in New York, Paul. Iran is your country. Tehran is your home."

"America is my country now too. And New York is my home, **not** Tehran. I love it here, but this is history for me. My future and life are in the States."

"That was a foolish mistake your father made years ago. He got lured away by the money he could make in the States. There are more important things than that, like family and traditions. You can correct that now by staying here."

"I won't," Paul said, looking frightened. "And I have to get Kate home. She's sick, and it's time for us to go."

"She can fly alone," his uncle insisted calmly, as Paul felt like he was talking to a wall.

"Are you telling me you won't give me my passports?" Paul asked, looking stunned.

"Yes, I am," his uncle said with a look of iron, as Paul stared at him in disbelief. "I think you need to spend time here. And you need to send Katie home."

"I'm not letting her fly home alone," Paul said firmly, as his uncle said nothing and quietly left the room, without another word to Paul.

Paul was in Katie's room two minutes later with a look of deep concern.

"What's wrong? You look like someone died," Katie said only half-joking.

"Someone did. Both my passports. My uncle won't give them back to me."

"Are you serious?" Katie looked horrified as he nodded and handed hers to her.

"They want me to stay," he said solemnly.

"For how long?"

"Forever, it sounds like. As far as they're concerned, I'm Iranian, and I belong here." It was the only thing that had worried his mother when they left—the possibility that someone would try to keep him there. As it turned out, she hadn't been wrong. "You're going to have to fly back alone. I don't want you to stay here. You're sick. You need to go home."

"I'm not leaving you here," she said with a look of panic. "What if we ask the Swiss embassy to help?"

"There's nothing they can do. I'm considered an Iranian citizen here."

"Your uncle can't do this to you," Katie said, starting to cry.

"Yes, he can. He's the head of the family. He says it will kill my grandfather if I leave again." Paul looked devastated as he said it. "And it will kill my parents if I don't. He thinks they should come back too."

"I'm not leaving Tehran without you," Katie said firmly, clutching her passport in her hand.

"Your aunt will go nuts. And your visa expires in two weeks. I want you to go back." And she still looked very sick. The virus she had caught had hit her hard.

"I'm not leaving you here," Katie said in tears.

"We have no choice," he said as he put his arms around her and hoped no one would see them. And this time no one did.

"I'll send a message to my aunt," Katie said with a look of defiance.

"There's nothing she can do," Paul said, looking defeated. His uncle made the rules and was calling the shots. And he wanted him in Tehran.

"You don't know Annie," Katie said, as she reached under her mattress and pulled out her BlackBerry and was relieved to see that the battery still had power. She texted Annie as Paul watched her. Her message to her aunt was succinct: "I caught bad flu. Paul's uncle won't give his passports back. I have mine. I won't leave without him. I'm sick. Paul is stuck. What do we do? Can you help us? I love you. K." She put the Black-Berry back under her mattress again, after turning it off, as Paul looked at her with a sad smile. He had the feeling that he would never get back to New York. He felt desperately sorry for his parents. And now he was sorry that he had come to Tehran with Kate. He was trapped, and in two weeks, when her visa ran out, she would have to go back. Annie and his mother had been right. The trip had been a mistake.

Chapter 21

Tom and Annie had spent a perfect weekend together. They'd gone to Da Silvano for dinner on Friday night. They went shopping on Saturday, and Tom had done some repairs for her around the apartment. They cooked dinner on Saturday night and made love by candlelight afterward, and on Sunday afternoon, after reading **The New York Times,** they went to a movie.

They'd had brunch at the Mercer with Ted and celebrated his liberation from Pattie. He had turned in his papers, dropped her class, and didn't mind getting an incomplete—all he wanted was to never see her again. When he took his withdrawal slip to his adviser's office, Pattie had seen him in the hallway and said not a word. She had played all her cards and lost and knew it. He felt like a new man, and he had decided to get his own apartment. He was tired of roommates. All he wanted now was to get back to his studies. He felt free and alive again.

Ted commented at lunch that he'd been trying to reach Liz all weekend.

"She's in London," Annie said cryptically.

"What's she doing there?"

"Meeting a friend," Annie said with a mysterious smile. She and Alessandro had agreed to meet there for the weekend, and Annie had encouraged her to go.

"Have you heard anything from Kate?" Ted inquired.

"I got an e-mail from her. She sounds like she's having fun. I guess I was wrong to be so worried," Annie said, sounding relieved. Tom was happy about it too.

"So did I. She sent me an e-mail. But it was so short, it didn't say much except hi, bye, and she loves me. When is she coming home?"

"In a few days," Annie said, happy that it was going well for her. Whitney had been right. She needed to let them fly on their own. Ted had gotten out of his nightmarish situation with Pattie, Liz had gotten rid of Jean-Louis, and Kate seemed to be doing fine in Iran. All was well in their world.

"I still think she was wrong to go," Ted said,

sounding like a disapproving older brother. But he had never been as adventurous as Katie, even as a young boy.

"Maybe not," Annie said generously. "If it goes well, it's a great adventure for her. And she'll feel very competent and able to take care of herself when she gets home."

"Paul's a great guy, but she doesn't know him well enough to go so far away," Ted commented, "and his culture is a whole other world." Annie didn't disagree, but she was happy that Kate seemed to be having fun. She and Tom went to the movies after that. She turned off her phone, and they cuddled and ate popcorn and enjoyed the movie, and then they went home. They were cooking dinner when she remembered to turn on her phone. It sprang to life instantly and told her she had a text message. It said that it was from Katie, and her heart nearly stopped when she read it, and she soundlessly handed it to Tom.

"What do I do?" she said with a look of panic. The fact that Katie was sick was bad enough, but she was refusing to leave Tehran without Paul, and he was stuck without either of his passports and couldn't leave.

"It doesn't sound good," Tom said with a frown. "Why don't you call Paul's parents and see what they think? They know the circumstances and the family in Tehran better than we do. Maybe Paul's uncle is just bluffing and trying to get him to stay." Annie called them immediately, and was grateful to find his mother at home. She read Paul's mother the text message from Katie and asked her what she thought. She was instantly as worried as Annie. Her husband was out, and she was candid with Annie.

"The family have wanted us to come back for years, and they think Paul should be there and not in the States. My brother-in-law is a very stubborn man. He could keep Paul there forever." She started crying as she said it. "That's why I didn't want him to go. They won't do him any harm. They love him and they think they're doing the right thing for him. They're trying to correct our 'mistake' of bringing him to the States. And I'm so sorry about Katie. I hope she's all right. My sister-in-law is a very sweet woman, and I'm sure she got a doctor for Katie and took good care of her."

"And now Kate is refusing to leave Tehran without Paul," Annie explained. It was a mess, and a difficult situation to resolve. She promised to call Paul's mother back, who said she would call the family in Tehran and try to get more information, and as soon as Annie hung up, she turned to Tom.

"How do I get to Tehran?" Annie looked at him

with wide eyes. She had no idea where to start, but she knew he did.

"You need a visa, which takes a couple of weeks to get, or longer." He looked pensive, then leaned down to kiss her. He felt sorry for her. Annie looked worried sick. "Let me see what I can do. I've got some friends in the State Department. Maybe one of them can help." He spent the next three hours on the phone, calling different people, and two of them promised to see what they could arrange the next day. They had to get the visa at the Pakistani embassy, just as Kate had, but Tom had explained the situation to them. He said she was a young American girl who was sick in Tehran, and her Iranian traveling companion was without a passport and unable to leave as a result. It wasn't a life-threatening situation, but it was extremely unpleasant for Katie and Paul, and they were stuck. He explained that her aunt needed to go over and bring her back, and Kate wasn't able to travel alone and needed medical attention as soon as possible in the States. He didn't know if it was true but hoped it would work as a compelling reason to get a visa immediately. He also explained that Katie's traveling companion was her Iranian boyfriend, who held American citizenship as well, and had parents in New York, who were also citizens. So this wasn't a romance that Katie had gotten involved with in Tehran. They had gone over for a visit to his family, and then Katie had gotten sick. And now his family was refusing to let him leave.

He knew that Katie wouldn't have asked for Annie's help unless she absolutely had to and had no other way out. Otherwise she would have figured it out for herself. She was a very independent girl. And they had no idea how sick she really was, or what she had, which worried him too. And there was nothing more they could do until morning. Annie lay awake all night and sent Katie a text message: "Working on it. Hang in. Be there as soon as I can. love, A." She had tried to call Paul's uncle, but the phone didn't answer, which upset Annie too.

She nearly jumped out of her skin when the phone rang at seven o'clock the next morning. One of Tom's friends had called the Pakistani ambassador in Washington and told him that this was a personal favor for a major journalist, and they needed two visas for Iran. Tom hadn't said anything to Annie yet, but he had made up his mind the day before and had asked for two visas instead of one. He wanted to go with her. He knew the area, the country, and the customs, and he knew she would have a hard time alone there.

She would do better with a man traveling with her, and he wanted to help. And he had the time.

The ambassador had agreed to give them both visas at nine o'clock that morning. All they had to do was pick them up at the Pakistani consulate in New York, and she could fly out on the next plane to London. They had to follow the same path that Katie and Paul had. The Pakistani ambassador had admitted to the middleman that the last thing anyone would want to deal with was a sick American girl, stuck in Tehran, with one of the most important American journalists begging for help on her behalf. It was a plea for assistance that they couldn't ignore, it was noninflammatory, nonpolitical, and a situation they wanted to resolve.

When Tom told her he was going with her, Annie looked embarrassed and guilty.

"You can't just drop everything and leave," Annie pointed out to Tom. "I can manage on my own." She was trying to be brave and not take advantage of him or even his connections, except to get her a visa and a flight. But she was deeply grateful for his help.

"Let's not be stupid," Tom said firmly. "I was bureau chief in that part of the world for two years. You can't do this alone. I'm coming with you. I'll call the network. You call the airline." He made it seem so simple, and it was certainly easier than trying to work it out alone. "We can pick up the visas on the way to the airport, and be on a noon flight to London, if they have one." Annie was praying they did. She wanted to get to Tehran as soon as possible. She had no idea how sick Katie was.

Tom called the network and told them he needed a personal leave of absence for three or four days, and Annie booked two seats on a one o'clock flight to London. She called her office after that and then she called Ted and told him what was going on. He was upset to hear it, and hopeful that Katie wasn't too sick, which was Annie's hope as well. Paul's mother called at that point. She had spoken to her sister-in-law, who said that Katie had had a high fever and severe dysentery, but she was better. And Jelveh had said they were keeping Paul with them because he should be in Iran, not the States. She said they were trying to make up for his parents' failures, which upset Paul's mother even more. She was crying when she told Annie that they refused to let Paul leave.

After that Annie packed a small bag that she could carry on the plane. She put in several scarves for her head. And an hour later they were on their way to the Pakistani consulate. Paul's father had called and given Tom all the details about where to find them. He had also given Tom both of Paul's passport numbers, and his brother's phone numbers again, where Paul and Katie were staying. They had everything they needed. There was nothing more that Tom and Annie could do now, except get there and find out how things really were. They were both sure that Katie would never have contacted Annie if she could have handled things herself. And Annie was infinitely grateful that Tom had come to help.

It was a long, agonizing flight to London, followed by a longer one to Tehran. The two of them spoke quietly and tried to guess what was going on. They were both worried that Paul's family might have discovered that Katie was more than just a friend, and that they were involved in a serious romance. Annie was worried too that while she was on the plane, she couldn't get text messages from Kate, since her phone was turned off. She tried not to panic on the two flights. And there was no text message while they waited in Heathrow before boarding the flight to Tehran. Annie had sent a text that said, "We're on our way. I love you. A." And there still was no response.

They were fingerprinted at immigration at Imam Khomeini Airport in Tehran, like everyone else, and they cleared customs easily. Tom had booked two rooms at a hotel. He had assumed they might be there for several days and had organized everything for them. He had even booked a room for Katie, just in case.

He was thinking about going to the police, but he didn't want to make things worse, and they had no legitimate claim to help Paul. His uncle had the right to keep his passport. And as soon as they cleared customs, they took a cab to the address that Paul's father had given them. They had no idea what they'd find there, nor what the attitude of Paul's family would be toward them, hostile or friendly. Clearly, something was wrong, since Paul couldn't leave Tehran. And Annie was increasingly worried that there had been no further messages from Kate. She was terrified that she might be sicker than they said. What if she had something potentially fatal like meningitis? Or had already succumbed? Tears sprang to her eyes every time the thought came to her mind.

When Katie had turned her BlackBerry on again, the battery was dead. She didn't know that Annie was on her way. And she lay in her bed, thinking about their situation, with Paul without a passport, and no ability to leave Iran.

Jelveh was still taking care of her and being motherly and kind, offering her tea, and small meals and rice, and herbs that she said would help her and give her strength, and Katie was feeling better. But she had no idea how to get Paul out of Tehran and back to the States, and neither did he. He came to her room constantly to check on her. And she told him there had been no further word from her aunt, since her own phone was now dead.

As Katie rested in her room, she heard the **adhan** that came right after sunset, as the muezzin called out the prayer. The **adhan** was a familiar sound now, since she'd arrived. She heard the last one of the day two hours later. Whenever Katie saw Paul, when he came to visit her, he looked seriously depressed. He was trapped.

It took Tom and Annie an hour and a half to get to the house from the airport. The traffic was terrible, and Annie looked tense as she sat in the backseat with Tom, wearing one of the scarves she'd brought with her. She had put it on in the plane before they landed, when the flight attendant gently reminded her to do so. All she could do was pray that Katie was okay and hadn't caught anything too serious or even fatal. She hoped they hadn't let her get dehydrated from the fever. She was worried sick about her.

The cab stopped finally in front of a large rambling house, and both of them got out. Annie wasn't even jet-lagged, she was so wound up, and she hadn't slept for the entire trip. Tom whispered to her as they got out of the taxi and reminded her to appear calm, patient, and strong, and not accuse them of anything, no matter how upset she was about Katie and Paul. Tom wanted to move with caution, and be as friendly and civil as possible until they knew what was going on.

Tom rang the bell, and a servant opened the door. He asked for Paul's uncle by name in a clear voice that exuded confidence and strength. It took a few minutes, and then Jelveh came to the door to greet them, looking gentle and sympathetic.

"I'm Annie Ferguson," Annie introduced herself. "I'm Katie's aunt, and I've come for my niece," Annie said, looking her right in the eye with a stern expression. But she met no hostility from Jelveh, who smiled at her. "She sent me a message that she's sick," Annie said, backing down a little. She turned to Tom then. "And this is Tom Jefferson. He's an American journalist. I'd like to see Paul and Kate." She wanted to see them immediately, but Jelveh appeared to be in no hurry. It had been almost two days since Annie had gotten Kate's text. She was so jangled, all she could do was pray she was still alive. If it was meningitis, she might not be. The thought made Annie shiver.

"Of course." Jelveh smiled at her. "She has told me all about you." And then, she asked them to wait for a moment. She disappeared and her husband came back to the door instead. He looked at the two Americans, nodded, and invited them inside. He took them into the living room and asked if they would like something to drink. He was extremely polite and seemed hospitable, and looked just like Paul's father, and Annie wanted to scream at them to take her to the two young people, but she remembered Tom's warning to be civil, calm, and patient. She was on their turf, on their terms.

"Your brother said you would help me," Annie said directly to him, wanting him to hurry, but he wouldn't. They had declined the offer of anything to drink. "I know my niece has been sick and I'm sure you've been very kind to her. But I was told that you took Paul's passport. His parents are very upset about it. I expect you to let both of them leave with me," she said firmly, hoping to convince him without a fight.

"Paul and Katie are both here," he said calmly. "And your niece is improving daily. She caught a very bad virus of some kind, but she's much better now. My wife has been taking care of her, and of course we will return her to you. We only kept her passport for safekeeping so she wouldn't lose it." Annie didn't comment but doubted that was true. "My nephew is a different story. This is his home, his heritage. He belongs here, not in New York. It was foolish and wrong of my brother to move away and leave Iran years ago. His son needs to be here, with our family. Paul will have a better life here. We want him to stay." Annie and Tom's hearts sank at the words. They could both tell that Paul's uncle was sincere and truly believed he was doing the right thing for him. It wasn't malicious or malevolent, only misguided, particularly since Paul had a life and parents in New York. But his uncle looked totally convinced of what he'd said. They didn't argue with him, and all Annie wanted now was to see Kate.

"Where's Katie?" Annie asked quietly. She wanted to see Kate immediately, but she wanted to get Paul out too.

"She's upstairs in her room." He looked anxious about Tom as he said it. He had the sense that Tom was an important person, possibly even a dangerous one, and he wasn't wrong. Tom was watching the scene in minute detail and hadn't spoken yet.

"Is she alive?" Annie asked with a look of terror. What if she had died while they were on the plane? Meningitis was her greatest fear, as it killed young people so quickly. But surely the uncle would have told her when they arrived if she was dead. Fear was clouding Annie's mind and jangling her nerves. They had said she was better, but was it true?

"Of course she's alive," he reassured her instantly.

"I want to see her," Annie said, fighting back tears of exhaustion and relief, and Tom stepped in. It was a tense scene. And Tom was wondering if there was more to the story than Katie had said in her brief text. Maybe they had figured out the romance between Paul and Kate and were upset and wanted to end it by keeping him in Iran.

"Have they committed a crime?" Tom asked bluntly.

"Not publicly, certainly," he reassured them, although his wife had told him that they were more than just "friends" as soon as she had discovered that herself. She kept no secrets from her husband. "Although they seem to be closer to each other than they admitted when they arrived. For a Muslim man involved with a Western woman of another faith, the punishment can be very serious here." Annie felt faint as she heard his words, and she squeezed Tom's hand. "For that reason, Paul was wrong to bring Katie here and pretend that

they were friends. But they're foolish and young."
He smiled at them both. "But an alliance between
them would not be wise. For that reason also Paul
should stay here. There will be no further danger
when Katie leaves. I returned her passport, credit
card, and traveler's checks to her. She is free to go.
I'm sure she'll be happy to see you." Annie and
Tom looked immensely relieved by what he'd said.
He had no reason to keep Katie there, nor did he
want to. She was not a hostage, she was a guest,
and they had treated her as one. "My nephew belongs here in his own country. He will not be leaving with Kate."

Tom looked angry when he said it. "That's a terrible thing to do to your brother and his wife. Paul
is their only child," he reminded him. "It would
break their hearts."

"Perhaps it will convince them to return," he
said softly. It was his fondest hope.

"That's not realistic, and you know it. They have
a life there now, and a business. It would not be
easy for them to come back." Paul's uncle nodded.
"And I'm prepared to make an enormous fuss if
you don't turn both young people over to me now,
with both of Paul's passports. His parents want
him back in New York and have asked me to bring
him." It was a show of bravado but their only
hope. Paul's uncle had every right to refuse Tom.

"I'm not sure he even wants to leave. He has strong ties to his homeland, and to us. To my wife and me, his cousins, his grandfather." His parents meant more to him, but Tom didn't say it. And Paul's uncle stood up. "I will take you to Kate," he said warmly, as though they were honored guests, and so was Kate.

A moment later all three of them were upstairs, and Paul's uncle knocked and opened the door. They saw Katie sitting up in bed, with Paul in a chair beside her. They were talking quietly and looking worried, and they looked stunned when Tom and Annie walked into the room. She had asked for Annie's help but didn't expect her to come. Katie let out a yell and leaped into her aunt's arms, as Paul smiled gratefully at Tom, who met his uncle's eyes with a look of ice.

"I want his passports now too," Tom said clearly. "Now. You can't keep him here against his will. I'm a journalist, and I'm prepared to see this through." There was a long, long hesitation, and then Paul's uncle left the room without a word. He was back five minutes later, with both of Paul's passports in his hand. He wanted him to stay, but he didn't want to cause his country embarrassment if Tom was going to create a scandal in the press, and he looked like he would. His love and respect for his country were greater than his desire to force his nephew to stay. The battle for Paul had been lost. And won by Tom. Paul's uncle handed him Paul's passports without a word, and with a look of sadness and defeat.

"Thank you," Tom said quietly, took them, and slipped them into his jacket pocket, as the young people watched the scene in awe.

Tom told them both to pack immediately. He didn't want to give Paul's uncle time to change his mind. Annie stayed to help Katie, and Paul went to his room to get his things. Tom had the passports and would not let them out of his possession now. Paul's freedom was in his hands.

Ten minutes later they were both downstairs with their bags. Katie looked shaky and wan and very pale. Jelveh had come into the hall by then, and she and her husband both looked grief stricken that their nephew was leaving. Paul's grandfather was out, so he couldn't say goodbye to him. And his cousins were in school. The girls had been sent to their rooms and did not emerge. Paul was not going to have a chance to say goodbye to anyone and looked sad.

Annie thanked them both for taking care of Kate, and so did Katie, and Jelveh was crying as she looked at Paul. She knew she would not see him again, and she hugged him as they left. His uncle had tears in his eyes as he turned away and refused to say goodbye, as the four Americans left the house. And Tom was touched to see that Paul was crying too when he got into the cab. He was thinking of the grandfather he would never see again. He looked longingly back at his uncle's house as they drove away. He was truly torn between his two cultures and two lives. He loved it here, and he loved his family. It had meant a lot to him to come back, and in some ways he would have liked to stay. But he knew he couldn't. It would kill his parents if he did. And Katie saw the agony on his face too. He was torn between his two worlds, and the people he loved in both. And whichever life he chose, he would be betraying the people who loved him on the other side of that decision.

He cried silently all the way back to the hotel. And no one said a word in the cab. The scene of his visible suffering was too poignant and too hard. Tom almost wondered if he had done the right thing by forcing his uncle's hand and making Paul leave with them. Maybe he wanted to stay. But Paul followed them into the hotel when they arrived. And he thanked Tom for helping him get his passports back and rescuing them both. Katie had really needed to go home, and she still didn't look or feel well, although she was better now. And although he hated leaving Tehran, he wanted to go back to his parents in New York and was grateful for Tom's help.

The hotel booked them on a flight to London three hours later. They didn't want to stay any longer. Tom and Annie's bags had gone to the hotel when they arrived. They had just enough time to collect them, leave again, and return to the airport. It had all gone much more smoothly than Annie and Tom had expected, because Paul's uncle had been reasonable. Annie was haunted now by the devastated look on Paul's uncle's face. They clearly loved Paul and would have liked him to stay. But his parents in New York would have been even more devastated if he had.

They called Paul's parents from the airport, and they were immensely relieved that he was coming home, and grateful that Tom had helped him. They knew that Paul might not have been able to get out otherwise on his own, and his uncle was a daunting figure for a boy his age. It would have been hard to prevail against him, and even Tom barely had. And they had played on Paul's uncle's love for his country and loyalty to Iran, not to create a public scandal in the press by refusing to let Paul leave.

Katie and Paul said nothing to each other on the flight to London. They were both looking pensive and shaken, and as the plane took off from Tehran,

Paul sat staring at the city that he loved and was so sad to leave. And after a while they both fell asleep, without saying a word. Annie covered them both with blankets and then went back to her seat and kissed Tom and thanked him again. It had been a strange odyssey, for all of them.

They were all exhausted during the brief layover in London. Katie still looked sick, and they all looked emotionally drained. This time on the flight to New York, they watched movies and ate dinner, and Paul and Katie chatted quietly for a while. It was the first time that Katie realized how torn Paul was about his two lives. She had wondered before they left Tehran if Paul was going to bolt and stay after all. He clearly felt far more Iranian than she had realized. In truth, he felt both. He had strong feelings of loyalty to both America and Iran, and it was tearing him apart.

His parents were waiting for him at the airport when they arrived, and his mother burst into tears when she saw him, and clung to him for a moment before she turned to thank Tom and Annie. The two young people were looking at each other sadly. Something had happened to them that day. They had been catapulted into adulthood and had seen how different their cultures were and how important to each of them. Katie was entirely American in every way, and Paul had a foot in two worlds. The situation they'd been in had been frightening for both of them, and far more than they could handle on their own. They were both grateful that Tom and Annie had come. And all each of them wanted now was to be with their families, in their own homes.

Katie kissed Paul lightly on the cheek before they left the airport. It was the first time they had kissed since the trip began, and neither of them was sure now if the kiss was hello or goodbye. They both looked sad as they left, and Annie could hear the sound of breaking hearts as they said goodbye.

Chapter 22

They were all exhausted when they got back to Annie's apartment. Ted was waiting for them, and he cried in relief when he hugged his sister. Annie put her to bed a few minutes later. Katie was asleep before she left the room. It had been an endless day, particularly for Katie, who had been so sick.

Tom stretched out on the couch as Annie and Ted talked quietly in the kitchen and looked for something to eat. Tom wasn't hungry, and he was too tired to think as he turned on the TV. He was watching the news on his own network, when they interrupted normal programming to announce a terrorist attack in Belgium. A bomb had gone off right outside the NATO building in Brussels, and fifty-six people had been killed.

"Oh shit," Tom said out loud as he called the network, and reported in.

"Where are you?" his producer asked him. They'd been calling him for hours. "I'm in New York. I got back two hours ago. I was in Tehran this morning," he said in an exhausted voice.

"Sorry, Tom. We need you."

"I figured when I saw the news." He sat up, guessing that he'd be in Brussels soon.

"Can you be on the midnight flight to Paris? We can get you a helicopter from Charles de Gaulle to Brussels, if that works for you."

"Sure." This was his life and what he did. He walked into the kitchen to tell Annie. "I'm leaving," he said, looking tired, but he smiled at her.

"Don't you want to stay here tonight?" She thought he meant that he was going back to his apartment.

"Very much. I've got to go to work. I have to catch the red-eye to Paris. There was a terrorist attack in Brussels."

"You're going **now**?" She looked stunned. She could hardly move. She couldn't imagine how he could do it after the day they just had traveling from Tehran to New York on two flights. "Can't you take a day off or something?"

"No, not when there's a breaking story like that one. I can sleep on the plane." Annie looked sorry for him as she followed him into the bedroom so he could grab some fresh clothes and pack a bag. She handed him an empty suitcase, and he filled it with on-air shirts and three suits, some jeans, and sweaters. He didn't know how long he'd be gone. "I'm sorry to leave you so soon," he apologized, and she smiled at him.

"After what you did for us, how can you apologize to me?" Her eyes were full of everything she felt for him, and he kissed her.

"My ex-wife hated this stuff. Every time I try to make plans or try to do something, I wind up on a plane flying halfway around the world in this business. My ex-wife said I was never there when it counted."

"You just were," Annie told him as she put her arms around him and held him. "You went all the way to Tehran to bring two kids home. I'd never have gotten Paul out without you. His uncle wouldn't have listened to me. I'd say that's being there when it counts. Wouldn't you?" He smiled at her, grateful for the praise. In his marriage, he'd always been made to feel guilty. Annie made him feel like a hero, and he was to her.

After he packed, he took a shower and changed. And she made him a sandwich. He leaned close to her and kissed her, as Ted and Katie drifted into the room.

"Where are you going?" Ted asked him when he saw the suitcase.

"Brussels, on a story. No rest for the wicked." Ted smiled and looked at him in amazement.

"I don't know how you do it."

"You get used to it," Tom said as he stood up and put an arm around Annie, although the last two days had not been normal fare, even for him. He hadn't been sure how it would turn out for Katie and Paul, although he didn't show it. But he was tired too. He'd been on four international flights in two days. "I'll call you," he said to Annie as he kissed her again, and they walked out of the room together. He picked up his suitcase and smiled at her. And then he laughed with a rueful look. "You know, that broken arm I got playing squash is the luckiest thing that ever happened to me."

"So was my ankle." She smiled back at him. "Take care of yourself. I'll see you on TV."

He saluted her and then was gone, and she walked back into the apartment and smiled at Ted. It had been an incredible few days, and Ted was happy for her and happy to have his sister home safe and sound. And it had all worked out because of Tom. There was no doubt in anyone's mind. He was an amazing guy.

The apartment was quiet an hour later. They

were all in their rooms, falling asleep. Annie glanced at the clock and realized that Tom was taking off at that moment. It felt good to know that somewhere in the world, he was there, and he'd be back soon. She couldn't imagine a life without him anymore. And she no longer wondered if there was room for him in her life. He was part of the landscape now. He was one of them. And there was just as much room for the kids as there was for Tom and Annie. It was their turn now.

Katie woke up feeling better the next morning. The trip to Tehran felt like a dream. It seemed so unreal and far away. She called Paul when she got up, and he sounded sad when he talked about leaving his family in Tehran, even though he was happy to see his parents again too and be back in New York. And he had been frightened when he thought of being trapped in Tehran against his will. He promised to come and visit Katie that afternoon. Katie could hear something different in his voice. He sounded quiet and distant.

It felt strange when he came to visit her at the apartment. The trip to Tehran had been exciting and fun, but his almost getting stuck there had shaken both of them. Katie had a sense now that she was in over her head, in a relationship that she wasn't ready for yet. They had talked about marriage as though it would be simple and easy. Now she realized how different their lives were and how much more complicated his was, torn between two families and two worlds, the old and the new. They both needed time to recover from the discoveries they'd made on the trip. It was a lot to digest, and she realized that neither of them was ready to be fully adults yet, and they both needed a break. Paul thought so too. It was too soon for either of them to make decisions about the rest of their lives. They needed time to just be kids, and things had gotten too intense for both of them. They needed time with their own families and friends in their own familiar worlds. Paul kissed her when he left, and they both knew that they needed time to grow up and just breathe. And Katie looked sad as she closed the door behind him.

They had taken a big bite out of life in the past few weeks and found it too much to chew. Life had turned out to be much more complicated than they thought, and they were both grateful to be home and just be kids again. Neither of them was ready to be a grown-up yet, and they were happy not to be. The dream of blending their two different worlds had turned out to be harder than they thought, no matter what their origins or religions. They had gotten much too serious much too fast and way ahead of themselves.

Liz came back from London two days later. And she couldn't believe all that had happened while she was away. She had dinner with them at the apartment. Ted was staying with Annie for a while until he found a new place, and Katie had told Annie that morning that she was going back to school as soon as the next term started. She had already given notice at the tattoo parlor. She was done there. She just wanted to enjoy being home with them. And she needed time to get over the virus she had caught in Tehran. Annie had taken her to the doctor and he confirmed that she was out of danger, but she still felt weak.

"How was London?" Annie asked Liz when she came to visit, and the look on her face said it all.

"It was wonderful. Alessandro is coming here next month, and I want you to meet him. He's a grown-up. It's so nice to be with a man who's not a kid. He's a man, and he acts like one. I love him, Annie." For the first time in her life, she knew it was true. She wasn't afraid to love him, no matter what the risk.

"That's what I always wanted for you," Annie said with a smile. Liz was a woman now. She wasn't a child anymore. "Do I hear wedding bells in your future?" Annie asked her. She hoped so, but she didn't want to push.

"Maybe. We're in no rush. If everything works out, I might apply for a job with Italian **Vogue**. But not yet. We want to see how it goes. I might help him open a store in New York."

"That all sounds good." Annie felt as though she had gotten Liz safely home. It had taken sixteen years. And she noticed that Liz had even gained some weight. She looked happy. She didn't look like she was running scared anymore. She wasn't afraid to lose him, or to love him. She was willing to take the risk. And Katie had figured out that she didn't have to take quite so many risks. Ted was enjoying being free again. They had all grown up. And so had Annie. They had each come through their rites of passage and grown as a result.

And what about you?" Lizzie asked her. "Where's Tom?"

"He's in Brussels. The poor guy had to fly over two hours after we got home. He didn't seem to mind. I guess he's used to it. That's how he lives. Running around the world, chasing the news." And she had the best of all worlds now. The kids she had raised, and a man she loved and wanted to be with. There was room for all of them in her life. And Tom knew it too. They were part of his life now, not just hers. They were all swimming in the same direction with quiet, steady strokes.

Tom called Annie that night, just after Liz left, and told her he was coming home. The story in Brussels had been covered. It was morning for him in Belgium, and he said he was leaving in a few minutes.

"What are we doing this weekend?" he asked her.

"Nothing that I know of. Why?"

"I was thinking that it might be nice to spend a couple of days in the Turks and Caicos again. I could use a little rest." It was a major understatement after the past week.

"Yeah, me too," she said, thinking of how wonderful it had been the first time they'd been there and how far they'd come since.

"Do you think the kids can survive without you for a few days?" he asked hopefully.

"I think so. Everyone seems to be back on track and relatively sane for the moment." And she felt that way too. She had never felt saner or stronger, and she was ready for a life with him.

"It's your turn now, Annie," he reminded her gently, and she thought about it and nodded.

"I guess it is." And then she corrected him with a slow smile. "It's our turn." She had given them sixteen years of her full attention, and now she wanted to share that with him. She was still there for her sister's children, and she always would be, but she had the time now to give him. The kids were grown up. They were taking over their own lives. They had made mistakes, and corrected them. And they had learned from it and survived. And so had she. He had come at the right time in her life, neither too late, nor too soon.

"I'll see you tonight," he said, sounding peaceful and happy. He couldn't wait to come home to her. He had something to come home to now. A woman, and a family. He was ready for that too. He never had been before.

Annie had just gotten back from the office and was making herself a cup of tea when he walked in.

"How was your flight?" she asked him as he kissed her. It seemed so normal for him to be there, as though he always had been.

"Long and boring. I missed you."

"I missed you too." Katie was out, and Ted had gone back to his apartment for a few days to pack up and move. Tom and Annie were alone, and it was peaceful. She finished her tea, and he followed her into the bedroom, and he was smiling when she turned around. "What are you smiling at?" she said as she sat down on the bed and kicked off her shoes and looked at him.

"I was thinking about how happy you make me," he said as he sat down next to her. "I remember when I thought there wasn't room for me in your life. I'm not worried anymore," he said comfortably, and lay back on the bed and pulled her down next to him. "This is where I want to be."

"Me too," she whispered, and he kissed her. She didn't feel pulled in ten directions. The kids had grown up, and so had she.

He drew her into his arms then and knew he was home. Finally. She was the woman he loved, and this was his home now, with her. And it had only taken a broken arm, a sprained ankle, and a lifetime for them to get here, and it suddenly all seemed so easy and just the way it was meant to be.

Annie had to give sixteen years of her life to her sister's children in order to be ready for him. Lizzie had to make her way through countless Jean-Louis in order to be brave enough to love Alessandro. Ted had to live through the insanity of Pattie to find out who he was and what mattered to him. And Katie had to defy everything and everyone and risk it all in order to find her freedom. They had each come through their growing pains and challenges, and so had Tom. He needed to be married to the wrong woman in order to recognize the right one, even if she didn't come packaged quite as he had expected and looked too busy for him when he got there. She didn't know it, but she'd been waiting for him.

The lessons they had all learned had been valuable and hard but well worth it. And the rite of passage, for each of them, had been the lesson they each needed to learn. There was a perfect symmetry to it, Annie realized, as she smiled into Tom's eyes. Even the sprained ankle and the broken arm had been part of a divine order that led them to each other. None of it had been an accident or a mistake. It hadn't been easy, but the rewards had been so great, for all of them. Annie was so grateful for how it had turned out. It could have been so different if they had faltered or refused the challenge—they would never have gotten here. But they had all been very brave. She smiled knowingly as Tom kissed her again. The circle was complete.

About the Author

DANIELLE STEEL has been hailed as one of the world's most popular authors, with over 590 million copies of her novels sold. Her many international bestsellers include **Big Girl, Southern Lights, Matters of the Heart, One Day at a Time, A Good Woman, Rogue, Honor Thyself, Amazing Grace,** and other highly acclaimed novels. She is also the author of **His Bright Light,** the story of her son Nick Traina's life and death. Visit the Danielle Steel Web Site at www.daniellesteel.com.